Skin

Paper

STONE

MÁIRE T.
ROBINSON

NEW ISLAND

D1579340

SKIN PAPER STONE
First published in 2015
by New Island Books,
16 Priory Hall Office Park,
Stillorgan,
County Dublin,
Republic of Ireland.

www.newisland.ie

PRINT ISBN:978-1-84840-3581
EPUB ISBN:978-1-84840-3598
MOBI ISBN:978-1-84840-3604

British Library Cataloguing Data.
A CIP catalogue record for this book is available from the British Library.

Typeset by JVR Creative India
Cover design by Mariel Deegan
Printed by SandBook AB

New Island received financial assistance from The Arts Council *(An Chomhairle Ealaíon)*, 70 Merrion Square, Dublin 2, Ireland.

10 9 8 7 6 5 4 3 2 1

About the Author

Máire T. Robinson lives and works in Dublin City. She holds a Master's Degree in Writing from NUI, Galway. In 2012 she was nominated for a Hennessy Literary Award in Emerging Fiction. The following year, she won the Doire Press International Fiction Chapbook Competition. Her début collection of short stories, *Your Mixtape Unravels My Heart*, was published as a result. This is her first novel.

Acknowledgements

A massive thank you to Eoin Purcell for his belief in the book at an early stage, and to Shauna, Justin, Mariel and all at New Island for their help and support with everything.

Jack Harte and Clodagh Moynan; and to Conor Kostick and the members of the group that formed as a result of his workshop at the Irish Writers' Centre who provided feedback on the first draft of the book – Hana, Michael, Rachel, Dearbhla, Jackie, David, Wes and Genevieve.

Thanks, as always, to Nuala Ní Chonchúir for her encouragament and kindness.

Dr Alison Forrestal of NUI, Galway for taking the time to meet with me and share her wealth of knowledge.

I'd also like to acknowledge some books that were invaluable during my research: *The Sheela-na-gigs of Ireland and Britain* by Joanne McMahon and Jack Roberts; Barbara Freitag's *Sheela-na-gigs: Unravelling an Enigma*; and Grace Bowman's *A Shape of My Own*.

All my friends for their support and interest along the way, especially Bridget Deevy, and my fellow historical site explorer, Benny Nolan.

A special thanks to my family: Catherine Robinson and Andrew Robinson, and to my extended family: Fran, Tony and all the Murphys. And last but not least, John Murphy – for everything.

Chapter 1

The baby's cry was an accusation. Moments before, he was resting placidly in his mother's arms. Now, in Stevie's clutches, he wailed at an inhuman pitch.

'There, there,' said Stevie, in what she hoped was a comforting tone. The baby looked like a potato. An irate, screeching potato. It hadn't been her idea to hold him, but there was no other option when Caitríona suggested it other than to smile and take the baby in her arms.

'Aw, he's just a little grumpy today,' said Caitríona. She made a clucking noise, as though her newborn son were an errant chicken. 'Who's a grumpy boy? You are!'

The baby's cries began to subside and Stevie gave Caitríona a relieved smile. Stevie was not surprised by the baby's reaction. She had perfected her routine for visiting friends with newborns. She knew the right gift to bring, the right cooing noises to make, and the arranged smile that would convey her sense of wonder at her friend's reproductive abilities. Stevie had everyone fooled. Everyone apart from the babies. It seemed that they sensed her discomfort, and wailed their protests accordingly.

Stevie had never bought into the notion of women 'glowing' during pregnancy. It was something people said, she suspected, to make them feel better: a consolation prize for the swollen breasts, varicose veins, constipation, and the all-round indignity of shuffling about like a giant watermelon on legs. It was only in looking at her friend now that Stevie realised how well Caitríona had, in fact, looked during the pregnancy. The contrast was stark. Caitríona was no longer Caitríona. If there were changeling children, perhaps there were changeling mothers too. Maybe the real Caitríona was away with the faeries glugging wine, chain-smoking, and throwing her head back in one of her unselfconscious throaty laughs, unaware that this other woman with a newborn in her arms had taken her place. This Caitríona had been ravaged, stretched, split open and stitched back together. She had given birth over a week ago, yet her stomach was still swollen in an effigy of pregnancy. There was an empty space, the former refuge where the screaming child was once silently curled up. Now there was nothing to fill it, like a plaster cast that keeps its shape long after it has served its function and been discarded from the recovered limb.

'How are you finding Galway so far, Stevie?'

'Yeah, it's … well, it's a nice change from Dublin anyway.'

'Have you spoken to Donal since?'

'Not really.' Stevie shrugged. 'There's not a whole lot left to say. I heard he's seeing someone.'

'Already? Jesus, he didn't wait long.'

'Yeah. That's him though. Can't be on his own.' Stevie tutted and rolled her eyes. 'Fuckin' eejit.'

Caitríona grinned and then sat forward and looked serious all of a sudden. 'Are you sure you're okay though?'

'Me? Yeah, I'm grand. It's none of my business what he does now.' Stevie cleared her throat and looked up from the spot on the carpet that she'd been staring at. 'But enough about me. What about this little fella? Have yous decided on a name for it? Jesus, sorry. I meant a name for *him,* his name?'

'Oisín.'

'Oisín, oh that's lovely.'

A sure sign that she was getting older, Stevie had discovered, was that when her friends told her they were pregnant, the first thing she said was *congratulations* rather than *oh fuck, what are you gonna do?*

She smiled down at the bundle in her arms. 'Hi, Oisín.' At this, the baby's roars started up again. Stevie held out the baby for Caitríona to rescue. Back in his mother's arms, his cries began to peter out, until he was whimpering like a dog that had been kicked and couldn't figure out why.

Caitríona unleashed a swollen breast puckered with blue veins, and offered it to the baby's quivering mouth. Stevie looked at her cup of tea with a newfound interest and crossed her arms over her own, almost flat, chest. Silence. Then the noise of the baby suckling.

'So when will yourself and Phil give him a little brother or sister?' asked Stevie.

She intended it as a joke, expecting Caitríona to groan and say something like, *Are you mad? Once was bad enough.*

Caitríona smiled. 'We're going to start trying again as soon as possible.'

'Really? That's great,' Stevie heard herself say.

Chapter 2

Joe Kavanagh turned into Buttermilk Lane. A busker's tune floated up and reverberated off the high buildings, bouncing back to his ears, plaintive and sweet. Even though it was just some cheesy guy with a tin whistle, each note soared and sang out sad and true. He wasn't one for the traditional music – the auld triangle, rebel songs, all that shite. Reminded him of home, where you couldn't have a pint and the craic without it getting to that time of night when the auld fellas got sentimental and dewy-eyed with the pints on them and the songs starting up. And them all shushing you to be quiet like you were at fuckin' Mass or something. Nah, he couldn't abide it.

Something about this change in the weather reminded Kavanagh of school uniforms and itchy collars: always that first week back when the sun would be scorching. Sunshine was a rare and blessed thing in Galway. It summoned the masses to outdoor worship. They walked along the Salthill promenade, squinty-eyed and joyful, lapping at their melting ice-creams. Dogs bounded with trampoline steps. Cats stretched in beams of sunlight and looked even more smug than usual. On sunny days, people liked to be close to water, and in the city there was a lot of it to go around. They sat on the grass beside the canal watching the eternal battle between duck and seagull. All manner of beatific worshippers sat by the river near the Spanish Arch – students, families with their children, crusties, winos, pill-poppers, and degenerates of every persuasion joined in holy union as they faced the sun. Tourists who had never experienced a winter in Galway sat in ecstatic contemplation. They had stumbled on some Celtic Shangri-La and were concocting plans to move to Galway immediately. Everyone felt connected under that sunlight, a palpable thing. On days like this, the city hummed.

Kavanagh saw the beggar-woman sitting in her usual spot at the end of the lane, hand outstretched, mumbling at passers-by: a living statue in a red raincoat, as much a part of the city as the buildings.

'Howaya, Mary?' he said, although he'd often walked past her without saying anything. 'Lovely day for it.' It tied in to this new feeling he had, walking around with a sense of pre-emptive nostalgia because things were starting to look different now that he knew he was leaving.

She looked up at him, her face hopeful, 'Spare any money?'

'No, sorry.' He felt guilty then when he saw her face fall. 'Ah, for fuck's sake,' he chastised himself. He shouldn't have spoken to her in the first place. That was the problem with optimism – it created all sorts of headaches. He rooted in the pocket of his jeans and handed her two Euro.

'Thanks,' she said, pocketing the coin and giving him a brief smile. 'Have you no paper money?'

He could feel the edginess creeping in as he cut through Eyre Square, and he had it in mind to head for a pint.

'Kavanagh!' a voice behind him called. He turned to see Maloney sitting on a low stone wall, a Buckfast bottle wrapped in brown paper clutched in his hands.

'All right, man. What's the craic?' he said, sitting beside him.

'Divil a bit,' said Maloney, squinting. 'What ya at yourself?'

'Ah, fuck all.' Kavanagh decided not to mention his plan to go for a pint. The last thing he needed was Maloney hanging off him.

'Any smoke on ya? Serious drought on, so there is.' Maloney's words seemed to emerge through his nose rather than his mouth. They were punctuated by an occasional whistle that sounded like the breeze down the chimney of Kavanagh's old house. Whenever he spoke to Maloney, he had the urge to grab him by the nostrils and force him to speak through his mouth.

Kavanagh shook his head. 'Sorry, man. If I hear of anything, I'll give you a shout.'

The late-August sun shone down on them, and Kavanagh closed his eyes and turned his face towards its warmth. He thought of Thailand. A beach. A hammock. The lap-lapping of waves and....

'Fuckin' pigeons. Rats with wings, hah?' said Maloney, nudging Kavanagh out of his reverie with a sharp elbow to the shoulder. He opened his eyes in time to see Maloney stand up and aim a kick at a mottled grey bird with his metal-capped boot. The pigeon leapt from the discarded punnet of curry-cheese chips it had been pecking at and landed a foot away on the grass, eyeing Maloney with one beady eye and then eyeing the punnet. Kavanagh shielded his eyes from the sun and looked at the offending bird. Its feathers gleamed in the sunlight like spilt petrol.

'Look at it. Fuckin' rotten yoke,' said Maloney, as he spat in the direction of the bird.

'Jesus, Maloney. It's only a pigeon, for fuck's sake. Keep your hair on.'

Maloney drank from the bottle again before offering it to Kavanagh. A tightrope of saliva still joined the bottle and Maloney's mouth.

'Ah no, you're all right, thanks.'

Maloney shrugged and took another swig.

'Lookit, he's still got his eye on those chips. The fucker.' Maloney took a step towards the bird, who looked up at him but didn't budge. 'You'll not get these,' he said, stooping down to pick up the container. The pigeon hopped off a few steps and looked back as if deciding on something, before taking off and flapping into the distance. The two men stared after it until it became a dot in the sky. It occurred to Kavanagh that a stranger passing by might look at him and Maloney and see no difference between them – two straggly wastes of space knocking back cheap booze in the afternoon – but he knew he wasn't like Maloney. Not a bit. No, he was a man who was going places.

Maloney shoved the chips under Kavanagh's nose. 'Here, d'ya want one?'

'Fuck off, Maloney,' he said, swatting the hand away.

Maloney shrugged, then threw the punnet in the nearby bin and wiped his hands together with a satisfied clap. 'Well, don't say I never give ya anything, ya cunt.'

Kavanagh sighed. 'Here, Maloney, have you heard of any work going?'

'Work?!' spat Maloney, as if the word offended his sensibilities. 'Fuck no. Are ya not signing on, like?'

'Ah yeah, I am. I'm doing a kind of apprenticeship, you know, but it doesn't pay. I'm learning how to do tattoos. You know the place on the docks?'

'Oh ya, it's that duck place, is it?'

'Duck place? Jesus, Maloney. Did they not teach you any Irish in school?'

'Ah, they did, yeah.' Maloney grinned. '*An bhfuil cead agam dul go dtí an leithreas?*'

'It's *dúch*, not duck. It means ink.'

'Oh, right, ya,' said Maloney. 'So, are you actually doing the tattoos, like?'

'Well, not yet, but eventually, yeah.'

'I got one done in Santa Ponza a few years ago.' Maloney rolled up his sleeve and showed Kavanagh his arm. Kavanagh squinted at an indistinguishable faded green blob.

'Here, what is it?'

'It's a fucking shamrock.'

'Oh yeah, course it is. I see it now.'

'Yeah, all the lads got them. Phelan was fucking out of it, man. He got it on his arse.'

Maloney laughed at the memory, hocked up some phlegm and spat it on the ground. It looked more like a shamrock than the thing on his arm.

'We'd some craic on that holiday.'

'Yeah? I'm heading off myself soon. Thailand. Just need to get some cash together first.'

'Thailand? Is it the ladyboys you're into or what?' Maloney snorted.

Kavanagh put his head in his hands. 'Jesus, I have to get out of here. Seriously. It's depressing.'

'Here, sell some more of that weed and you'll have the money like ... that.' Maloney tried to click his fingers, but no sound emanated. He tried again, frowned at his fingers and then looked at Kavanagh, a sly smile creeping onto his face. 'Oh sorry, man. I forgot. Sure you can't be doing that any more what with Pajo an' all coming after ya.' Maloney gestured towards Kavanagh's eye, where a purple bruise was faintly visible, fading to a dull yellowish colour at the edges.

'This? Walked into a door, Maloney.'

'I heard it was good shit.'

'Who told you that?'

'Ah, no one. Just I heard it was better than Pajo's fucking dried-up twigs and sticks, is all. Can you sort us out with some?'

'I dunno where you're getting that from, Maloney. I wouldn't know anything about that.'

He looked at his wrist, although he wasn't wearing a watch. 'Listen, I better be heading off anyway, yeah? I've to meet someone. Take it easy.'

'All right, man. Sure I might see ya later for a pint.'

'Yeah, grand,' said Kavanagh as he headed off. 'Ya will in yer shite,' he muttered.

'Sound, man, sound.' Maloney's nasal farewell floated after him on the breeze.

That was the problem with Galway, he thought to himself. Too many shifty fuckers that you shouldn't even be giving the time of day to. Fuck it. He'd walk around and he might bump into someone else to go for a pint with. There was always someone to go for a pint with.

*

Kavanagh stumbled inside and headed straight for the kitchen. He could hear the low, familiar noise of his housemates, Gary and Dan, playing *Grand Theft Auto*. The place stank of weed. It wouldn't even occur to them to open the bloody window. Pair of clowns. He grabbed a can of beer from the fridge and popped it open, taking a long drink. Then he saw it on the kitchen table: the brown parcel that was addressed to him. He lunged for it and tried to pry open the cardboard box that was sealed shut with layers of brown tape. He squinted at it

and tried to get his eyes to focus. After fumbling with it and cursing at it for a spell, he found the edge of the tape and started to peel it back, but it broke off in his hand.

'Fuck!' he cried impatiently.

'All right, Kav?' came a lazy voice behind him.

He turned to see Dan standing in the doorway eating a packet of crisps.

'Oh yeah,' Dan pointed at the parcel. 'That arrived earlier. I signed for it.'

'Cheers, Dan.' Kavanagh grabbed a sharp knife from the block on the counter and sliced through the tape.

'Very discreet packaging for a dildo supply shop.'

Kavanagh shook his head. 'I am surrounded by idiots.'

'Speaking of idiots, are you having some trouble opening that box there, Kav?'

'Fuck off.'

Dan adjusted his glasses, folded his arms, and stood back to watch as if 'Man Attempts to Open Box' was some new avant-garde form of entertainment.

'Here, what's in it anyway?'

'A gun.'

'Yeah right,' snorted Dan. Then he took a tentative step closer. 'Is it? I wouldn't put it past you.'

Kavanagh wrestled the box open, peeled back the layers of bubble wrap and pulled out the implement. He looked at it and then pointed it at Dan. 'See? It's a tattoo gun.'

'Oh, is that what they look like? Why do you need that? Do they not have them in Dúch?'

'We-ell,' said Kavanagh, 'Finn won't let me use his. Says I have to learn by observing first.'

'Makes sense,' said Dan.

'Nah. The best way of learning something is to actually *do* it. Fuck this watching shit.'

10

'So … you're gonna do tattoos with that yoke?'

'Yeah, that's the idea, Dan.'

'On who?'

'Everyone.'

Dan shook his head. 'Not on me. Tattoos are lame.'

'You're lame, Dan. I do need some practice though. Next time you're asleep …'. He pointed the gun at Dan and made a buzzing noise.

'What, you're gonna set bees on me?'

Kavanagh rolled his eyes. 'That's the noise the machine makes. I could tattoo you a bee though, if that's what you're into. Right …' he moved the gun close to the centre of Dan's forehead, 'here.'

'Keep that yoke away from me, and my beautiful, beautiful face. If you're looking for someone's face to experiment on, I'd go with Gary's. I mean, let's be honest, it could only improve things.'

Kavanagh laughed, grabbed a couple of cans from the fridge and put them in the pockets of his hoodie. He put the tattoo gun back into the box and carried it with him as he headed towards his bedroom. 'Right, I've work to do. Later,' he called over his shoulder.

Kavanagh placed the box on his desk, and took out the pot of black ink that he had ordered alongside the tattoo gun. It was a rotary machine that, according to the user reviews, *Gives good results and is handy for lining and shading. Sweeeeeeet!!! 4.5 stars.* Another plus point was that it was the cheapest one he could find. The gun was lighter and smaller than the ones in the tattoo parlour. It felt good in his hand. He switched it on and heard the familiar hum of Dúch, but in miniature. He took another long swig from the can, took a deep breath and then rolled up his trouser leg. Now he would finally see what this tattoo business was all about.

Chapter 3

Stevie walked the length of Shop Street amongst the meandering stream of pedestrians. Buskers competed with each other for airtime like a radio being tuned in. The sounds of a djembe drummer overlapped with the operatic warblings of a raven-haired woman singing along to a blaring backing track, before fading into an acoustic guitar version of 'Fields of Athenry'. A balloon modeller fashioned a pink balloon-dog for a little girl. A group of young lads heckled a man posing as a statue in an attempt to trick him into moving.

'Push him over!' said one.

'He's only standing there. He's not doing anything,' said another, shaking his head in disapproval.

'Let's rob his money,' said the first, making a sudden lunging movement towards the hat full of coins that was lying at the man's feet. Stevie smiled to herself as she saw a faint flicker of panic betrayed on the man's silver-painted face.

She was new to Galway, and was still taking it in. What she enjoyed most was strolling around the city streets. She saw it as it was, but she also saw the old Galway underneath, like a faint pencil sketch visible beneath a thick layer of paint. At the Spanish Arch, where youths sat and stared dreamily at the brown churning river, hiding their beer when policemen on bicycles came by, she saw the old fish market in her mind's eye, and the shawled women with red petticoats selling the Claddagh fishermen's catch. She saw the noblemen and women in the old Lynch townhouse that the bank now occupied. Crowded tenement houses were still visible to her, despite their modern guises. Beneath the restaurants and craft shops of the cobbled passageway of Kirwan's Lane, she saw candlelit figures in windows as the clip-clop of horses down medieval laneways sounded in her ears. It was all there for her. She could see it all.

Stevie headed towards Neachtain's and saw that all of the outdoor seats were filled with people drinking pints. She had arranged to meet up with Orlaith, an old friend from Trinity, who had become a secondary school history teacher, and had also recently moved to Galway. They would have to sit inside. It was no harm; a breeze was setting in, and it looked like rain was on the way. Stevie thought to herself how strange it was that just a month ago she had felt so lost. Since then, something had imperceptibly shifted. Stevie could now feel the deliciousness of time stretching out before her, time on her own. She had been warned that undertaking a Ph.D. could be a lonely business, but now she looked forward to languishing in its solitude – the hours spent in research, the silent reverie, connections made, ideas sparking – as she weaved her way through history.

When she moved to Galway, Stevie had worried about living on her own. For the first two weeks, she had hardly slept. Unwanted thoughts invaded her mind, which triggered a succession of emotions, a domino effect of grief, regret and anger, until she would be weeping into the darkness, or conducting arguments in her head, denouncing the shadows on the edges of her mind, trapped like a helpless witness as scenes repeated themselves, an endless churning vortex she couldn't escape. Sometimes, during these moments, she heard her own voice in her head, a coolly detached observer: *This is it now, Stevie. You really are fucking losing it.*

She drank then to help her sleep, and it worked a bit. But one glass of red wine led to two, three, a whole bottle, until she was bumping into chairs or dropping glasses or just about managing to stop herself from ringing Donal. The following day she would be groggy. By the time she had woken up, the best part of the afternoon was already past. Her thoughts were slippery, and she didn't have the strength to clutch them to her. Everything slowed down, and the most simple task seemed monumental. These days she could sit in a café for an hour or two while she read a history book, or watch people flowing past, content in her own company. Now, when she thought of her time with Donal, and the fact that she was no longer with him, she felt huge relief, like shrugging off a wet wool coat, like she had been holding her breath without realising it, and now she was inhaling a steady stream of oxygen.

She stepped into the cool darkness of the bar. Temporarily blinded as her eyes adjusted to the indoor light, she heard Orlaith before she saw her, that old, familiar laugh. She was sitting at the bar, chatting to the barman. Orlaith was strikingly beautiful with jet black hair, pale skin and hazel eyes. She couldn't blend into the background if she tried.

'Hey, Orlaith!' Stevie called, and before the second syllable had left her mouth, Orlaith had spun around, leapt off her bar stool and ran to hug her. 'Oh my God, you're here! I can't believe it. This is brilliant. Here, what are you drinking?'

*

They wanted the night to spin out of control, take them where it willed, carry their puny bodies on its whim. Stevie and Orlaith travelled from pub to pub, trading stories, filling in the blanks of the years between then and now, all the while shedding their possessions like old skin – an umbrella, a hat, a ten Euro note – sacrifices they offered up to the night. They passed a woman with one shoe hobbling along Shop Street, and greeted her like a long-lost friend. They wanted the night to spin out of control, and they would not question where it brought them. Obedient, they would go where it led. They bellowed into the night, and new friends came crawling from alleyways in response, their numbers swelling under that inky sky, all spinning. They took the pills in that last pub, and now the lights were changing. Their bodies were becoming melodies. They had basslines for fingers, and their pupils were the taut skins of snare drums. The night was spinning out of control, but they would cheat the night and they would not sleep. They would float.

In the taxi, they headed towards Salthill, and Stevie looked out at the rain bleeding into the passing lights, an ever-changing art exhibition that flickered and danced in the car window for her alone. This was what she had needed all along. It was so clear to her now.

There were decks at the party, and Stevie and Orlaith submerged themselves in the music coming from the speakers.

Stevie felt the bass pump through her body. She was the bassline, rhythmic and charging, filling up the room with love. Inhaling sharply on her pipe, she realised she had already smoked it all. She dug out her pouch of tobacco from her bag, refilled it and lit up, before grabbing Orlaith in a bearhug of an embrace.

'Thanks for bringing me out!' she shouted in Orlaith's ear.

'No, thanks for coming out,' beamed Orlaith. 'It's so great to see you again. I love you.'

Their words flowed out of their mouths, rolling and scattering like marbles.

'I love you too,' said Stevie.

'I love this song,' said Orlaith.

'I love it too,' said Stevie.

'What is it?' said Orlaith.

'I don't know,' said Stevie.

'Teaching has ruined nights out for me,' said Orlaith, looking furtive all of a sudden, eyes darting around the room from beneath her thick black fringe. 'I'm always worried I'll bump into one of my students.'

Stevie grinned. 'You're a pillar of the community now, Orlaith.'

'I know, Stevie. How the fuck did that happen?'

Their dancing was all-consuming, but then they wanted to talk so they sat on the sofa. Stevie had to tell Orlaith the problem with Donal, and she had to listen and stroke Stevie's arm, and every so often Stevie would say, 'I'm talking too much am I talking too much you don't have to sit here listening to me I know I'm talking too much…'. And Orlaith would smile and light another cigarette, and say, 'No no no tell me tell me everything.'

It seemed they hadn't been talking for very long, but it was four in the morning already, and people were starting to leave the party

That's when Stevie noticed the two girls in the corner of the room. They were floundering, their feet like mice stuck in a glue trap, their mouths the startled O's of demented carol singers, their hands reaching, reaching for something only they could see – some invisible tormentor hovering in mid-air.

'Oh no, oh no, oh no,' said one of the girls in a dull unblinking monotone.

A stocky man with a shaved head and meaty arms looked at the girls and laughed. He smoked a joint, and passed it to the even larger man who stood silently grinning at his side.

A woman with peroxide-blonde hair and black roots was pointing at the two girls. 'He gave them ketamine, Walshy!' she shrieked, nudging the small weasely-looking man who stood beside her. 'They thought it was coke.' She threw back her head and cackled. 'I can't believe you did that, Pajo! You're some bollocks.' Walshy laughed along with her in a high-pitched squeal.

'I never said it was coke, Jacqui,' shrugged Pajo, smirking to himself.

And even though empathy filled Stevie's every pore, she could feel nothing but revulsion for Jacqui and Pajo and their posse of friends who were grouped beside the two girls like an ugly pack of hyenas. It was like they had sucked all of the air out of the room. Stevie could feel her love buzz start to cave in on itself.

She turned to Orlaith, who was staring at the girls. 'Ah God, Stevie. Look at them.'

'I know. It's fucking horrible, but there's nothing we can do. They'll just have to wait until it wears off.'

'I took that stuff once.' Orlaith shook her head. 'Never again.'

'Do you fancy a glass of wine?' asked Stevie. 'I've a bottle in my bag around here somewhere.'

'Oh my God, yes. Let's have a drink.' Orlaith jumped up from her seat. They made their way through the room of people, faces dripping with sweat, to search for a bottle opener in the kitchen.

*

Kavanagh sat at his kitchen table, rolling a joint and watching Dan pacing up and down the length of the tiny room, like a caged zoo animal.

'Did you see them in there?' Dan said in an urgent voice to Kavanagh and Gary. 'It's yer man, Pajo and his sidekicks.'

Gary nodded. 'Walshy and Hulk.'

'Yeah, Little and Large ... or Little and Fucking Humongous.'

'I know, I know,' said Gary, 'fucking ropey buzz. Look, could you ... I don't know ... go out there and tell him the party's over or something?'

Dan shook his head. 'You want me to tell Pajo Donnellan to leave? Are you fucking mental?'

Gary shrugged. 'Yeah, I suppose we can't really do that. We could.... Ah, fuck! I don't know. Ropey buzz, man.'

'Fucking tell me about it. I'm not going back out there 'till they leave. We'll be stuck in here for the night. Here, give us a smoke, Gar.'

Kavanagh wasn't thrilled to hear that Pajo was in their flat either, but he had no intention of drawing attention to the fact. He smoked his joint and silently looked around the kitchen, his unwitting prison. Two girls were riffling through the kitchen drawers, talking away to each other a mile a minute.

'Can I help you there, ladies?' said Dan to the girls.

'Oh, do you live here?' said the dark-haired girl. 'Great party! I'm Orlaith and this is Stevie. We're just looking for a wine opener.'

'I'm Dan. Yes, I do live here,' Dan smiled, 'for my sins.'

Orlaith looked at him blankly.

'Right,' said Dan. 'Anyway, a wine opener. Yeah, there must be one around here somewhere. Here, Gary, where's the wine opener?'

Gary plucked something from the sink and held it out, 'Here,' he said.

Dan shook his head. 'Gary, that's a fucking potato peeler.'

Gary looked at his hand in surprise. 'Oh yeah. Sure that's no good to you. Unless … would you like some potatoes?'

'No, thanks,' said Orlaith.

'Wait, wait, I have it here,' said Dan, rooting around in the sink. 'Here you go, ladies.' He presented them with a spatula.

'Oh, no. We're looking for a bottle opener,' said Orlaith earnestly. 'But thank you.'

Gary looked at Dan, shaking his head as they both started laughing.

Kavanagh stood up and reached for the bottle. 'Here, give us that. I'll open it for you.'

Stevie handed him the bottle wordlessly.

'Saw this on YouTube.' Kavanagh took off his shoe and put the bottle into the foot-hole, then drew back his arm and banged the shoe off the wall.

'What are ya at?!' screeched Gary, still holding the potato peeler aloft.

'Yeah right, Kavanagh. That'll never fuckin' work,' said Dan.

They watched, mesmerised, as, sure enough, with each tap the cork began to edge out of the bottle.

'No way,' said Stevie.

Kavanagh looked at her and smiled. 'Once more,' he said, keeping his eyes locked on hers as he drew the shoe right back and smashed it with accidental force against the wall.

'Oh, careful,' said Orlaith, 'you might break …'.

As the word 'break' left her mouth, the sound of glass breaking filled the kitchen, as though Orlaith had summoned it. Kavanagh's left hand around the top of the bottle crushed the splintered glass. Red wine spurted onto the floor. Still staring at Stevie, it was only when the cold liquid seeped into his sock that Kavanagh noticed the broken glass.

'Oh fuck!'

'Are you okay?' asked Stevie, as Kavanagh looked from his foot to the remnants of the broken bottle in his hand and dropped the remainder to the floor. 'Jesus!'

Blood poured from his hand and splashed onto the tiled floor, where it mixed with red wine. Gary let out a girlish screech. They all stood in silence staring at the blood dripping from Kavanagh's arm for what seemed like an eternity. Stevie stepped forward and took Kavanagh by the arm and led him to the sink to rinse off the flecks of glass. His blood flowed into the sink and seeped into a used teabag that was sitting beside the plughole. Stevie could feel the throb of his pulse, and she glimpsed the tattoos on his arm, the pictures distorted under the flow of water.

'I think you need to go to the hospital,' Orlaith grimaced as she gestured towards Kavanagh's arm.

'Yeah,' said Stevie. 'I think so too.' The clean towel she had wrapped around the wound just moments ago was already soaked red. There were spatters of red on Stevie's white top that could have been blood or wine.

'Ah no, it'll be grand,' said Kavanagh.

'Seriously, you look like you need stitches. Jesus, it's a shame.' Orlaith shook her head.

Kavanagh looked at her in confusion. 'It's all right. I'm not gonna die.'

'I mean it's a shame about the wine.'

'I'll come with you,' said Stevie, 'to the hospital.'

'Would you do that?'

'Sure. Let me just grab my bag.'

*

As Kavanagh stood by the door, waiting for the girl and trying not to drip blood on the floor, he felt his heart sink as he saw Pajo approach.

'Well, well, if it isn't my old pal Joe Kavanagh,' said Pajo. Hearing his full name pronounced like that gave Kavanagh the stomach-lurching feeling of his youth when it could mean only one thing: he was in trouble. His insides curdled.

'What brings you here?' said Pajo.

'I live here,' said Kavanagh.

'Really?' smirked Pajo, 'Well, that's good to know. Very good indeed.'

Kavanagh could have kicked himself. 'Look, I'd love to stay and chat, Pajo, but I appear to be bleeding to death.'

He held up his bloodied hand, and was satisfied to see Pajo take a step backwards as he looked at it in horror. Kavanagh turned and opened the door without giving Pajo a chance to respond or to ask him what had happened. Outside, he stood in the rain for a bit and waited for the girl. He didn't know for how long, he wasn't wearing a watch, but it felt like forever. A taxi approached, and Kavanagh took one last look towards the door. No sign. His legs felt like they might give way. He hailed the taxi and headed for the hospital.

*

'Where is he? The guy with the hand?' Stevie made her way into the kitchen, her bag on her shoulder. 'I was supposed to bring him to hospital.'

'I told you already. He left ages ago,' said Orlaith. 'Jesus, you're even more fucked than me.'

'Should I go after him?'

'Are you mad? It's lashing rain.' Orlaith grabbed Stevie's hand. 'Come on inside and dance with me.'

Chapter 4

'Jesus, my head,' Pajo heard Jacqui say as she sat up in bed, stretched her skinny arms and yawned. She looked at him with a lopsided smile that she probably imagined was endearing.

Pajo squinted and shielded his eyes. 'What time is it?'

Afternoon light was creeping in through a gap in the blinds, casting long shadows on his bedroom wall. It made Jacqui's dyed-blonde hair look even more bleached-out than usual. Her eyes were dark with smudged eye make-up.

She checked the time on her phone. It was lying next to a pile of clothes strewn on the ground. They were hers. Pajo's clothes were folded in a neat pile on a chair at the end of the bed.

'Half one,' she said. 'I could use a cup of tea. Do you want me to make you one?'

Pajo shook his head.

'I can make it and bring it in to ya, if ya like?'

'Nah, it's grand. I'm getting up now anyway.'

'Yeah, me too.' She smiled at him again.

'Yeah, I've got shit to do today, so …'.

'Oh … sure.' Jacqui looked at her nails, which were bitten down to the quick. 'I'll just … get going then.'

'Right.' Pajo yawned, stretched, and got out of bed. Jacqui riffled through her clothes, pulling on her underwear under the covers. She sat on the edge of the bed, plucked her jeans from the floor and put them on.

'It was a good night though, wasn't it?' She pulled on her top. 'The look on those girls' faces was gas.'

'Hmm?' said Pajo as he checked his phone.

'Right, well ...' she pulled on her boots and stood up by the end of the bed. 'I'll just ...'.

Pajo looked up from his phone. Jacqui was standing there wide-eyed, looking at him like she was some sort of simpleton.

'Got everything?'

She nodded and patted her handbag on her shoulder. 'So, I ...'.

'Here, I'll let you out,' he said. 'The door's locked.'

'Oh right, thanks. Thanks, Pajo.'

He unlocked the front door and opened it for her. A blast of daylight shone in.

'Oh God,' she said, putting her hand up to shield her eyes as she shuffled outside and laughed nervously. She turned to look at him.

'Okay,' she said. 'Will you call –?'

'I'll see you around, yeah?' he interrupted, making to close the door. In that instant, he saw her face fall. Maybe he had pushed her too far. He'd have to reel her back in a bit.

'Aren't you forgetting something, Jacqui?' He smiled.

'What's that?'

'Are you not gonna give me a goodbye kiss?' He tapped his cheek with his middle finger.

She smiled uncertainly and stepped towards him. She went to kiss his cheek, but then kissed him on the mouth instead, her chapped lips rubbing against his.

'That's my girl. Bye darlin'.'

She beamed, visibly bolstered by this tiny kindness as she tottered off into the daylight.

He closed the front door and boiled the kettle for tea in the kitchen. Jacqui was all right to have around, but he didn't want her getting ideas. He'd rode her a few times, and she was a good fallback if there was no one better around. He wasn't a good-looking guy, he knew that, but he appealed to a niche market. If there was a whiff of drugs or violence in the air, and they saw that he was at the centre of it, there was a certain type of woman who couldn't jump on his dick quick enough. That was just the reality of it. He could spot these girls a mile away. They were attracted to the potential danger of the situation. It got their blood pumping, made them eager, let them escape the crushing ordinariness of their lives. Or maybe he was a means for them to act out their self-loathing. If these girls wanted him to confirm what shitty and worthless people they were, he was happy to oblige.

One of his favourite things was taking photos on his phone. He'd managed to amass quite a collection. These girls always let him do what he wanted. Maybe some of them regretted it afterwards, but he never heard if they did. Some were so out of it they probably didn't even remember. He was never in the photos, at least his face wasn't. When he told them what to do, they listened. He liked them on their knees on cold bathroom floors. They swallowed what he gave them like good girls. He liked to cum on their pretty faces, to watch it drip down their cheeks, get in their hair.

The kettle whistled, and he filled up a cup with boiling water. Life was survival of the fittest. It was foolish to pretend otherwise – that power didn't exist and wasn't there to be used. He hated the word 'bully'. Nobody accused tigers of bullying antelope. They tore them limb from limb because it was in their nature to do it, because they could.

A tiger couldn't be anything but a tiger. No matter how you tried to dress it up, people were animals acting out their nature, fulfilling their own needs.

He had learnt this early on, had seen how the pack mentality was already in the boys back when he was in school. They congregated in the yard at break time, perfecting the art of cruelty. At first he was on the wrong side of it, and his mam made him go with her to the principal's office. They both looked at him like he was a stray dog in the rain. The mortification of it, being seen as a victim, as powerless. He despised them for it.

The truth of it was that he didn't want to punch anyone, but he recognised that if he wanted to change his situation he needed to do so with his fists. At the start of secondary school he signed up for boxing training, but he soon realised that he wasn't cut out for it. His reactions were slow; he was a stocky, lumbering thing. When he tried to work the skipping rope, it tangled around his giant feet. None of that mattered. A watcher, he took in what he needed, saw how the men in the gym carried themselves. All he needed to do was assume the posture. Then the boys in school heard he was a boxer, saw it in the way he carried himself. One fight – that was all he needed – one fight, and his reputation would precede him.

He got his chance with Eamon Devlin, the boy who was always looking for trouble. He had hair on his face by the age of 12 and was smoking twenty Johnny Blue a day by the age of 14. He was riding women – he claimed – by the age of 15, and getting served in the over-18 club with his fake ID. Word of the fight after school spread, as it always did in these situations, and the crowd of boys encircled Pajo and Eamon in the yard. Pajo could hear them shouting encouragement, mostly to his opponent, who everyone assumed would win. Eamon started the fight in the traditional manner, by shoving Pajo hard and *yelling, 'Come on!'* Pajo puffed out his chest, drew up his fists, and that's when he saw the look in Eamon's eyes, that flicker of fear and uncertainty, that slight step back. It was only a fraction of an inch, but a perceptible one to Pajo. It was all he needed. He knew then that he had already won. He landed a clean punch on Eamon's bristly jaw. *Smack.*

'Awwww –!' came the collective groan of the crowd. Eamon lunged at Pajo, pushing him hard again and trying to connect with his face, but Pajo blocked every scrappy throw.

'Hit him!' the boys cried in frustration. Pajo landed another punch, this time on Eamon's left eye.

'Ooh –!' groaned the crowd, a hint of *schadenfraude* audible in their voices. Eamon changed tack now and lowered his head, charging at Pajo like a disgruntled goat as he pummelled blows into Pajo's sides – the actions of a desperate man. Pajo knew he just had to bide his time. Winded now, he manoeuvred himself so he would be out of the way of Eamon's fists. He weaved into a better position as Eamon looked up. His eyes were two wide saucers that Pajo was determined to smash as he threw his final punch. *Smack!* Eamon fell to the ground in slow motion. He didn't get up. Pajo stood over him, fists still clenched, his heart caught in his chest. Eamon groaned, rolling over onto his side. You could almost see a ring of cartoon stars around his head. Pajo knew he had done enough.

Nobody bothered him after that. He discovered that the threat of violence was far more effective than the violence itself. Now he could control their reactions on tap, like Pavlov's dog. They had all seen the fight. With a flex of his muscles, a snarl of his lip, he could inspire the same terror again without getting his hands dirty. As he grew older and got into dealing, he discovered he could get others to do the dirty work for him. There were plenty of fellas like Hulk who were tightly coiled springs who only needed a guiding hand to direct their violence; and plenty of fellas like Walshy with a sly, conniving talent for finding out who was up to what and passing on what he needed to know. He mostly dealt hash in those early days, the odd bit of acid. Then it was pills, speed and coke – always something to be bought or sold, and he was the man who could get his hands on things.

He brought his tea into the sitting room and looked out the window as he drank. His view from the penthouse apartment looked down over the Spanish Arch and towards the Claddagh. Seagulls hovered like drones looking for targets. He could see himself reflected in the floor-to-ceiling window, and he liked what he saw. He'd been going hard at the gym, and it was paying off. He was muscular, solid, the product of discipline.

You couldn't let anyone get away with anything, even small fry like Kavanagh. They'd roughed him up once for dealing weed. Pajo was convinced that there was a rival supplier in Galway. He had heard rumours but couldn't get to the bottom of it. He thought Kavanagh might be behind it, but it turned out he didn't know anything. They'd put him in his place, and Pajo hadn't given him a second thought since, but something about last night was niggling at him. It had him thinking back to when he was younger and that first fight with Eamon all those years ago. He couldn't figure out why it was on his mind now when it was something he hadn't thought about in years. Then it clicked with him – last night he had seen the look of fear in Kavanagh's eyes, but then the little runt had surprised him with his bloodied hand, had knocked him off guard. It was a long time since that had happened to him and he didn't like the feeling. No, he didn't like it at all. He would have to keep an eye on that Kavanagh.

Chapter 5

Quay Street, nine a.m. Delivery trucks trundled along the cobbled street, ignoring pedestrianisation like war tanks rolling into enemy territory. Workers scrubbed away the evidence of last night's carousing like furtive murderers. Steam rose with the smell of disinfectant. The city was shedding its filthy skin. A newly mopped floor and here was Kavanagh, his arm in a sling – a testament to his mouldiness and stupidity – strolling through it with filthy shoes. Girls floated past him like fragrant ghosts, their skin fresh, their hair glinting in the morning light. A barman rolled seats and tables out of Neachtain's. Kavanagh had spoken to your man somewhere before but couldn't remember his name. The barman nodded to him in greeting. Kavanagh nodded back. 'Hoywa now?'

'Didn't think you'd be up at this hour, Kav.'

'Oh, you know me, fresh as a daisy. Any chance of a pint?'

'No, sorry, man, just coffee. Come back at twelve.'

A bell clanged out nine times. Everywhere, people were on their way to somewhere, except him. A failed actor from last night's scene who refused to leave the stage even though the new backdrop had been wheeled on. They'd given him a painkiller at the hospital. A pint would be a nice addition, would see him right.

Kavanagh saw his life as a line graph: a steady segment across the x-axis of *MEH-MEH-MEH,* interrupted by an occasional rise to a peak of *CRAIC! CRAIC! CRAIC!* This was usually followed by a sharp plummet into *DOOM DOOM DOOM,* until the line crept slowly back up to *MEH,* where it languished and lingered in a not particularly exciting fashion, until the next dip or peak. Right now, he was in a dip. In fact, the dip was so low it may have slid right off the bottom of the chart.

Lately, the peaks had been few and far between. He felt like life was the scaggy tail-end of a party he was trying to squeeze any last bit of craic out of as the same scratched record played on a loop. He wasn't really drinking or taking drugs to get high any more, it was just to keep along that steady line of nothing-muchness. He didn't quite know what he had been expecting his life to turn out like, but it wasn't this. Yet he didn't know how to go about fixing it. He'd had a series of jobs over the years since art school that he would be enthusiastic about at the start, but they never really stuck, or he never really stuck with them.

When he had gone to Thailand the previous summer for his friend Nogsy's wedding, a glittering alternative life beckoned. It seemed to him that you could live well there, live it up even, with little money. Nogsy was a different person out there. He was tanned for a start, and his new wife, Kannika, her family, and everyone at the bar called him Niall. It jarred in Kavanagh's ear. He had a surfboard. *A fucking surfboard.* Kavanagh laughed at that for a good half hour. *Fuck off, Nogsy. Are you serious?* He was all about the outdoors now, and he brought Kavanagh climbing what he said was a hill, but looked very much like a fucking mountain to Kavanagh. He trailed behind Nogsy, a cigarette in his mouth, sweating his balls off, the muscles in his legs screaming.

'Come on, bro. Not far to go. There's a killer view from up here.' Nogsy bounded ahead.

That was another new thing about Nogsy, or Niall. He'd picked up the habit of calling people *bro*. There was no irony in it. It was unnerving. Maybe Nogsy had always been this Niall character. Maybe this upbeat, positive surfer was always in him – a mutation waiting for the right conditions to spawn. Maybe Galway had been the wrong environment for Niall to prosper. Maybe he'd had no choice but to bitch about college projects and skip lectures with Kavanagh to chain-smoke and watch reruns of *Murder She, Wrote*.

Nogsy had never been the strongest artist in their class, but now he didn't make excuses or put other people's work down like he had done in college. When they finally got to the top of the hill/mountain, they sat looking at the view of the bright blue sea dotted with lush green islands stretching out on the horizon until it met a clear sky. They started chatting about the old days and what their classmates were up to. Nogsy was still finding the time and the enthusiasm to paint, despite his bar work.

'I know I'm never gonna be the best painter,' he shrugged. 'But that doesn't really matter. I just love doing it, you know? I can't *not* do it, so it's enough for me.'

'Sure,' said Kavanagh. 'That's great.'

'Thanks, bro. What about you? How's your work been going?'

Kavanagh started to spout on about the great series he was planning: his blue Galway paintings.

'I'm glad you're keeping at it, bro. You had more talent than the lot of us put together.'

Nogsy worked in a tourist-trap pub on Bangtao Beach. Kavanagh sat at the bar as Nogsy worked and got chatting to the people who came in. It was pleasant. There was a friendliness to it. *We're all on our holliers, lads!* Out of habit, he kept looking at the faces coming in the door to see if he knew anyone. He had to keep reminding himself that he was in Thailand. There was an air of unreality to it, sitting there with Nogsy, just like the old days but in this different environment – the familiarity of the company jarring with the utter alienness of his surroundings.

Kavanagh headed out by himself when Nogsy was tied up with preparations for the wedding. It was then that he came across the tattoo shop, right on the beach. The range of flash displayed on the walls was eclectic, with the usual standards he was used to seeing mixed with designs he had never seen before – from traditional Thai tigers, dragons and gods, to intricate Maori-inspired curves and spirals. The first day Kavanagh called in, a guy was getting a large tattoo on his back of a Thai warrior sitting astride a three-headed elephant. He couldn't help but look at it taking shape, casting glances at the man's back as he looked at the designs on the walls. The owner of the shop introduced himself. His name was Logan, and he was from New Zealand. When Kavanagh told him that he lived in Galway, Logan's face lit up. He had visited Ireland a few years before. Next thing, he was offering Kavanagh a beer and they were chatting, watching the three-headed elephant come into being on the man's back.

For the next few days, while Nogsy was busy with wedding preparations, Kavanagh hung out with the guys in the tattoo parlour, drinking ice-cold beers and playing darts. It was a busy spot filled with young Brits on their gap years, Irish guys and girls on their way to or from Australia, and people of all nationalities and walks of life. Girls in bikinis flitted in to get butterflies on their ankles, or roses to adorn their shoulders. It was all peace and love, like the Age of

Irony had never happened. National symbols were popular too. They did a great trade in Welsh dragons, shamrocks, and maple leafs. Travelling abroad seemed to stir up patriotic fervour in young people that could only be sated by having their national identity inked onto their flesh.

Kavanagh lamented how far from Thailand he was as he leaned on top of a bin and struggled to roll himself a cigarette with his free hand. He thought of the party, making his way to the front door as he trailed blood after him, waiting for the blonde girl in the white top to reappear so that they could leave together. He had been trying to impress her with the bottle trick, but instead had engaged her with his idiocy. It wasn't his style to chat up girls. Girls were like bees buzzing around at parties. If you sat still long enough, they would come to you. But this girl wasn't noticing him. Still, he had gotten her attention eventually, and she would have left with him and everything if it wasn't for Pajo.

An Atlantic breeze whistled through the laneways, and the drizzly rain carried the smell of a lost day at the seaside. It was always like this at the arse-end of summer the weather couldn't make up its mind – one minute it bathed Galway in sunshine, the next it spat rain. He heard the strains of 'Galway Girl' coming from a shop. Somewhere in Galway at all times, someone was playing 'Galway Girl'. Fucking 'Galway Girl'. If he heard that song one more time. *Been all over this world … ain't seen nothing like a Galway girl.* Yeah, ain't seen nothing like her tearing the arse out of it, elbowing her way to the front of the queue in Supermac's at four in the morning. Right about that, Steve Earle. He used to like Steve Earle and all. Jesus, that fuckin' song. Been all over the world? He had in his hole. Hadn't been to Thailand, that was for sure. Kavanagh realised that his mistake was coming home. He had been in paradise, sleeping in the beach hut, drinking with the guys from the tattoo parlour. It was all there, this life that he could be living now, and he'd left it. He'd gotten sucked straight back into this bottomless hole. He vowed that he would get the money together. Maybe he could convince Alex to let him sell weed again. If not, then as soon as his hand was out of this bloody sling, he'd find some type of work – any type of work – and save enough money to get the hell out of Galway once and for all.

*

When Stevie woke it was dark. After the party she had shuddered home, crawled into bed fully dressed, and slept through the remainder of the day. The wind howled outside and rain lashed the windows. The wind sounded like it could rip off the roof of the flat. She imagined indifferent children of gods, peering in at her doll's house, pointing to the tiny books in stacks on the floor and her desk piled high with papers, at her small form tucked up in her doll's bed. She got up and looked out of the window. She could hear the river but couldn't see it. The dark waters blended into the black night as the tree cast shadows into the room. The outside was threatening, reaching with gnarled fingers toward her throat, rapping at the window to be let inside. She heard a dripping noise and saw that water was coming in through one of the windows. She would have to call the landlord about that. There was some part of her that wanted to surrender to the elements, to strip off her pyjamas and stand with bare feet squelched in the grass by the river, to feel the jagged, biting rain cut into her bare skin. This thought brought Pam to mind – Pam with her scars on top of scars – and she felt her loss with a sharp pang.

Stevie had never given much thought to her body until it started to change and become an alien entity. She had always been something of a tomboy. Her Christian name, Stephanie, was discarded at a young age and left to gather dust along with the abandoned dolls under her bed. Her body existed as a functional form then. With skinny legs, she ran through fields and played soccer with her brother and his friends. Her freckled arms were thin as matchsticks, but she used them to punch back as good as she got, perfecting the art of dishing out dead arms and Chinese burns.

It all started around her fifteenth birthday. Her breasts began to grow, then her hips and thighs widened. Even her stomach seemed rounder and more pronounced. Whereas before her body was just there, she was now conscious of it. She tried not to think about it, to cover it up, but it was always complaining, telling her that it was too tired, or too hungry, or too fat fat fat. Food became different. It took on a new significance. She couldn't eat certain things, but she couldn't explain why. Bread became impossible. On her way to school each day, she began to throw away her packed lunches, lobbing them over a wall into some bushes. At dinner time she moved her food around her plate and put as little as possible in her mouth. She grew to enjoy the empty feeling in her stomach, to ignore her body's cries for food, instead savouring one apple cut up into tiny pieces and chewed methodically. She could move about now with a new lightness, an airy energy. Not eating had given her this feeling, and she liked it, so she became even more determined to avoid food. She shaved herself everywhere, clogging up the plughole with wet, dark-blonde hair.

Stevie felt her cheeks flush when the girls in school joked about their periods. Hearing them say they were 'on the blob', or 'on the jammy rag', made her stomach turn. By the time she was 16, she was always cold. She started wearing two thermal vests under her school uniform, a pair of tights and two thick pairs of socks. She no longer played soccer with her brother and his friends. Her periods stopped.

With each successive year of secondary school, student numbers fell as teenage mothers-to-be dropped out. Stevie's mother tutted and shook her head when she heard about them. 'You have to be so careful. It's different for girls. Your whole life would be ruined.' Stevie wondered what it would be like to have young parents. Her mum and dad still called the radio 'the wireless' and insisted the family eat fish on Fridays. Her friends didn't have parents like that.

When Stevie collapsed one day at school, her mother came to collect her and brought her to the doctor. Then there was a conversation that she couldn't follow. To her, it was just noises falling out of mouths, sounds reverberating off walls, and yet she knew that this conversation meant that everything was at risk. Her private territory, this secret that belonged to her, was now public. It had been given a name and now they wanted to take away this thing that had kept her company, made her feel strong. The doctor sent her into hospital, where they told her parents they would have to keep her in overnight and arrange a psychiatric evaluation.

'We just want you to get better,' said her mother. 'Your poor father is heartbroken.'

That night Stevie dreamt of the bushes on the way to school. They glowed a septic green, oozing months of uneaten sandwiches, lovingly prepared and wrapped in cling film.

It was in the psychiatric unit that she befriended Pam, a strawberry blonde with an upturned nose and a sprinkling of freckles on her face. They sat together in the day room, smoking cigarettes and drinking cup after cup of black coffee. They talked about everything except the reasons they were both there. Stevie couldn't figure out why Pam was in the unit until the day she reached up to get a book from the shelf and Stevie caught a glimpse of the inside of Pam's left arm – a messy patchwork of scarred skin, old wounds faded to white intertwined with newer red marks. She had an urge to leap from her seat, grab the arm and cover it in kisses.

One day, Pam said she wanted to do Stevie's hair. 'It'd look lovely in an up-do. You know, like for a debs.'

Stevie wasn't that keen on the idea, but she allowed Pam to sit her in a chair as she laid out a hairbrush, hairspray and clips on a small table beside them.

'You've gorgeous hair, do you know that?'

Stevie shrugged. 'Yeah?' She had never given much thought to her long dirty-blonde hair, and kept it that length more out of laziness then vanity.

'It'd look lovely with some highlights. Bring out the blonde more.' Pam started to brush the tangled mane. 'Do you know what you want to be, Stevie, when you finish school?'

'Dunno really. I like history.'

Pam wrinkled her nose. 'You mean like wars and stuff?'

'No, like really old stuff. Ancient artefacts and things like that.'

'Yeah? That's deadly, Stevie. You could work in Dublin Castle or something. I want to be a hairdresser. I want my own salon some day.'

'Are you sure that's a good idea, being around all those scissors?'

Pam set down the brush and her right hand instinctively flew to adjust her left sleeve, although it already covered her scarred skin. Stevie was about to apologise, tell Pam it had just come out, she didn't know why she'd said it, when Pam surprised her by snorting with laughter.

'Yeah, Stevie, and you should be a chef.'

They both erupted into a fit of giggles then, which they couldn't stop. As one trailed off, the other let out a hoot and the two of them started again.

'Oh my God!' Stevie clutched her stomach. 'I'm gonna die.'

Tears were streaming out of Pam's eyes. 'Oh Jesus, stop. I'm gonna piss myself. I'm gonna tell Dr Doyle on you, Stevie. You're a bad influence, so ya are.'

'Now, Pamela,' said Stevie in a man's deep voice, 'we can only help you if you want to help yourself.' She raised her hand to her face and mimed adjusting a pair of glasses. 'You must commit to recovery, Pamela. Are you committed?'

'We're all fuckin' committed around here, Dr Doyle.'

*

Stevie filled her pipe with tobacco and lit up. Wide awake now, she flicked through the pages of a history book, but couldn't focus on it. The fridge hummed. She felt like an intruder in her own home, like she could be caught at any moment and chastised for trespassing. *But this is my house,* she thought.

'This is my house,' she said aloud, and the voice that came back to her in the dark was strange. She began to hum a song, but her voice sounded odd and tuneless. Stevie stood up and walked over to the map of Ireland on the wall. One of the first things she had done when she moved in was to hang it up. It was the type of map that hung in primary school classrooms around the country so that children could learn the names of the provinces, the counties, the mountains and the rivers. The map served a dual purpose. Not only could she plan the sites she would visit for her research, it also hid a patch of damp that stained the peeling wallpaper. As a child, Ireland had looked alive to her. A mutated entity with straggly limbs bent backwards: the watery eye of Lough Neagh, the button nose of Downpatrick. When she had seen a map of the world for the first time, she was surprised at how tiny Ireland was: a dot of an island, off another island, off Europe.

When she was 17, Stevie went on a class trip to the National Museum and looked in wonder at the Ardagh Chalice and the Tara Brooch. She had learnt the story of the brooch in primary school, how a little girl had discovered it when playing near her home. It had inspired the 10 year-old Stevie to go out and dig the soil near her house, but all she uncovered were rusty nails and snail shells. Standing in front of the brooch at 17, she felt so far removed from her 10 year-old self as to be looking back on another person's life, or remembering a scene from a film. Most of her classmates were bored by the museum tour and barely looked at the exhibits. As the guide led them around, they whispered to each other and tried to make each other laugh, silenced occasionally by the icy glares of the teacher that promised retribution. Stevie didn't join in the giggling or elbowing. Since coming back from the psychiatric unit, she was no longer part of the group. Nobody said anything to her face, but she knew they talked about her. She could tell from the way they would fall silent sometimes and throw meaningful looks at each other when she walked into the classroom. She was marked now, separate. The guide led them to an exhibit, a stone carving of an emaciated female form with an oversized skull, legs splayed, and genitalia on display.

'Jaysus, what's that thing?' a girl in her class said.

'It's your ma,' said another classmate, and laughter erupted followed by an angry shushing from the teacher.

'This is a sheela-na-gig,' said the guide. 'They were primarily found on churches from the eleventh to the thirteenth century. Then there was an expansion of their use on castles and other stone structures during the fourteenth to the sixteenth century.'

Stevie listened, enraptured, as the guide pointed out some more examples, and explained how the sheela-na-gigs had only come to the attention of historians relatively recently, as many of the carvings had been destroyed or hidden away in the seventeenth century, following an order from the papal authorities for their removal.

'However, many sheela-na-gigs were found buried in graveyards or concealed in walls or gate pillars, suggesting local people held the figures in high esteem, and were unwilling to follow the orders of the Church to destroy them.'

This had planted the seed of interest for Stevie, and over the years, the more she learnt about them, the more the sheela-na-gigs appealed to her – the seeming anomaly of these lewd stone carvings reclining brazenly over the entrances to churches and sacred buildings, pagan fertility symbols in houses of God.

Standing in front of the map, Stevie traced her finger over the red marks she had drawn onto it. She had stuck small red stickers on the places she planned to visit for her research. Each dot represented a sheela-na-gig she would catalogue. Standing back, she surveyed the map – a mutant child with measles. There were clusters of dots in certain areas. She had joined up some of the dots with lines, plotting a trajectory for the trips she would make. Eventually she would visit them all and duly cover the walls of her flat with photographs, maps and notes on index cards.

Already, she had stuck up some photocopied pictures of sheela-na-gigs so she could compare their similarities and differences in appearance. They were as individual as people with their variances in size, shape and expression, but they were all unmistakably the same, unmistakably connected. Carved from stone, they were for the most part bald with large skull-like heads, some smiled, some grimaced, and others had neutral expressions. They stood or squatted in an act of display with thighs spread and one or both hands pointing to or touching exaggerated genitals. Most either had no breasts or the drooping breasts of old women. Some had been carved to show emaciated ribs, others displayed scratches on the head and body.

Stevie made a cup of tea and sat down. As she surveyed the map and the pictures, she felt her unease start to retreat. There was something reassuring about seeing her work surrounding her: a constant visual reminder of what was done and all that was left to do, and her incubated within the walls of it like a womb.

Chapter 6

'I brought you some milk.' Kavanagh stood scanning the coffee table for a space that wasn't taken up by overflowing ashtrays, Rizla papers, chocolate wrappers or empty cups. There wasn't one. He placed the carton on the floor.

'Ah sound, thanks, man,' said Alex.

Alex seemed to survive on a diet of tea and chocolate. Kavanagh couldn't remember the last time he'd seen him outside. He was watching a film that was projected onto the white wall in front of them. A lady in a ball-gown sat beside a man wearing a monocle at a candlelit dining table.

'Which one is this again?' asked Kavanagh.

'*Smiles of a Summer Night.*' Alex's curtains were always drawn, and he was always watching some film or other, invariably something by Bergman. He seemed to be in one of his quieter moods tonight. Sometimes you couldn't stop him talking. An armchair philosopher, he would theorise and pontificate for hours to his rapt audience of one. Other nights they would smoke quietly, and Alex would look surprised to see that Kavanagh was still there when he stood up to leave.

'Cup of tea?' said Alex.

'Sure, thanks.' Kavanagh began removing a pile of books from the sofa with his free hand so that he could sit down.

'Stick on the kettle there so,' said Alex, without taking his eyes from the film.

In the kitchen, Kavanagh cursed his sling as he struggled to fill up the kettle. He found two cups in the sink and gave them a cursory rinse under the tap. Squeezing the teabag against the edge of the cup was tricky, and he nearly knocked over the cup with his first attempt. Trying to carry the two cups of tea in one hand turned out to be a mistake. One tilted downwards and tea splashed onto both his jeans and the floor.

'Ah, fuck!'

He set one of the cups down on the counter and brought them in one at a time.

'Thanks,' said Alex, as Kavanagh placed the cup beside him. 'I fucking love Bergman.'

Kavanagh smiled to himself. 'Really, Alex? You don't say.'

'Here, skin up there if you like, Kav.'

'Ah, I can't really.' Kavanagh took a sup of tea and nodded towards his sling.

Kavanagh knew that there were a few others like him who called up and chatted with Alex and left with wrapped packages to distribute to friends. He didn't know who these people were. They were never there when Kavanagh arrived. Alex juggled his friends like a seasoned adulterer, making as little reference to the others as possible, and referring to them only in the vaguest possible terms.

'You know there's a drought on. You could make a killing, Alex.'

'Hmm?' Alex continued to look at the film.

Kavanagh sighed. Alex wasn't motivated by money. He didn't need it, or seemed not to at any rate. So Kavanagh tried flattery.

'You have no idea, Alex, of the shit these poor Galwegians are smoking. The dregs of Spain and Amsterdam. Yours is the best stuff in the whole country.'

Alex laughed at that and looked at him. 'Come off it, Kav.'

'You'd be acting in the national interest.'

'Too risky …' Alex turned back to the film. 'Since … you know. I've heard things about that lad. You should stay well out of his way.'

When Kavanagh had the run-in with Pajo and his goons, he had tried to lie about the black eye, but Alex had seen straight through him.

'Look, Kav, let's just keep it small, yeah? A cottage industry, isn't that what they call it?'

The plants were notoriously difficult to maintain, but Alex had no problems with them. They thrived under his care in the little room beneath the lamps he had set up for them. Kavanagh wondered if Alex spoke to them about Bergman when he was on his own. Maybe they shared his passion for cinema and were growing taller and taller in the hopes of peeping out into the sitting room and viewing the films for themselves.

'How's the painting going?' Alex asked.

'Ah, it's not. But I'm working on some tattoo designs. Gotta get some practice in before I head over to Thailand.'

'Yeah? That's cool, man.'

'Man, I should have just stayed over there.'

'You'll get back there if it's meant to be.'

'If it's meant to be? I wouldn't have had you down as a fatalist, Alex.'

Alex grinned. 'Sure, what's for you won't pass ya. When God closes one door, he opens a window.'

'Always opening windows, that fella. Letting all the heat out.'

It was only much later, when the credits had rolled, the ashtray had been filled and Kavanagh was standing up to leave that Alex looked at him properly for the first time as he handed him the package of weed. 'Jesus, man. What happened to your hand?'

Chapter 7

Jacqui Maloney stood manning the entrance to the dressing rooms. She absent-mindedly checked the number of items a teenage girl in the queue was holding before handing her the corresponding number tag and resuming her daydream about Pajo. She imagined him surprising her after work, waiting for her with a bunch of bright yellow flowers. Then he would bring her out to dinner, and in that candlelight, would lean in and whisper….

A woman exiting the dressing rooms distracted her from her reverie. She let out a loud sigh as she walked towards Jacqui.

'No joy, love?' Jacqui reached to take the clothes back from the woman.

The woman shook her head and tutted. 'Why do they always look nicer on the hanger?'

Jacqui smiled in recognition. 'Tell me about it.'

Jacqui knew from experience whether customers would buy the items they tried on or hand them back to her. She had gotten the job straight after she finished secondary school – same shit, different day. She had been working there the longest of the floor staff but had never been promoted to manager. Never expected it. Young ones who had started years after her now told her when to go on a break. She was passed over, and yet she had some sort of seniority because she knew everything, and she could explain to the new people in her slightly impatient way that these were not the right hangers and those shirts were folded all wrong. These fly-by-nights, college students, part-timers who never stuck it out for long – they were tourists here while she was a permanent resident.

She rezipped and rebuttoned the items of clothing as she fixed them on the hangers ready to go back out on the shop floor. The world of the shop was different from the real world: under the fluorescent lights they sold aspirational dreams in Lycra, knock-offs of designer trends in polyester, the latest Milan fashions mass-produced in Mauritius. Jacqui spent her days stocking items that were all out of whack with the seasons: bikinis, flip-flops and beach bags for a summer she knew was never going to arrive. She was putting Christmas decorations on shelves before Hallowe'en had even passed.

Jacqui tried to resume the daydream, but she felt stupid all of a sudden. She knew in her heart that the man she was imagining was not the real Pajo. This scenario she had concocted would never happen. That was okay, she told herself. There were different types of love, not just the soppy sort that you saw in films. She loved Pajo, and nobody could take that from her. The important thing in life was whom you loved, not who loved you back. She had decided this early on and had spent a lifetime perfecting the art of unrequited love. She beamed it, a one-way channel.

Growing up, the person she loved the most was her father, although she had never met him. All she knew of him was the dismissive shake of her mother's head when Jacqui asked questions about him. But Jacqui heard things through the thin walls at night when her mam and her Auntie Sharon sat up sometimes listening to music, drinking wine and smoking. She tried to piece it all together from the snippets that floated up with the cigarette smoke – stolen gifts to her hungry ears. Her mother was still young, and in the company of her sister she was younger still, laughing and gossiping and singing along with the radio as Jacqui listened, her ear pressed against the coldness of the wall.

She knew that her father was somewhere in the city, and that her mother used to work with him before Jacqui was born. She had heard her mother saying something about his car and the leather seats. Jacqui would sit on the wall by the roundabout at the edge of the estate and study the passing cars. Maybe her father was driving one of them. Dreams of her father were elaborate and all-consuming. She became convinced that he was keeping an eye on her, some benevolent man who would reveal his presence when the time was right. One of these days he would pull up at the side of the road and call, 'Jacqui!' and she would sit in the front seat beside him with music playing. He might bring her into town to Griffin's for tea and a chocolate eclair. Every birthday and Christmas she thought to herself, *maybe this year.*

When she was 8, her mam started vomiting in the bathroom in the mornings even when she hadn't been drinking the night before. Then she told Jacqui she was going to have a new brother or sister.

'Does this mean my dad will visit?'

Her mother shook her head. 'I'll explain when you're older.'

Jacqui cringed now whenever she looked back on the time she had spent trying to make her father appear through sheer will. She was so focused on this phantom parent who never materialised that she didn't appreciate the parent she did have. Her mother was gone, and now it was too late.

'Jacqui!' She heard a familiar voice calling her from across the shop floor. She looked up with a start to see her younger brother making his way towards her. He was with some crusty guy, one of those straggly winos from Eyre Square. They were talking loudly and staggering about the place.

'Hey, Jacqui, howya?' He was standing in front of her, a dazed look on his face. She was so mortified she could barely look at him.

'What are you doing here?' she hissed in an angry whisper.

The security guard came over. 'Is everything okay, Jacqui?'

'Grand, it's grand, Kev,' she said. She could feel her cheeks burning.

'S'grand!' said Maloney, slurring his words. 'Just having a chat with my sister. Nothing wrong with that, is there?'

Jacqui looked around in embarrassment. Shoppers passing by were rubbernecking like they were passing a traffic accident.

Jacqui looked at Kev, a look that said *please don't make this a bigger scene than it already is.* He nodded, then backed away. 'If you need me, just shout.'

Jacqui waited for him to walk away. She grabbed her brother by the elbow and marched him over into the quietest corner she could find. 'What the hell do you think you're doing?'

'Well, we were passing, you know, and I hadn't seen ya for a while, and …'.

'I'm in work now.'

'I know. It's just that me and Grover…'.

'Who the fuck is Grover?'

'My friend over there.' He nodded towards the man he'd arrived in with who was perusing a rack of women's pyjamas. 'He's got six dogs!'

'I don't care how many dogs he's got. What do you want?'

'See, the thing is we're a bit short of money and we kind of owe this guy …'.

Jacqui shook her head. 'I'm broke. Pay day's not until tomorrow.'

Maloney's face fell. 'Even like a few quid would help, like …'.

Jacqui reached into her pocket and handed him a €20 note. 'This is the last time. I mean it.'

'Thanks, sis. I'll pay you back,' said Maloney. 'Here, Grover!' he shouted. 'Let's go, yeah?'

Chapter 8

There was something reassuring about returning to education in September. *I must be institutionalised,* Stevie thought to herself as she put her books, pencil case and notebook into her shoulder bag. She had enjoyed going shopping for them during the week, but then she was the type of person who could spend hours in stationery shops mooning over diaries and fondling envelopes; the type of person who got a giddy thrill from picking out a stapler. Although she hadn't always enjoyed her school years, there was something reassuring about the routine of it.

After graduating from her history degree in Trinity College, she had struggled. Her *Indiana Jones* fantasies of unearthing artefacts in exotic locales were soon put to rest. Archaeological digs meant crouching in mud and dirt, shivering in ditches, pipe-smoking in drizzle. Her frame was slight and she felt the cold easily. Her muscles would ache from the brute strength required to heave dirt and rocks and wheel trundling wheelbarrows. Besides which, this type of work was sporadic at best, and hardly a reliable stream of income. There seemed few options post graduation other than to train to become a teacher, as Orlaith, Caitríona and several other people from her class had done. Stevie tried to visualise it, but it was an image that refused to appear.

Others in her class had gone off travelling to Australia or the States, but that wasn't an option for Stevie.

She spent a few years office-temping, manning reception desks, battling with switchboards and dutifully shuffling bits of paper as a desk-monkey in a succession of businesses. This was during the boom years when companies had money to burn and thought nothing of bringing in temporary staff at exorbitant rates. There was always some task that the staff either didn't want to do or didn't have time to do themselves. It was usually menial in nature: inputting data, filing, or preparing batches of letters or FedEx parcels. Stevie didn't mind this type of work. In fact, the less taxing, the better. Once she got a handle on what she was doing, she fell into a rhythm where she could do the work but let her thoughts drift completely free. She re-watched historical documentaries in her mind. She stretched herself to recall facts she had memorised for college exams, important dates and discoveries. Sometimes she had conversations with characters from the past in her mind's eye. Druids would confide in her their visions. Monks in their round towers would confess to her their fears of attack as they toiled with ink over vellum pages. She could have gone on like that quite happily, an oracle to lost worlds in the midst of temples of modernity where deals were done and gods of prosperity worshipped.

Then, over the years, the jobs changed. From six-month contracts in multinational bastions of glass and light in Dublin's financial district, she was offered a day here or there in one of the business parks on the outskirts of the city, in places like Sandyford or Bluebell. Whereas before the work had been consistent, sometimes with a few different jobs to choose from, gaps began to grow between assignments of a week, two, sometimes more. Then the gaps between assignments started to get longer. Things were changing. She realised the full extent of this shift when she had a two-week assignment in Bray in a computer company and the workers were threatening to strike: a large part of the company was being relocated to Hyderabad in India. Every day the news was filled with stories of multinationals shutting down their Irish bases. It was around this time that Stevie decided to actively pursue going back to college for her Ph.D., an idea she had been toying with on and off for years. Maybe academia was the way to go after all.

Today was an induction session at the university for all new Ph.D. candidates. Her supervisor, Dr Bodkin, had asked her and the other medieval history students to arrive early so that they could meet each other before the session. Stevie had only been to the university once before, for her initial meeting with Dr Bodkin. She walked over the narrow Salmon Weir Bridge. The footpath was full of other students heading in the direction of the university. Cyclists and cars flew past in a steady stream. In the River Corrib below, a fisherman in waterproof trousers waded, casting his reel into the fast-flowing current that sparkled with dappled light. The bells of the imposing green-roofed cathedral rang out as Stevie passed. In the canal, three swans floated by, a startling splash of white against the dark background of the water. A group of canoeists in wetsuits were gathered at the edge, about to enter.

Stevie turned right and walked down the path to the university. Across the playing fields, she looked towards the quadrangle, a beautiful building at the front of the campus, all stone and creeping ivy. She had been impressed by its imposing structure the first time she had visited. The rest of the buildings on campus were somewhat less impressive, a hodgepodge of architecture that had been built at various stages over the years with seemingly little thought to any kind of overall stylistic coherence. So it was that Soviet-bloc-style towers made unlikely neighbours with Portakabins and the odd two-storey building that looked like it had been transplanted from some suburban housing estate.

Inside the main concourse, Stevie stood in line for tea from the ground-floor kiosk. The smell of burnt cheese wafted through the line. It seemed the students travelled in packs for safety and all dressed the same. The boys wore hoodies and jeans or tracksuit bottoms. The girls wore hoodies, short skirts, thick black tights and Ugg boots. Stevie was conscious of the noise her high heels made on the tiled floor. She had wanted to make a good impression, so had erred on the side of caution and worn her office temping wardrobe of trousers, high heels and a blouse instead of her usual day-to-day clothing, which generally consisted of some variation of black jeans, converse, a white top and a black cashmere sweater. She realised she was probably overdressed and began to feel slightly ridiculous, like she was playing the part of a secretary in a trashy TV show. Some of the first year students looked so young and fresh-faced with expectant eyes. Stevie realised it was ten years since she had been in their position. A whole decade since she had started her undergraduate degree, just before her nineteenth birthday, and here she was, 29 years old, about to embark on another three years of study in a new city where she hardly knew anyone.

The history department was in one of the two tower blocks. Stevie travelled up to the top floor in the creaking lift. A large, draughty window overlooked the grey cement courtyard below, dominated by a bright yellow modern sculpture, an eyesore of tangled metal, like some piece of debris washed up on a beach. Stevie looked at the people below, milling about, bathing their faces in sunlight, or sitting on benches reading, smoking or chatting. Beyond the campus, rows of grey houses stretched out into the distance.

She knocked on Dr Bodkin's office. The door swung open and a middle-aged blonde woman in tortoise-shell glasses beamed at her.

'Stevie! Lovely to see you again.'

'You too,' smiled Stevie. In their previous meeting, Dr Bodkin had shown such enthusiasm for her subject, and for Stevie's proposed research, that at times she had literally rubbed her hands together gleefully. She had that quality that Stevie knew to be rare in academics: knowledgeable without being an insufferable know-it-all.

'Welcome, welcome,' said Dr Bodkin, shaking Stevie's hand. 'The troops are here. Let me introduce you.'

She ushered Stevie into the office that she would be sharing with the other Ph.D. candidates, where they each had a locker and shared use of some computers and a printer. The room was bright, with a view of traffic whizzing over the Quincentennial Bridge and the River Corrib below, snaking off beyond the horizon.

'Stevie, I'd like you to meet Adrienne. Adrienne is researching poetry and the bardic tradition.'

'Hi, Adrienne. Nice to meet you. That sounds really interesting.'

'Thanks,' mumbled Adrienne, looking at a spot on the floor and fiddling with the sleeve of an oversized purple cardigan that swamped her tiny frame. She had a pale face, dark hair, and squinty eyes framed by her most prominent feature: two thick caterpillar eyebrows that looked like they were plotting a way to crawl towards each other and meet in the middle of her forehead.

'I'm Gavin,' came the booming voice of a stocky man who was bulging out of a T-shirt that was printed with the words: 'Historians Do It For Posterity!' He had blonde hair, but his patchy beard was red, causing a visual disconnect. He looked like one of those paintings you might see in an Anglo-Irish 'big' house – a moneyed, buffoonish expression that betrayed years of inbreeding and a penchant for blood sports. He held out a sweaty paw for Stevie to shake. 'I'm researching medieval weaponry.'

'Nice to meet you, Gavin. I'm Stevie.'

'I asked you to come here a bit early today so that you'd have a chance to meet each other and talk about your research,' said Dr Bodkin. 'Pretty soon you'll all be so busy with your own modules and studies that you may not see each other from week to week, so it's nice to touch base now before things get too hectic.'

'Are you the girl who is researching sheela-na-gigs?' Gavin asked.

Stevie nodded. 'Yeah, that's me.'

'Yes, they are rather interesting, aren't they?' he bellowed. 'Mysterious objects. Do you subscribe to the notion of the Romanesque theory?'

Dr Bodkin caught Stevie's eye and smiled. Something told her it was going to be a long day.

Chapter 9

Finn looked out the window of Dúch. The street outside was quiet. There was still no sign of Kavanagh. When Kavanagh had approached him and said he wanted to learn how to become a tattoo artist, Finn had agreed to take him on as an apprentice. He had shown Finn a few drawings and they weren't half bad, and he had warmed to Kavanagh straight away, seen something of himself in the fellow floundering art school graduate who was trying to find his way. But now he was beginning to have his doubts.

This is how it had been going for the last couple of weeks: Kavanagh would come in late, oftentimes smelling like a hangover. He would pace, look out the window, pace, sit down for a bit, yawn, pace, repeat – like a dog that needed to be walked. He seemed to know everyone and he kept seeing people he knew walking past the shop. He would leap up and run to the door and yell *Howya Jim?!* or *Howya Mary?!*, and proceed to have lengthy conversations on the footpath. He would offer to go and pick up Finn's lunch or coffee, but would invariably get the order wrong. Throughout the day he would 'just pop out for a bit', disappearing for large swathes of time, and return stinking of weed. It was hard to be angry with him though because he seemed genuinely interested in tattooing. Whenever Finn was working on a client, Kavanagh hovered behind him and studied the process intently. He looked at the displays of designs and traced his fingers over the lines as if committing them to memory.

Finn asked him to work on some designs of his own. He could see that Kavanagh had talent, but it was unfocused. He was lazy. There was no finesse. No additional time spent. He seemed happy with just being okay. Maybe it was his fault. Maybe he needed to be more like his old mentor, Eight Ball, authoritarian and menacing, but it just wasn't in his nature. The thing was, for Finn, it was a difficult process to explain logically. For him, the tattoo was already there. It was underneath the skin. If he explained this to people it would sound strange, so he didn't, but he had met other tattoo artists who had experienced the same thing. It was a conversation, a type of communion. They almost entered a trance-like state where everything disappeared but the needle and the flesh. Finn told himself that everyone had to start somewhere, and he remembered being as clueless as Kavanagh. Well maybe not quite as clueless, but pretty green.

Finn was fresh out of art school and still called Fionn when he spent a year in San Francisco, learning his apprenticeship from a bald-headed, old-school hard-ass who went by the name of Eight Ball. It was a fortuitous encounter, and he seized it while he had the chance. He was hovering in the doorway, looking at the tattoo designs on the wall. The range was beyond anything he had seen back home in Ireland. There were all of the classic American designs: flags and eagles and Sailor Jerry pin-ups. He knew he wanted a tattoo, but it needed to mean something. A good-luck amulet he could carry with him, like the boys going off to war who got their tattoos in Honolulu's Chinatown before shipping off to Japan. As he was looking at the designs, an argument was breaking out in the shop.

'Fuck you, man,' spat a kid who couldn't have been more than 19 as he backed out of the shop. His hands were balled into fists, his cheeks flushed, his voice trembling.

'Get out of here before I kick your skinny ass,' yelled the older bald man. He reached for the nearest thing to hand, which happened to be a half-drunk cup of Coke. He flung it at the kid's retreating back. It landed on the footpath, where the lid came off. Coke splashed up the back of the kid's legs and ice cubes puddled at his feet.

'You're an asshole, man,' said the kid.

With that, the older man seemed tickled. He let out a belly laugh. 'Tell me something I don't know.'

The kid pushed past Finn and stomped off down the street, pausing for a moment to give the place the finger and spit on the ground.

'Sorry about that,' the man said to Finn, beckoning him into the shop. 'Kids these days, huh?'

It turned out the kid had been Eight Ball's apprentice, and now there was a vacancy, so Finn came to be Eight Ball's new apprentice. All he did for the first six months was clean, pick up the lunch orders and watch Eight Ball at work. The buzzing noise of the needle was constant. Some days it could cut right through him and sounded like the sickening noise of a dentist's drill, but if the mood was right and he was feeling upbeat, he heard it as a hummingbird flitting about in the summer sun.

Eight Ball was old-school, unapologetically so. 'You fucking black T-shirt kids,' he would rant in Finn's general direction. 'You can't design. You got your stencils. You got your needles preloaded. Think you know it all now but you don't know shit.'

Finn would present him with one of his designs, and he would look it over, then look at Finn and shake his head. 'This ain't it, man. Not even close.'

But something, stubbornness perhaps, kept Finn coming in, day in, day out. He was soaking everything up like a sponge. He saw the intricacies of Eight Ball's designs, the attention to detail he put into every tattoo. He thought he would probably see out the entire apprenticeship without ever laying his hands on a tattoo gun. Then one day, seemingly out of nowhere, Eight Ball looked at him, placed his hand on Finn's shoulder and said, 'You're ready.'

The Americans found it hard to get their heads around the word Fionn. *Dude, your name's Fun? What did you say? Oh, Fee-yone? Huh?* For a time, Eight Ball called him Funyun. *Adapt or die*, he thought to himself one day as he looked Eight Ball in the eye and said, 'Call me Finn.' So he came back to Ireland four years later with a new name, a West Coast twang, and a sleeve of the best tattoo work that side of the Atlantic.

Finn was doing some sketching when he saw Kavanagh come into the shop. He glanced at the clock on the wall. He was over an hour late. He saw that Kavanagh's arm was in a sling, a sheepish look on his face.

'Sorry, I should have rang. I, uh, had a bit of an accident.'

'What happened?'

Kavanagh relayed some story of trying to open a wine bottle at a party and ending up in the hospital getting stitches.

'Wait, you put the bottle in your shoe?' said Finn.

'It works, honestly,' insisted Kavanagh, as Finn laughed. 'Well, it's not supposed to break, obviously. So, yeah. I'm out of action for a while.'

'Well, look, take it easy for a bit until you're recovered.'

Kavanagh nodded. 'Okay. Also, I … uh … ordered a tattoo gun, a miniature one, online. '

'You what?'

'Yeah, I wanted to get a bit of practice in, you know?'

'Have you used it?'

'Yeah, wanna see?'

'Sure.'

Kavanagh rolled up his trouser leg and showed Finn an intricate Celtic knot on his calf.

'I only had black ink, so …'.

'Did you trace this out?'

'No, I did it freehand.'

He could see that Kavanagh wanted some kind of validation. It was a decent effort, but the shading was off and it looked flatter than it could have done. Finn shook his head and heard his old mentor's words emerging from his own mouth, 'This ain't it, man. Not even close.'

'I know, I know,' said Kavanagh.

'Look, I mean, it's not bad for a first attempt, but you should have waited … I don't think you get this whole apprentice thing. I take this seriously. If you want to learn about this stuff, you have to watch and learn and try to take in all you can.'

Kavanagh nodded. 'Fair enough, yeah. I hear what you're saying.'

'So, give it some thought over the next few weeks. If you're really serious about this and you want to come back, give me a shout. We can have a chat about it.'

Kavanagh nodded. 'Okay.'

'And keep that shit clean. Did you cover it with cling film?'

'Yeah,' Kavanagh lied.

Finn grabbed a bunch of antiseptic wipes and placed them in Kavanagh's good hand. 'Here, take these with you.'

'Thanks, Finn.' Kavanagh ambled towards the door. 'I'll be in touch,' he called over his shoulder.

Chapter 10

The shop was full of second-hand furniture, like the mismatched home of some ragged family. A kitchen table and four chairs stood beside an outdated velvet sofa with ornate wood panelling, and a children's desk painted with flowers. Nestled at the back, Stevie spotted a bookcase – dark wood with three shelves. They were spaced widely apart, perfect for her taller history books.

'Excuse me, how much for the bookcase?' she asked the man behind the counter.

'Twenty Euro.'

'Twenty? Okay.' Stevie nodded.

'But for you, twenty-five.'

'Oh, twenty-five …?'

'Ah, I'm only coddin' ya!' The man laughed a booming laugh that filled up the shop and caused all heads to turn towards them. He leaned towards her and in a low conspiratorial voice said, 'Are you a student, are ya?'

'I am, yeah.'

'How much do you want to pay for it?'

'Well, I …'.

'Sure, give us a fiver.'

'A fiver?'

'Yeah.'

'Are you sure?'

'Ah yeah. Call it a student discount. Do you need a hand bringing it to your car?'

'Oh, no thanks. I've no car but I'm just around the corner.'

'Grand, I'll move it for you now.' He picked up the bookcase and left it by the door for her.

'Thanks a lot.' Stevie handed him the money.

'No worries. Here, do you like this fella?' The man pointed to a religious statue beside the till of a small porcelain boy wearing a a crown and a garish red and gold cloak.

'Oh, yes, he's very …' Stevie searched for the right word.

'Isn't he?' The man nodded in agreement and looked at the statue in open appreciation. 'That's the Child of Prague. He'll keep an eye on ya.' He reached for the statue and put it in a plastic bag.

'Oh, no, I….

'He comes with the bookcase.'

'Oh right, okay. Thanks.'

'Sure you can manage now with that?'

'Ah yeah, fine thanks.'

Stevie was surprised by the weight of the bookcase. The man had made lifting it look so effortless. She could feel his eyes on her so she summoned all her strength, turned to smile at him before lifting the bookcase, then shuffled crab-like out the door. She managed to get around the corner before lowering the bookcase to the ground, the muscles in her arms screaming with relief.

A familiar figure walked towards her. He smiled at Stevie as he held up his right hand, which was resting in a sling. 'Well, if it isn't Florence Nightingale.'

'Oh, hey, you're alive!' said Stevie. 'I was worried about you. It wasn't too serious I hope?

'Nah, just got some stitches. I'll live. I don't think we were properly introduced. I'm Joe, but everyone calls me Kavanagh.'

'Nice to meet you. I'm Stevie.'

'Stevie,' he repeated, smiling at her. 'I like that.'

'Thanks. I'd, ah, shake your hand, but, you know ...'. She laughed and gestured towards his sling.

'Here, I'll help you with this, if you like. Where are you headed?'

'Wood Quay.'

He picked up one side of the bookshelf and winced.

'Oh, mind your hand.'

'Ah, it's grand.'

They got to the end of the street before he stopped. 'Smoke break?'

'Sure.' Stevie accepted a cigarette from Kavanagh's packet. They lit up and leaned on the bookcase.

'I hope I'm not keeping you.'

Kavanagh shook his head. 'Nah, I'm just on my way home. I was at the dole office. They're on at me to do a FÁS course.'

'Oh yeah? In what?'

'Fuck knows. Welding or some shit. This sling should buy me a bit of time anyway. They never have courses in things you might actually want to learn.'

'Yeah, what they should really offer is a FÁS course that teaches you how to avoid having to do FÁS courses.'

'I'd sign up for that,' said Kavanagh. 'It's not like I'm *not* looking for work, ya know? It's just there's fuck all out there at the moment.'

'Tell me about it. That's mainly why I decided to go back to college. I was doing a bit of office temping. A day here, a day there, but it was going nowhere.'

'Everyone's going back to college these days. We must have the most educated dole queues in the world.'

Kavanagh flicked away his cigarette butt and smiled. 'Right.' He smacked his good hand on top of the bookshelf for emphasis. 'Let's get this show on the road.'

*

They placed the bookcase against the wall in Stevie's flat, and Kavanagh took in the small but cosy surroundings.

'Nice. So who do you share this place with?'

'Just myself.' Stevie pulled back the curtains and light poured into the room.

'Aw man, I'm a bit jealous now, I have to say. I've Gary and Dan to put up with.'

'Oh, those guys. Yeah, I met them at the party. The spatula twins.'

Kavanagh laughed. 'I'll tell them they have a new nickname. They'll be delighted with that.'

'Ah no, they seemed sound.'

'Yeah, they're not the worst. I can see now why you need this.' Kavanagh gestured towards the stacks of books and folders piled up on the floor. 'Are you a writer or something?'

'No, I'm studying history.'

'Oh.' Kavanagh felt his heart sinking like a stone. 'Like my father.'

'Really?'

'If you start talking about DeVelara and the Free State, I'm out of here.'

Stevie laughed. 'It's the medieval stuff I'm into. A bit before Dev's time. Is your dad a teacher?'

'He was. Actually, he used to teach at my secondary school.'

'Oh. That must have been ...'.

Kavanagh nodded. 'Yeah, it was pretty fucking embarrassing, but I wasn't in his class so I suppose it could have been worse.'

Kavanagh had cultivated a lack of interest in history to avoid having to take his father's subject. Seeing his father in the halls was bad enough; actually sitting in his class and listening to a continuation of his dinner-time historical lectures would have been too much to bear. The boys called him 'Spittalfields': he was so passionate about his subject that he was in the habit of frothing at the mouth during his nationalist tirades. Kavanagh wasn't sure if his father knew about the nickname, but all things considered he had got off lightly compared to the teacher with the nervous tick that the students called 'Twitchy Ferguson', or the unfortunate geography teacher who was lumped with the succinct but cutting 'Stench'.

'So, would you like a cup of tea?' asked Stevie.

'How about a pint?' Kavanagh smiled. 'I suppose I kind of owe you a drink after smashing up your wine.'

*

'Best seat in the house,' said Kavanagh as they sat in the snug in Neachtain's. They placed their drinks on the small round table that had an old map of the world under its glass top. 'That's the great thing about daytime drinking – no packed pubs. Your choice of seats.'

Someone was playing jazz standards on the old piano in the corner. The plinky-plonky strains of 'All of Me' drifted over to them.

'Looks like this is my new local.' Stevie took a sip of wine.

'Oh yeah?' said Kavanagh. 'Do you come here a lot?'

'Well, this is my second time. I only moved here recently for college.'

'Ah, you lucked out so. This is my favourite pub. There's a couple of nice ones down the west as well.'

'Down the west?'

'Over the river.'

'Oh yeah, I know where you mean,' said Stevie.

'It's a small place really. More a town than a city in a lot of ways.'

'Yeah, I like it though. How long have you lived here?'

'Too fucking long,' said Kavanagh. 'But I've concocted an escape plan.'

'Oh yeah?'

'Thailand.'

'Oh right, you're gonna move over there?'

'Yeah. That's the plan anyway. See, I was over there last year. A friend of mine was teaching over there and he married a Thai girl so I went over for the wedding. Man, I should have stayed put. It's like something out of a film. White beaches, palm trees … monkeys.'

Stevie laughed. 'Monkeys?'

'Have you been over there?'

'No, I haven't.'

'I learnt to swim over there and everything. Well, kind of. The water was like a bath. I'm telling ya, I've drank cups of tea colder than that sea.'

Stevie traced a finger around the edge of her wineglass. 'It sounds amazing.'

'It is. I can't wait to go back.'

This was how it had been for Stevie with friends over the past few years, always someone moving some place, or someone coming back from some place, an endless rotation

of leaving dos and returni
England, America. One con
seemed every person her age
musical chairs. She sat and s
turned to travel, which it inva
everyone was looking outward:
Stevie felt like she was at odds w
she was in a permanent state o
past, at the secrets in the moss
revealed. Travel was such a part ... ... vernacular for people
her age that there was almost a presumption that she shared
these experiences: the J1 visa in America, crammed into an
apartment with college friends, or backpacking around South
Asia, or taking a year out in Australia. So she demurred if the
topic came up. She asked questions, feigned interest. 'Oh, I've
heard it's lovely there,' she would say. And if anyone asked her
directly had she been to a particular place, she would say 'not
yet', which was more hopeful than a flat out 'no', and implied
a desire to go, which in reality wasn't there. 'Oh, you know,
money …' she would say, and they would smile knowingly
because everyone was broke these days and now it was okay
to admit it, even revel in it.

'When are you heading back?' asked Stevie.

'As soon as I can get the money together. It's tough
though. You'd think there'd be more jobs out there for an
art school dropout with the use of only one hand.'

'You're an artist?'

Kavanagh winced. 'Well, no. Yeah … well kind of.
I mean, I used to paint but I'm not doing so much these
days. What I'm really interested in is tattoos. I'm doing an
apprenticeship at the moment.'

'Oh, cool. Do you have many yourself?'

He grinned. 'Yeah, one or two. How about you?'

her head. 'No, I was planning to get one at
member, back when I started in college.'

were you gonna get?'

vie cast her mind back to when she was 18 and
d herself drawing a blank. 'Do you know, I can't even
remember. I think I wanted to get one on my back.'

He rolled up his trouser-leg to show her an intricate black Celtic knot on his calf. 'This is my most recent. I did this one myself.'

'Wow, it must be difficult to tattoo yourself.'

'Yeah, it's a bit awkward all right. I wanted the practice though. It would be better only I was a bit hammered at the time.'

As he was pulling down his trouser leg, she thought she caught a glimpse of a tattoo above the one he had shown her. 'Is that another one?'

'Oh …'. He looked sheepish for a moment, but realising she had already seen, he pulled his trouser leg back up, farther this time. 'You mean here?'

She saw a row of deep black lines on his leg that looked like scratch-marks.

'That was when I'd just got the tattoo gun. I didn't know how deep you were supposed to go with it, you know? I needed to kind of warm up and get used to using it before doing that proper one.'

'Wow,' said Stevie. 'That's …' but she couldn't articulate what it was she wanted to say. His body was not a temple, it seemed, but something to scratch and claw at. The marks were like something you'd scrawl on paper then scrunch up and throw away, and yet there they were, a permanent mark on his skin.

'Can I …?' she surprised herself by saying it as she reached out her hand. It was a compulsion, like wanting to run her fingers over rough-grained wood. She would rather risk getting a splinter than never knowing how it felt.

'Sure,' he said.

She touched his leg, tracing the lines of the tattoo scratches. When she went to pull her hand away, he placed his hand on top and wrapped his fingers around hers. They sat like that in silence for a while until he leaned towards her and then his mouth was on hers.

*

In the moment of waking to the sound of pigeons cooing and the morning sun slanting in through the window, he was a boy in the old house in Clare. He heard the familiar creak of the bed springs as he turned from the harsh morning, trying to clutch the last fragments of sleep as they fled from him. But he was not a boy. He knew this by the hangover that beat at his temples. He opened his eyes and took in the small room and the figure of the woman lying in bed beside him. How had he ended up here? Had she invited him back? He tried to remember leaving the pub.

Her hair was fanned out on the pillow under her, dirty-blonde and tangled. Her arms were stretched over her head like a ragged mermaid caught up in a net. He scanned the room to look for his clothes, a force of habit, and then looked back at her face. She was still asleep, or at least appeared to be. But it was only his T-shirt that was strewn on the floor beside the bed. He was still wearing his jeans. She opened her eyes and he looked away, then back at her.

'Morning,' she said. 'Would you like some coffee?'

He found it best to avoid these moments, the awkwardness of the morning after when the intimacy of the previous night evaporated as the hangover set in. The last girl he had slept with ... not slept with – banged, rode, fucked – had asked for some water from the glass he was drinking from, and when he had handed it to her she wiped the rim of the glass before taking a sip. He noticed the gesture and it had made him horrifically sad. He tried to remember that girl's name now, but couldn't. Maybe he should have left before Stevie had woken up, but it was too late now.

'Morning. Don't suppose you've anything stronger?'

Stevie laughed but then realised that he was serious. 'Oh right. Yeah, I've a bottle of wine, I think.'

'Please tell me you have a corkscrew.'

'Oh, I don't need one. I learnt this great trick recently for opening a bottle of wine with a shoe.'

She got up out of bed and he saw that she had also slept in her clothes. He looked at her long, slim legs as she padded barefoot towards the kitchen.

'Where's the bathroom?' he asked.

'Same place it was last night.' She laughed and pointed towards the bathroom door.

It was coming back to him now. They had stayed in the pub until closing time. Drinking pints, kissing, exchanging stories, laughing about him breaking the wine bottle, more kissing. He had told her about the hospital, waiting in the A&E department in the chaos of the noise of the walking wounded. He could just about remember stumbling out of Neachtain's at closing time. Chips on the way to her place. Vinegar dripping down their arms. Then smoking joints and talking about ... what? Everything. Nothing. Music, art, tattoos. Yeah, that was it. She was interested in the tattoos. He remembered drunken kissing, clamouring, half-hearted grappling with clothing, but both of them too drunk to do anything other than pass out.

Stevie boiled the kettle and got the wine from the kitchen press. When she came out of the kitchen he was sitting on the sofa, looking at her pictures of the sheela-na-gigs and the map.

'So, this is what you're studying?'

'Yeah, I've just started really. I've been interested in them for a while though.'

'Yeah?' He stood up and walked over to the pictures. 'They're pretty cool. Are they stone carvings?'

'Yeah, they're called sheela-na-gigs.'

'Oh yeah, sheela-na-gigs. You were telling me about them last night.' An image came to mind of her gesturing towards the map and talking animatedly as his drunk brain tried to follow what she was saying. Something about driving around Ireland....

'Doesn't PJ Harvey have a song about them?' he asked.

'Yeah, she does. Do you like her?'

'Ah yeah. Sure you can't beat a bit of PJ.'

'I used to listen to that album all the time when I was a teenager. I think my family thought I was insane.'

Kavanagh laughed. 'Yup, mine too. Did we have this conversation last night?'

'Yeah, probably.' Stevie poured them each a glass of wine. 'Wine for breakfast is either a really, really good idea, or a really, really bad one.'

'I'm gonna go with really, really good idea,' said Kavanagh.

'Yeah, sure it's made with grapes so it's probably one of your five a day.'

Kavanagh nodded in agreement. 'It's heart healthy. All those lads in Sicily drink it like water and they live into their hundreds.'

He stood up and walked over to the map of Ireland on the wall and traced his finger over the lines drawn onto it. 'So, is this all the places where they are, the sheela-na-gigs?'

Stevie nodded. 'I'll be visiting all of those sites in the next year.'

'All of them? Jesus, there's loads.'

'I know! I had no idea there were that many until I started studying them. But quite a few have been moved from their original locations to the history museum in Dublin, so I've already catalogued those ones.'

'So what are they exactly?' asked Kavanagh. 'Are they Pagan symbols or something?'

'Yeah, maybe. That's one possibility anyway, that they were something that was left over from the change in Ireland from Paganism to Christianity.''

Kavanagh stepped back from the pictures and cocked his head to the side. 'So ... are they basically like giant vaginas? I mean, in your expert historical opinion?'

Stevie laughed. 'Well, I suppose you could say that. They probably have something to do with childbirth, but it's a bit of a mystery. There's loads of different theories about them.'

'Right,' said Kavanagh.

He sat down on the sofa beside her and then they were kissing again. Stevie was enjoying kissing him. Just kissing. There was a clumsiness to it, as if they were teenagers. She had forgotten what that was like, the giddy new thrill of it, washing machine kisses on an endless spin cycle. The feeling of waiting for something to happen next – worrying that it would, then worrying that it wouldn't. Tongues probing, hands roaming, doing everything but, not in bed but in dark corners of house parties, or drunken suburban laneways, or under the cover of darkness in blameless fields. His stubble was scratching her chin and she knew it would leave a mark, but she didn't care. Yet there was a tenderness in it too, all this kissing.

She took his hand and led him back into the bedroom. It felt strange to have this man touching her, this man she barely knew, when she hadn't slept with anyone other than Donal in years. It was like a foreign language she had learnt but forgotten, and it now felt strange and muddled on her tongue. He must have sensed her reticence. He took it slowly, waiting for her lead, kissing every inch of her until she grabbed him towards her. It was painful when he first entered her and she tensed. He sensed this and slowed down until they found their own rhythm, a mutual language their bodies could converse in, and then she was on top of him. Stretching, reaching, her hips thrusting over and over until they collapsed – spent, tipsy and sticky. They dozed through the morning, stretching out the wine, the kissing, the smoking. They kept the curtains drawn to keep the outside world from flooding in.

Chapter 11

Stevie set off on the first of her research trips to visit sheela-na-gig sites, all the while praying to the Automobile Gods that her tiny car wouldn't break down over the course of the week. It was a hatchback that had seen better days. Duct tape covered a tear in the back seat like a bandage. Air whistled through a gap in one of the back windows. The engine grumbled its protest if she went above fourth gear. Still, it was hers to travel wherever she needed to, and it felt good to be on the road, singing loudly with the window rolled down. For this trip she was focusing on sheela-na-gig sites in Galway and the Midlands. She had an AA map of Ireland on the dashboard, a handwritten itinerary and printouts of her hotel and B&B bookings in the glove compartment, and her new digital SLR camera in her bag. Her first visit was to Ballinderry Castle just outside Tuam. From there she would travel to Roscommon to visit a further three sites. Then it was on to Longford, Westmeath and Offaly, before making her way back to Galway. Altogether, she would squeeze in visits to ten sites in five days.

She was making good time as she neared Tuam. It felt great to be on the road, singing loudly with the window rolled down, and she was enjoying the scenery, seeing the cattle and sheep in the green patchwork fields as she passed. The sun shone but there was a touch of autumn in the crisp air, and on the side of the road wild blackberries hinted at their own withering.

Stevie parked at Ballinderry Castle and headed on foot towards the squat limestone structure up ahead. It stood on a slight hill surrounded by trees. She had read that the castle was built in the sixteenth century by the de Burgo family on the shores of a Lough that had since disappeared. Over the years it had passed through many hands and had been occupied by various forces. Cromwell's army had briefly occupied the castle, and later Parnell had stayed there. It had even been used as a British military outpost during the Troubles. Stevie smiled as she thought to herself that the only constant presence throughout this span of time was the sheela-na-gig on the wall.

From the top of the hill she surveyed the surrounding area, but she could see nobody, and the only noise was the faint rustle of the breeze and birdsong from the trees. She couldn't see the sheela-na-gig at first as she made her way around the perimeter of the castle. Then her heart leapt as she spotted it on the archway of the main doorway, on a keystone that projected outwards. She had seen drawings of the figure in a book, but had imagined it to be larger. She realised that it could easily be missed by visitors to the castle unless they were specifically seeking it out. Retrieving her camera from her bag, she started to take some photographs of the carving. It had a large head with a neutral expression. Two plaits protruded from either side, which could have been hair, or some type of headdress. The figure was standing with legs spread wide open, and two hands were joined around the genitals. Stevie had read that this particular example was unusual and important as it featured an intricate background of Celtic-style patterns. Also, unusually for a sheela-na-gig, a rush of liquid was depicted between the legs, which could have been urine, menstrual blood or some other substance. This was where the uncertainty came in, thought Stevie, as she zoomed her camera in to take a photo of the liquid. It was impossible to know for certain one way or the other. All they had were theories.

Stevie felt like skipping as she made her way back down the hill. After all of her hours of researching, reading and planning, she had started at last. There was something special about seeing the sheela-na-gig not as a picture in a book, or even an exhibit in a museum, but *in situ,* where it had been for centuries. She knew that the task ahead of her was enormous, and that she was only at the start, but she had taken that first step and felt excited by the possibility of it all.

As she drove to the next site, Stevie thought about the figure and mulled over the many possible explanations of why it was there. She had started to make her way through all of the texts and research on sheela-na-gigs both in Ireland and the UK. One explanation claimed that the figures existed purely for defensive purposes, that their presence at entrances to sacred buildings had a talismanic purpose that prevented evil spirits from crossing the threshold. Then there was the Romanesque theory, which proposed that the aim of the sheela-na-gigs was to provide a visual warning to the illiterate against the sin of lust. Similar imagery of female exhibitionists could be found in Romanesque-style churches in western France, Normandy and Spain, so perhaps in an Irish context the sheela-na-gigs had acted in a corresponding way. It was also possible that they represented a Celtic goddess such as the hag-like *Cailleach* from Irish and Scottish mythology. Perhaps they were a hangover as a result of the change from the Pagan worship of several gods to the Christian worship of one: an uneasy link between folk belief and religion, where an assimilation of pagan artefacts was necessary to placate the superstitious. It was possible that it was a combination of all of these things, and that the figures served a number of functions, or that their function had started as one thing and evolved over time.

It was this ambiguity that fascinated Stevie, the fact that so much was mysterious, unknown, and perhaps unknowable. One school of thought that particularly interested her was the midwife theory, that sheela-na-gigs had somehow been used to aid women during childbirth. Many of the figures were found in small rural churches, and the quality of the stonework varied greatly, suggesting they were not the work of skilled craftsmen but that of amateur carvers, placing them in the realm of local tradition.

Stevie had read that women in the medieval period would have spent most of their adult lives either pregnant or nursing infant children, only to bury a large number of their offspring who died from malnutrition or disease. She could picture the women in labour, their wild eyes appealing for mercy like startled horses as the midwife made a poultice from herbs. To her, the sheela-na-gigs seemed to belong in such a setting. Perhaps back then there was comfort in the statues, the ritual of it, the sympathetic magic. Maybe they were touched for luck, fingers poked into idol holes, prayers offered up, to inspire the feeling that these things could somehow be controlled – pain made bearable, death staved off. She wondered if that was what it was all about: as some flowed into the world and others flowed out – birth, life, death, birth, life, death, birth – an endless cycle through the spread legs of a stone statue.

*

The roads were quiet as Stevie drove towards the B&B in Roscommon later that evening. Birds floated by like ghosts haunting the darkening sky. Having driven past it, realising her error and backtracking, she finally pulled up outside the B&B , which was cast in a faint dusky light. The proprietor, a Mrs McGarry, was looking out the window as Stevie parked, and as she approached the front door it flew open.

'Oh, hello. Come on in out of the cold. Is it just yourself, love?'

'Just me,' smiled Stevie.

'Oh, you poor pet. Come on in. I'll show you to your room.'

Stevie followed Mrs McGarry as she walked up the creaking stairs. The old woman leaned heavily on the bannister, favouring her right leg. Stevie tried not to look at the limp and instead looked at the back of Mrs McGarry's head, which resembled a perfectly solid helmet of permed curls.

'Here we are, pet.' She turned the key in the lock and opened the door.

Mrs McGarry shuffled into the room on her bad hip. She surveyed the single bed, the threadbare carpet, the faded wallpaper, turned to Stevie and raised her hands with palms facing upwards in a gesture that said, *Well, what do you think?*

Stevie forced a wide smile. 'Oh, it's lovely.'

'Now there's no television here, but there's one in the common room downstairs. You can come down once you're settled in and watch the soaps if you like.'

'Oh, thanks, but to be honest I'm quite tired after all the driving. I think I'll just have an early night.'

'Right you are. There's a little kettle there now if you'd like a cup of tea.'

'Great.'

'Breakfast is served from eight until nine tomorrow. Will I put you down for the full Irish?'

'Oh no, not for me thanks. Just a bit of cereal is fine for me, if it's going.'

'Toast?'

'Oh, no thanks, just …'.

Eggs?

Just the cer…'.

'I could do you a scrambled egg on toast, or a boiled egg, or a poached egg, or a rasher? Are you a vegetarian, is it?'

'No, I'm not. I just don't eat much in the mornings.'

'Ah, sure you haven't a pick on ya! Sure I'll do you the full Irish. It's included in the price, you know?'

'Well …'.

'Sure you know the way, if it's put in front of you in the morning you might change your mind.'

'Right.'

'Night so, love.'

'Night, Mrs McGarry,' Stevie said to the retreating curls.

'Dolores, love. Call me Dolores.'

Maybe I'll have a bath, Stevie thought, as she brought her washbag into the bathroom. The sink gurgled and choked like a dying man, and a cloying smell of dampness cloaked the air. *Maybe not.* Brushing her teeth, Stevie saw that her reflection appeared gaunt in the mirror above the sink and the dark circles under her eyes were highlighted by the poor lighting overhead. She headed back into the bedroom and sat down on the bed. As she had suspected, the mattress was soft and offered little support. She ran her hand over the starchy bed cover and grimaced: a severe case of Catholic quilt. The light in the room was cast from a single bulb that gloomed in a pink chintzy ceiling lamp. She tried to find the switch for the bedside lamp and ran her hand around its base to no avail. She checked the top of the stand near the bulb and still couldn't find it. Then she ran her hand along the flex and finally found the switch. She flicked it on. It sparked for a brief moment and then the bulb died with a popping sound at the exact moment a spider scurried across the wall and disappeared behind a picture of the Sacred Heart. Stevie let out a startled shriek and clamped her hand over her mouth. The garish image of the crucified Jesus looked down at her reproachfully. She could go downstairs and ask Mrs McGarry – Dolores – if she had a spare bulb, but she could hear the strains of the *Coronation Street* theme music. She didn't want to deprive the poor woman of her soaps and force her to scuttle around the house on her bad hip looking for a light bulb amongst the cobwebs and religious pictures. She unpacked her pyjamas and her notes, then smoked a furtive joint out the window as she checked her phone. No missed calls or messages. She still hadn't heard from Kavanagh. He'd said that he'd call when he was leaving her place that evening. He had looked her in the eye and kissed her on the lips and sounded like he meant it. Maybe he had at the time but had changed his mind since.

She closed the window and changed into her pyjamas. She planned to read over her notes in bed, but tiredness came over her like a wave. Wrestling with the sheets that had been tucked in tightly, she turned down the bed before sinking under the covers and drifting off to sleep. She half woke to hear the plaintive sound of a cat looking to be let in. In the dream it was on the windowsill and she had forgotten to close the window after smoking the joint. In the dream she could sense it there, just outside, and she tried to rouse herself from sleep to go and close the window, but she was weighed down by her own heavy limbs, immovable as stone. She knew in the dream that it was too late now and that the creature would come flying in through the curtains and onto the bed, an angry mewling ball of mangy fur, knife-like claws scratching, a cat's body with the cold stone face of a sheela-na-gig.

Chapter 12

The kitchen of Flanagan's was filled with a cacophony of voices and clanging pots, the smell of boiling cabbage, and an invisible wall of soggy heat. Kavanagh lugged giant saucepans with encrusted brown-sauced rims into the sink before dousing them with detergent and setting to work on them with the power-sprayer. He loaded and unloaded the industrial-sized dishwasher in a constant dizzying routine of clinking plates, soap and steam. Despite the back-breaking work, it felt good to be using his hand again. He no longer had his arm in a sling, and there was a faint scar where the stitches had been. He was vaguely disappointed that they hadn't left more of a mark on him. The smell of the kitchen was nauseating, and the various cooking odours were doing his hangover no favours. He had been dying for a cigarette break, but when he took one the tobacco on his empty stomach had made him heave, and he thought for a moment he would vomit. At least, poised over the sink all morning, he was standing in the right spot for it if he did. His feet ached from standing all day. Part of the bonus of working in the restaurant was the free meals they had offered, but the smell was so off-putting he couldn't imagine taking them up on it. It was unbelievable that people actually came here of their own free will and paid for this food.

The restaurant was a newly-opened tourist trap on Quay Street that served 'Traditional Irish Fare' according to the sign over the door, which featured a grinning leprechaun playing a harp surrounded by a border of shamrocks. A giant pot of gristly Irish stew boiled on the hob. Plates of fatty bacon and lacklustre cabbage were served up with a generous splatter of curdled parsley sauce. Microwaved plates of stodgy apple crumble wept beneath mounds of synthetic cream. Simon, the owner, lived out in Barna some place, and according to the staff was never really there except to count the takings at the end of the day. His surname wasn't even Flanagan. It was Dudley-Tompkinson, but then if he opened a restaurant called Dudley-Tompkinson's, people would probably have expectations of tiny sandwiches with the crusts cut off and Eton mess. Best not to confuse people.

'Good lad, Joe,' Simon had wheezed, resting a manicured hand on Kavanagh's shoulder after he offered him the job. 'It's minimum wage to start with, but play your cards right here and we'll have you moving up the ranks in no time. Six months down the line and you could be managing this place.'

Kavanagh nodded and plastered on a smile to go with his poker face. *Six months down the line I'll be sending you a postcard from Thailand, you fat fucker.*

'Kitchen porter' was his official title. In the hierarchy of the kitchen, he was on the lowest rung. That didn't bother him at all. He had always found it strange that people were so defined by their jobs. His father, the teacher; his brother, the accountant. Why couldn't people just *be*? As soon as they were telling you their name, they were telling you what they did. He didn't know where that left him. Was he Joe Kavanagh, the artist? To call himself an artist seemed ridiculous. It was such a loaded word. He didn't know if it was something you did or something you were. If it was something you stopped doing, was it something you ceased being?

He remembered when he was still a young lad whose balls hadn't dropped, not yet old enough to be self-conscious or embarrassed by his own earnest pursuits. During the summer holidays he used to head out with his painting set and easel and paint the long grass and the sheep.

'Do you know what you are, Joe?' Colum, his older brother, would ask when he arrived home with his paintings from the day. 'You're a real *kunstmaler*.' He'd put the stress on the first syllable and smile like someone who knew more than Kavanagh. He had started studying German at secondary school, and he knew that Kavanagh had no idea what he was calling him, but could only presume it was something derogatory.

'You don't know what that is, do you, Joe?'

'Yeah, I do,' Kavanagh would lie. The trick was not to show that he was upset. If he concentrated very hard, he could keep his expression neutral. Then he wouldn't have won, but he wouldn't have lost either.

Colum would smirk. 'What is it then, smart-arse?'

'Why should I tell you if you already know? Sounds like *you* don't know what it is.'

And Colum would walk off laughing, amused at having tormented his younger brother. Kavanagh had no idea what the word meant. He even thought that it might be something Colum invented. It was only later when he started secondary school himself that he heard the word again in German class. He was surprised, considering the way Colum had spat it at him with such disdain, to find out that it was an innocent word that meant 'artist'.

Working in the kitchen, he found his thoughts wandering off in all kinds of directions. Something about the dull repetition of tasks made his mind drift back to the past. It would be better if he had someone to chat with. The other lads working there seemed fairly sound but they all spoke to each other in Polish. He was the minority party in the kitchen. So unless they decided to address him in English, he couldn't really join in their conversation. He could barely hear them anyway over the radio and the general noise. Besides, he was expending most of his energy on trying not to puke, so he wasn't too bothered.

He found himself thinking about Stevie, replaying their morning together. Her straddling him, her long legs wrapped around him, her blonde hair falling over him as she bent down to kiss him. The softness of her lips. Shit, he should ring her. He hadn't rang her still and the days were getting away from him. Kavanagh sprayed a saucepan with a water jet. He sighed as a particularly stubborn layer of gelatinous brown liquid refused to give up its embrace of the saucepan's rim. *Think of the money, think of the money, think of the money,* he repeated to himself.

Chapter 13

Stevie let herself into her hotel room, dropped her bags and looked out the window. She could see the River Shannon below and Athlone town in the distance. The room hadn't cost much more than the basic B&Bs she had stayed in on the rest of her trip, but she noticed that there was a flat-screen television on the wall, and the receptionist downstairs had been keen to point out that the bath had a jacuzzi function. The hotel was one of those Celtic Tiger follies, built back in the time when people took weekend breaks to rural idylls just for the hell of it. Now it stood barren and pristine, trying to tempt punters with recession-buster midweek offers and relaxation-spa and golfing deals. The breakfast order form on the desk had already been filled in: *one orange juice, one Rice Krispies, one white coffee, one fried egg, white toast.* Stevie imagined that she was this person in an alternate universe, a parallel 'her' who ordered these things: a person who drove a large car that never broke down and planned foreign holidays, perhaps.

She ran her hand over the bedspread and then sat down on the king-sized bed. The covers felt soft and inviting, the mattress firm and supportive, unlike the cramped bed with the banjaxed springs in the last B&B. The bed was far too large for one person, she thought, as she patted the other side of the made bed. It was an invitation for sex. An invitation she couldn't accept. She imagined what it would be like if Kavanagh were there with her, but pushed the thought from her mind. He wasn't going to call, best to forget about it. The blankets and sheets were all tucked in under the mattress in some unnecessarily complicated manner, and there were far too many pillows and little cushions on top. She grabbed them and threw them onto the chair, then turned down the bed.

Downstairs in the bar, Stevie had a bowl of soup as she read over her notes. The place was practically empty apart from an older couple sitting by the window that overlooked the car park. Stevie watched as the woman examined her cutlery, bringing it close to her spectacled eyes and squinting at it before placing the knife and fork back on the table. Then she lifted up her side plate and examined the bottom of it before placing it back down. She leaned forward and touched the flowers in the vase that stood in the middle of the table and said something to her husband, who was staring into the middle-distance. He didn't reply. She picked up the cutlery and started the whole routine again. Stevie felt a sudden sense of happiness that she was alone, that she no longer had to make small talk. She remembered sitting with Donal in a café just before they broke up and neither of them had a word to say to each other. Had they stayed together, maybe they would have ended up like this couple. Being content in her own company was preferable to feeling lonely in someone else's. A giant television beamed a soccer match into the room as the lone slack-jawed barman stared at it and the young lounge girl wiped a cloth over and over the same clean countertop.

Back in her room, Stevie flicked on the television but couldn't concentrate on anything. Her mind was full of the sheela-na-gigs. She loaded the photographs she had taken onto her laptop and scrolled through them one by one: the plaited hair of the Rahara sheela-na-gig; the two sheelas at Scregg Castle in County Roscommon – the tiny one with its legs in an acrobatic pose, and the second figure with the same cow-like ears as another in Kilsarkan, County Kerry, that she had seen a photograph of; the weathered Abbeylara sheela; the strange four-eyed sheela of Taghmon Church in Westmeath; and the sunken, compressed oval figure of Moate Castle with a wide mouth, teeth, and a protruding tongue.

Her mobile phone rang, piercing the silence of the room, and she scrambled to retrieve it from her bag. She saw 'Kavanagh' displayed on the screen. She cleared her throat and told herself to sound casual.

'Hello?'

'Hey, Stevie. It's Kav.'

'Oh, hi. How are ya?'

'Sorry I haven't rung sooner.'

'Oh, that's okay.' She hoped her voice didn't betray the amount of times she had checked and rechecked her phone since she had last seen him.

'I started a new job and I've just been up to my eyes.'

'Ah, fair enough. That's great about the job. Where are you working?'

'In the sudsy bowels of hell. You know that new Irish restaurant on Quay Street? The one with the leprechaun on the sign?'

'I know the one. I've passed it all right.'

'Just passed it. You've never gone in?'

'Can't say I have. Am I missing much?'

'A party on a plate, that's what you're missing. The best food in Galway. How the place doesn't have several Michelin stars is beyond me. The toasted ham *sangwich* is a triumph.'

Stevie laughed. 'I'll have to check it out when I'm back so.'

'Oh, are you away somewhere?'

'Yeah, I'm doing a bit of research, visiting a few sites.'

'Ah shite. I finally have a night off. I was seeing if you wanted to meet up for a pint later.'

'Ah, I would, only I'm in Athlone. I'll be back tomorrow evening though.'

'Sound. Sure I'll give you a ring then. Maybe we could do something?'

'Sure. Sounds good. Talk to you then.'

Stevie went back to looking at the photographs. Faintly, she could just about hear the sound of a television coming from another room, the ping of a lift, the tiniest wisp of two voices laughing. A hotel room was a strange place to be alone.

Chapter 14

'So, I'm meeting up with that girl tomorrow.' Kavanagh passed the joint to Alex.

'Yeah? That's deadly, man. Where are ya bringing her?'

'Just gonna bring her to Neachtain's for a few pints, I think. She said she likes the place.'

'Nice one.'

'Why, do you think I should bring her somewhere else?'

Alex shrugged. 'Ah … nah, I think Neachtain's is good. You can always go on somewhere else after.'

'Should I buy her something?'

'Yeah, buy her a pint anyway, I suppose, and a kebab from the Charcoal Grill on the way home.'

'No, like something … I dunno. Flowers or something?'

'Flowers?' Alex took a long drag of the joint as he considered this. 'Yeah, I suppose.' He exhaled a steady stream of smoke that floated upwards. 'Flowers. Yeah, sure why not?'

'But I'm meeting her there and she'd have to carry them around with her all night.'

'Yeah, that would be a bit shit really when you think about it. They'd probably start to wilt.'

Wild Strawberries was projected onto the wall, and they watched the black and white figures. Kavanagh had seen this one before. This was the bit where the professor guy was at his old cabin in the countryside. Kavanagh found he was tired from the long hours of work, and the joint was making him even more drowsy. He couldn't muster up the energy to read the subtitles, so he stopped trying to follow any narrative and instead looked at the images, letting them wash over him as though each frame were an individual painting.

'If you were American now,' said Alex, 'you'd bring her on a date, bowling or playing miniature golf or something.'

Kavanagh grimaced. 'A date? Irish people don't go on dates, do they? Have you ever gone on a date?'

'Only to the pub.'

'Is that a date though? Is going to the pub not just going to the pub?'

'I dunno. I think it's going on a date to the pub.'

'This has all gotten very confusing all of a sudden,' said Kavanagh, taking a drag from the joint and passing it back to Alex.

'Ah yeah, the pub is grand I'd say. Sure see how it goes. Maybe next time bring her somewhere special. Here, you should bring her to your restaurant. Wine and dine her. Sure you'd get the staff discount.'

'Yeah, we could feed each other bacon and cabbage. Pure romantic, Alex.'

'I don't know. I'm the wrong person to be giving advice. I haven't had much luck meeting ladies.'

'Well, actually leaving the house would be a step in the right direction.'

'Sure, send them up to me, send them up to me. I'll leave the door on the latch.' Alex laughed. 'If they look like Bibi Andersson all the better.'

'Who? Bibi … Bibi …'. Kavanagh repeated, the words feeling strange on his lips. 'This is some strong weed.'

'Yeah, it's HPW.'

'HPW?' The sounds emerged slowly from Kavanagh's mouth, floating towards the ceiling and popping like bubbles.

'High-powered weed. The good stuff.'

'Oh …' Kavanagh tried to grasp the thought as it floated away from him.

'That's Bibi …' Alex pointed at the film.

Kavanagh looked at Alex's lips making random shapes and tried to focus on the sounds. 'Huh?'

Alex laughed. 'Who's Bibi Andersson? Jesus, do you listen to a word I say?' He shook his fist at Kavanagh before gesturing towards the film.

'Ah!' said Kavanagh, with all the delight of Newton discovering gravity. He pointed at the film. 'Your one there?'

'Yeah,' said Alex. 'That's her. She's in *Persona* as well, and *The Seventh Seal*.'

Kavanagh felt the fog of his mind starting to clear. 'I haven't seen *The Seventh Seal* yet. Is it any good?'

'You haven't seen *The Seventh Seal*? Seriously? Jesus, what have we been doing all this time? Right, we're gonna watch it straight after this. I can't believe you've never seen it!'

'So it's about a seal then, is it?' Kavanagh looked at Alex with rapt attention. 'I love films about animals. And there's seven of them? Jesus, that sounds class altogether.'

'Fuck off, Kav.' Alex tried to contain his smile.

In the film, Bibi was sitting under a tree and smoking a pipe as she chatted to the professor dude. 'Actually, do you know who looks like Bibi?' said Kavanagh.

'Who?' said Alex.

'Stevie.'

'The girl you're meeting?'

'Yeah. She even smokes a pipe.'

'Fuck off. She does not smoke a pipe.'

'No, seriously. She used to do archaeology and they can't smoke when they're on digs because of the ash or something, so they all smoke pipes.'

'Wow. If things don't work out with you two can I have her number?'

Alex was in good form tonight. Kavanagh decided to seize the opportunity. 'Here, Alex, there's a couple of Polish fellas I work with, sound lads. They were asking me could I sort them out with some weed. What do you reckon?'

Alex thought about this for a moment, shifting position in his chair and leaning back. 'How did they know to ask you?'

'Eh, I don't know really. I didn't think of that. I suppose I just have that look about me, you know? I look like a reliable sort, capable of getting things.'

'Capable of getting stoned anyway. I dunno, Kav. What do you reckon? Do you think it's safe enough?'

'Ah yeah, it'll be grand,' said Kavanagh. He could tell from Alex's body language that he wasn't convinced. 'Sure who would they be telling?'

Alex shook his head. 'I don't want Pajo showing up at my door.'

'I can appreciate that. He'd ruin your beautiful wood floor by dragging his knuckles over it.'

Alex laughed. 'Yeah, I think it's best to leave it for a while. Just to be sure.'

'Okay, that's fair enough.'

Chapter 15

Stevie discovered that Christmas was a season that suited Galway. The days were short and the nights were long. Open fires and pints of stout beckoned. It seemed as though the city collectively awakened from the temperance of November and *Mí na Marbh*. Even though she hadn't partaken in November's tradition of avoiding alcohol, she could feel the spirit of abstinence that prevailed throughout the month. She had found it difficult to leave the comfort of her home in November and do battle with the endless drizzle and darkness. December felt different – it brought the warmth of fairy lights and Christmas trees to counteract the coldness. The season of the dead was over, and now it was the turn of the living as people returned home to see friends and family. Eyre Square was transformed with a Christmas tree, market stalls, and a German beer hall where people sat at long tables drinking Weissbier and clinking heavy glasses as they toasted each other over the din. Caro-singers attempted wobbly harmonies and shook their collection buckets like maracas on Shop Street. The balloon modeller switched tack and revealed the festive balloon figures in his arsenal: children clutched balloon Rudolphs and Santas. They skated at the ice-rink on Nimmo's Pier, their bandy legs like newborn deer on the unfamiliar surface. They laughed and fell and cried and got back up again as they moved around the rink in circles – a juddering circuit of unsteady dancers – exhaling into the crisp winter air dotted with stars hanging in the cold Atlantic night.

Stevie put down her book as she saw Orlaith enter the bar, trailing a dripping umbrella after her.

Orlaith dropped her bag and umbrella on the floor as she slumped down in the chair opposite Stevie. 'I apologise in advance if I'm shit company.'

'Rough night?'

'Staff Christmas party. Did the dog on it. Myself and the geography teacher were up dancing on tables at one stage. Fucking morto. Then the PE teacher was trying to get me to do that lift from *Dirty Dancing*.

Stevie laughed. 'Does he look like Patrick Swayze?'

'No, his deformed cousin maybe. He's surprisingly fat for a PE teacher as well. You'd think they wouldn't allow that.' Orlaith rested her arms on the table and put her head in her hands. 'Oh God, why do I do these things to myself?'

Stevie laughed. 'Because you're an idiot?'

'You're not supposed to say that. You're supposed to tell me it's not that bad. Reassure me. Lie.'

'It's not that bad,' said Stevie.

'I'm seriously shame-spiralling at the moment. You know when you're in the horrors and stuff keeps coming back to you, a series of mortifying images?'

Stevie nodded. 'Oh yeah. Sometimes I think my life is just a succession of shame-spirals and I'm just spinning away through it all like a particularly mortified starling.'

Orlaith groaned and then lifted her head up and rested it on her palms. 'I was supposed to do my Christmas shopping today, but if I do I know I'll end up punching someone.'

'The shops are manic, so that's a very real possibility. Online shopping, it's the only way to go.'

'Stevie, you're a fucking genius. Why didn't I think of that?'

'Hair of the dog?'

'Oh God, no. I'll just have a pint glass of coke, thanks, Stevie.'

Stevie smiled and stood up from her chair.

'Actually …' called Orlaith, 'maybe a hot whiskey would be good. I can feel myself getting a bit of a cold.' She put her hand up to her throat and gave an exaggerated cough.

'Good call. A hot whiskey should nip that in the bud. Sure, it's medicinal. I might have one myself just to be on the safe side.'

'Getting sick just before the holidays too. Bloody typical.'

Stevie ordered the drinks at the bar. 'Fairytale of New York' was playing over the speakers. The Christmas CD must be on a loop. The same song had been playing when she came in. She set the drinks down on the table and sat down.

'Deadly, thanks.' Orlaith took the hot drink in her hands to warm them. 'Sorry I haven't seen you in so long. School has been flipping mental with exams and everything.'

'I can imagine.' Stevie stirred the whiskey and watched the granules of brown sugar dissolve at the bottom of the glass. 'Yeah, I've been pretty busy with research and visiting some of the sites. I still have so much to do though. I haven't even made a dent in it really.'

'Ah, it's early days. Give yourself time. Have you been talking to Caitríona recently?'

'No, I've been meaning to call her actually. How's she getting on? How's baby Oisín?'

'Oisín's doing well, but they had some bad news. Phil lost his job.'

'Oh no!'

'Yeah, she said they're thinking of moving to Canada if he can't find anything in the next few months.'

'Oh wow. That's a big decision with the baby and everything.'

'It mightn't be so bad. Apparently there's loads of engineering work over there so Phil would definitely get something. Sure I might follow her over myself.'

'What about your job here?'

I'm only on maternity cover. And everyone keeps telling me how lucky I am to have anything. You're not allowed to complain about your job these days.' She rolled her eyes. 'Anyway, who knows what'll happen in the next few months? I mightn't have a job this time next year.'

'Would you want to live over there?'

'I dunno,' said Orlaith. 'I was thinking it might be nice to go and live in a big city. I mean, Dublin's small in the grand scheme of things, but could you even call Galway a city?'

'Of course it's a city.' Stevie found that she felt protective of her adopted home.

'More like a glorified town. There's nothing to do here besides drink. They don't even have a museum or an art gallery.'

'Ah, they do. The museum's really cool actually.' she and Kavanagh had visited it just last week. They had stood arms entwined, marvelling at the view from the top floor of the river and the Claddagh stretching out beyond. 'Besides, how often did you go to galleries in Dublin?'

Orlaith smiled. 'Yeah, fair enough, but at least I knew I had the *option* of going. How are you finding it here anyway? Have you heard from Donal at all since?'

Stevie shook her head. 'I haven't, no. I'll probably see him when I'm home for Christmas though.'

She realised that she had barely given Donal a thought. She traced her finger over the brown sugar particles that had fallen on the table. Something prevented her from telling Orlaith about Kavanagh. The last few weeks had been filled with them spending time together, but somehow to give voice to it, to explain it in words, would be to jinx it, to burst this bubble that contained the two of them. She hadn't spoken about him to anyone.

She smiled to herself thinking about him. It had thrown her off guard how quickly it had happened, this feeling of closeness. It made sense, their being together, the fact of it. She loved the moment after they had made love before they drifted off to sleep. They fit together, their two bodies entwined, and she found herself smiling as she ran her fingers over his skin and the images that were there. She had committed them to memory, and as they lay together in the dark she traced the lines of them – the cobalt tiger with paws that stretched across his shoulder onto his arm; the flames along the length of his right forearm that remained unquenched by the blue swirls of water that mingled with them; the Celtic knot on his leg and the marks above it....

'Do you reckon something might happen?'

'What? Sorry …'. She looked at Orlaith in surprise.

'Donal. When you see him do you think you might end up together?'

'Oh, God no. Sure he has a new girlfriend now, was I not telling you? We'd just be seeing each other as friends.'

Orlaith laughed. 'You can't be friends with your ex.'

'Of course you can.'

'Oh, Stevie.' Orlaith shook her head in disapproval. 'Absolutely not. There's always feelings on one side or the other.'

'There really isn't with us though. It was an amicable break-up.'

'No such thing. That's like saying it was a neutral war. Besides, why would you even *want* to stay friends with an ex? I remember reading this interview with Julie Burchill once and she said she never stays friends with her exes. She said why would I keep an orange I'd already sucked all the juice out of?'

She pointed towards Stevie's nearly empty glass. 'Same again?'

'I thought you were just having the one.'

Orlaith smiled. 'A bird never flew on one wing.'

Chapter 16

Bing Bong – Jacqui Maloney to the checkouts, please! – Ksssssshhh – That's Jacqui Maloney to the check …–kssssssshhh – thank …–kssssssshhh – you.

Jacqui sighed and finished hanging up the stack of T-shirts on the rail. That new girl hadn't a clue how to use the intercom properly. She weaved her way through the busy shop floor as she made her way to the checkouts. Festive music blared throughout the store and the place was heaving with shoppers. Jacqui used to love the buzz and bustle in the run-up to Christmas, but this year was different: it would be her first Christmas without her mother. Last year she had sat with her in the hospice watching bad television with one eye and the clock with the other. Her brother arrived in half an hour before visiting hours were over for the evening with no explanation as to why he was late. She scowled at him, ready to give him a bollocking, but when she saw her mother's face light up, she bit her tongue.

When her brother was born, she pretended he was hers. She pushed him in his pram around the estate. Everyone smiled at her and everyone wanted to meet him. They laughed at his scowl. He never smiled. She was patient with him when he roared and screamed as a child. He always had snot running down his nose no matter how much she wiped it with a tissue.

He hit the other children in the playground. Nothing was ever his fault. Then there was the trouble with the guards as he got older, the warnings. He wasn't 18 yet, so they couldn't touch him, and he knew it. Then there was his carpentry apprenticeship, an honest trade, and he seemed to be doing well. Their mother was hopeful, but then he fell out with his boss over God knows what. All he'd done since then was hang around, drink and do whatever drugs he could get his grubby hands on. Not that Jacqui was an angel by any means, but Maloney didn't know when to call it quits. That's all his life was now and he accepted it, seemed to languish in it.

Carol, the duty manager, was waiting for her at the checkouts. 'Hiya, Jacqui. Someone's after toppling a display in the kids' section. Would you mind sorting it out for me?'

Jacqui nodded and strolled off. The place was in a heap with baby shoes strewn all over the floor. She picked up the shoes and placed them back on the stand with great care. So tiny and perfect. She liked working in the children's section. Mothers came in with their babies and they picked up the little clothes and shoes.

A small boy dropped his teddy bear and started to cry. Jacqui longed to take him up in her arms, rock him gently and whisper *hush hush little baby*. She picked the toy up off the ground and smiled as she held it out to him. He took it in his little hand and he smiled at her, a chubby-cheeked grin that showed his one tooth.

'Thank you,' said the child's mother. 'He's forever dropping that thing.'

'No bother. Isn't he a dote?'

The child's mother smiled. 'Say bye-bye.'

'Bye-bye,' said the boy, waving his pudgy hand.

'Bye-bye,' said Jacqui. She could feel a lump in her throat. She laughed and smiled at them both and busied herself with tidying the tiny clothes on the hangers as the mother pushed the child off, away from her.

The thought of having a baby had crept up on her recently. She imagined what it would be like to be a mum, to be part of a new family, one she had created herself. She had dreams of pushing a pram down Shop Street. Maybe she would have a little girl and she would bring her to Griffin's for cake. Every day she would tell the little girl that she was beautiful, and she would mean it. Or she would have a little boy who looked just like Pajo, and everyone would say, *isn't he the spit of his father?*

Chapter 17

As the coach trundled along the motorway towards Dublin, the radio droned over the speakers and Stevie looked out the window at the snow-covered scenery passing by – houses, trees, fields – changed by their christening of cold whiteness. She had the peculiar sense that the coach was not moving, rather that it was the landscape that was rolling past while she, the coach and its passengers remained static as the stagnant air became more stagnant still, and they all inhaled and exhaled as one unsettled entity.

The coach stopped at Eden Quay and passengers piled off, bundled up in warm coats. The driver wished people a Merry Christmas as he unloaded their luggage from the storage hold and they shuffled off along the icy streets, their breath visible in the cold night air. As she waited on O'Connell Bridge for a bus to her parents' place in Monkstown, Stevie realised she had made the right decision to leave her car in Galway. The paths were icy and treacherous. For some reason, the footpath on the bridge over the River Liffey had been gritted only halfway across. A man sat on a piece of cardboard at the division like a shabby gatekeeper at a toll bridge, asking for a fee that nobody passing would pay as he blew on his hands and rubbed them together for warmth. The side of the bridge just beyond where he was sitting was covered in glittering ice. A girl walking past the bus stop skidded. Her hands reached out and grasped at air as she fell backwards like an unsteady toddler, and landed with a smack on the footpath, her two legs sprawled in front of her. She sat in stunned silence for a moment before her boyfriend helped her up and she started to laugh as they inched their way along the path, arms entwined.

The bus lumbered south through slush-filled streets and on into the suburbs. Snowmen stood in white gardens and Christmas trees were visible in front windows. Smaller roads off the main bus route were not gritted, and the empty snow-covered paths had an eerie glow under the streetlights. Stevie reached the shortcut to the housing estate where her parents lived. It was filled with about fifty identical pebble-dashed houses. They could be reached off the main road by car, but there was a gap, in the wall beside the green that was a quicker way to reach the houses on foot. Stevie climbed over the gap and after a couple of shaky footsteps found that it was safer to slide her feet along the icy path than to make any attempt to walk at her normal pace. This familiar ground where she had played countless games of football and rounders as a child was different now, cast with a strange spell – otherworldly, dreamlike – but at the same time, potentially dangerous. It was impossible to continue wheeling her suitcase when she got into the estate. The snow was too thick, so she lifted it up and walked along carrying it by the handle until she reached number thirty-four.

Fumbling for her keys in her bag, she realised she felt strange about simply letting herself into the house where she had grown up but no longer lived. She was about to ring the bell when the door flew open.

'Stephanie!' said her mother. 'Come in out of the cold.'

'Hi, Mum.' Stevie gave her mother a hug.

'Oh, you're frozen. I wish this snow would melt. I'm sick of it now, so I am.'

'I know,' said Stevie as she shrugged off her coat. 'It kind of makes getting around fairly difficult.'

'Well, you're home now. You don't have to go anywhere for the next few days. I've the fire set and I'll light it later.'

'Oh, lovely.'

'You're looking well, love. Very healthy,' said her mother as Stevie hung up her coat on the coat stand. Stevie's father appeared from the kitchen. 'Hello stranger,' he smiled, opening his arms wide for a hug.

Stevie sat at the kitchen table with her father. She wasn't hungry but accepted her mother's offer to make her a toasted sandwich to avoid any looks of concern passing between her parents. She knew that on some level they still blamed themselves for not noticing her illness earlier all those years ago. They had brought her up well, protected her from harm, not realising that the real danger was not something external, but would come from within her. They didn't expect this specific threat, so when it did arrive they couldn't recognise it.

After her stay in hospital, the counselling sessions and the slow recovery back to what seemed like normality, they still couldn't figure out the *why* of it. She grew up like everybody else. She was not the victim of trauma or bad parenting or neglect. This was just something that had happened: some mysterious thing that had entered her life, and as a result, their lives.

It was always there. She could see the worry in her parents' eyes, the glances they exchanged, no matter how many years had passed. She could see it in friends, the way they appraised her figure. A voice in her head had told her not to eat and she had listened to that voice. That voice was her friend, her confidante. That voice knew exactly what to do, or not to do. That voice could see into the depths of her soul. She had hushed that voice to a whisper and then quieted the voice altogether, but she knew it was still there, like a faint electrical hum, waiting to rise to a pitch.

'I never use this feckin' yoke.' Her mother pulled a George Foreman grill out of the press and gave it a wipe with a cloth. 'Great news. Your brother has managed to get a flight tomorrow morning.'

'Brilliant,' said Stevie. 'I was worried he wouldn't get home for Christmas.'

'Did you see the news with all the poor people stuck at the airport?'

'No, I don't have a TV. I was reading about it though.'

'There were no flights at all the last few days,' said her father. 'The runway was closed. It's funny to think that a little bit of snow could cause such chaos. They ran out of grit and everything, so they can only do the main roads.'

'Will we have a little nightcap for ourselves?' asked her mother.

'Seriously?' said Stevie. Growing up, there had never been alcohol in their house. She knew that her paternal grandfather had been 'a bit too fond of the drink' and that her father had always avoided it, perhaps out of fear that he would follow in his father's footsteps. He never talked about it much, and as far as Stevie could see, her mother had no interest in it either.

'Well, it is Christmas.' Her mother rooted in the press and produced a bottle of Baileys. 'Now, do you have ice with this?'

'Yes,' said Stevie.

'No,' said her father at the same time.

Her mother looked at them both in confusion. 'I have a measure glass here somewhere.' She opened another cupboard. Stevie watched as her mother poured a shot of Baileys with great care into the tiny glass. If Stevie were pouring it she would have foregone the measure glass altogether and poured about twice as much.

'How's your course going, Stevie?'

'Good, Dad, thanks. Although it's not exactly a course. I'm doing research.'

'But you can always do the H.Dip. afterwards, can't you?' said her mother. 'That's what Rita's daughter did and now she has a great job. There's always jobs in teaching.'

'Not so much these days. The new teachers have it hard now with the pay cuts,' said her father.

'Your cousin James was let go from his job, did I tell you that?'

'No, I didn't hear that.'

'Yeah, the company closed down. I.T. or something I think he was in. Now I'm sure he'll get some sort of redundancy package, but you'd wonder will he get another job, and poor Fiona with one on the way.'

'That's awful,' said Stevie.

'That's their other baby now.' Her mother pointed at a photo that was stuck to the fridge. 'Mason, they called him. Where do they get these names at all? He's 2 now, would you believe? It seems like his christening was only yesterday.'

The fridge was covered in photographs of other people's babies. They were her cousins' children and the children of the sons and daughters of her parents' friends. To Stevie, they all looked the same. Every time she came home there were more photographs.

'Whose is this baby?' Stevie pointed to what looked like a new addition from the last time she was home, a

Thank You card with a picture of a scowling baby on its cover.

'Oh, that's Marian's daughter's baby. You remember Marian, my friend from work?'

'Oh yeah.' Stevie didn't remember Marian, but it was easier to pretend she did to spare the lengthy explanation.

'So you'll be seeing your friends now over the Christmas?' said her mother.

'Yeah, I'll probably go to the pub on Stephen's Night if the weather clears.'

'And will Donal be there?'

'Probably, yeah.'

'He was a lovely fella.'

'I'm sure he still is, Mum. He didn't die.'

'But we never see him any more, do we, Peter?'

Stevie's dad shrugged. 'That fella had worms. He'd eat you out of house and home.'

'Yeah, Mum, you only liked him because he ate your food.'

'And why wouldn't he? You think I'm a good cook, don't you, Peter?'

'Stevie knows what's best for her.'

'Thanks, Dad.'

'So, is there anyone new on the horizon?' asked her father. 'A Galway man maybe? Not as good as a Wicklow man, of course, but better than a Dub at any rate.'

'The bloody cheek of you!' said her mother.

Stevie laughed. 'How many Baileys have you two had? No, sure I've no time for a love life these days.'

'Am I ever going to get any grandchildren at all?' said her mother.

'Well, you might. Maybe from Tom.'

'Sure Tom is only a baby!'

'Mum, he's 27'

'Poor Tom, all on his own over in London.'

'Ah, break out the tiny violins!' said her father.

'When I was your age, your father and I were married and we were even considered old, weren't we?'

'Sure you were an old maid.'

'I was not!' She slapped him on the shoulder and let out a girlish laugh.

'Well, I'm sorry to disappoint you but I have no immediate plans to marry or start a family.'

'Sure you never know, sometimes you don't plan these things,' said her mother. 'They just happen.'

'So you don't think a person should be married first before they start having children?' said Stevie, thinking of all those teenage warnings about single motherhood and lives being ruined.

'Ah, sure it's all backwards now. They're living together and having babies and *then* getting married. You don't want to leave it too late either. You don't want to be an auld one like me.'

'With age comes great wisdom,' said Stevie, for want of anything else to say.

'With age comes great arthritis,' said her father with a wry laugh.

Both of her parents were retired now. They seemed different to Stevie, more relaxed without the pressure of the daily nine-to-five, but they also seemed older, more fragile. She saw that her father's hands were cold-looking, his knuckles swollen. He reached for his glass in a way that was stilted and almost mechanical. It reminded Stevie of one of those arcade games where the mechanical claw lurches and judders as it attempts to clasp its prize.

Chapter 18

Kavanagh listened to the satisfying crunch of snow underfoot as he made his way to Alex's flat on Christmas Day. The church bells chimed and the streets were empty apart from the odd car that crawled past on the sludgy roads. Kavanagh's clothes were unsuitable for the weather. His feet had turned to lumps of ice in his Converse, and he could feel the wet creeping into his socks. The heavy snow had arrived two days ago, and with grit in short supply the country had all but come to a standstill.

Kavanagh had called his mother on Christmas Eve. 'Ah, the roads,' he said. 'You know yourself ...' and let his voice trail off. 'I'll be down in the New Year.'

Since his father's death four years ago, the house had been haunted by his absence. It was too much reality for Kavanagh to take. Over the course of the previous three Christmases his mother had made frequent references to his absent father throughout the day.

'God but your father loved pulling the crackers, do you remember?' she said as Kavanagh and his brother Colum tried to get into the spirit of things by putting paper crowns on their heads.

'Ah, but your father was some man for the sprouts,' she said as she stared wistfully at the Brussells sprout on the end of her fork.

Last Christmas Kavanagh had gotten nicely stoned to get through the day, but then he had to put up with Colum's disapproving looks and he had become paranoid. Sitting on the toilet he felt his heart thumping in his chest and he became convinced he was having a heart attack, just like his father. His father had died on the toilet. 'Just like Elvis,' his aunt shook her head and said to Kavanagh and Colum at the funeral with something that sounded close to awe. The paramedics had to break down the door. Now, when Kavanagh thought of his father, sometimes an unwelcome image materialised of the man lying on the bathroom floor with a quiff, massive sideburns and a white sequinned jumpsuit bunched around blue lifeless ankles.

When he was growing up, it wasn't so much that Kavanagh's father disapproved of his son's love of art, it was more that he lacked any kind of interest in it. 'That's nice,' he would mumble absently when Kavanagh's mother showed him her son's latest painting, his eyes taking on the familiar glassy quality they displayed when his wife would talk about her bridge game with Sheila Brennan or how so-and-so's daughter was marrying so-and-so's son from the village, but hadn't invited Mrs what's-her-name to the wedding.

The young Kavanagh spent hours sketching his surroundings: the long eyelashes of cows, the rusted iron roof of the shed, the light and shade of hay bales biding their time in the fields. His older brother was his father's son. Colum's art was in practicalities: feeding the cows, stocking the shed, saving the hay. He had the same interest in Irish history and even traversed the land with the same slight limp in his left leg.

*

Alex's house had the familiar earthy smell of his plants, but there was a waft of brandy that gave the place a Christmassy feeling. The warm blast of air was welcoming after being outside in the sleety cold. Kavanagh shrugged off his damp coat and stamped the cold from his feet. Alex had taken one of the larger cannabis plants from the other room and placed it on the table. It was decorated with a single threadbare string of red tinsel.

'Nice to see you getting into the Christmas spirit, Alex.'

Alex picked up the plant and handed it to Kavanagh. 'That's your Christmas present. It was either that or some socks.'

'Brilliant, thanks. Hopefully I won't kill it.'

Kavanagh opened his rucksack and took out a small canvas. 'I, eh, got you something as well.' He handed him the painting. 'Merry Christmas, Alex.'

Alex looked at it intently. 'Wow, you painted this, man?'

'Yeah.'

'Seriously? For me?'

'Yeah. It's just something … you know. Your walls are a bit bare, in fairness.'

It was a small oil painting in various shades of blue, a night scene of the Claddagh with a shadowy boat docked in the bay and the dark outline of the houses on the Long Walk. He had painted it a couple of years earlier, but only found it under his bed the other day when he was tidying up.

'Fucking hell. That's class.' Alex placed the painting on the mantelpiece with great care before turning to face Kavanagh. 'Here, do you want some eggnog?'

'Eggnog? Seriously?'

'Yeah. It's pure Christmassy, like. I had an American girlfriend once, Barbara, she used to make it.'

Kavanagh wrinkled his nose. 'Jesus, I dunno. Has it got eggs in it?'

'Yeah. It's fucking eggnog. Course it's got eggs in it.'

'Raw egg, like?'

'Yeah. Here, I'll get you a glass.'

'Jesus, I don't know about this. Did you make it yourself?'

'Of course,' called Alex from the kitchen.

'I suppose I'll have to try it so since you went to all the trouble.'

Alex handed Kavanagh the glass and he sniffed it gingerly. 'Ah, brandy. You should have said.' He knocked it back. 'Here, whatever happened to her?'

'Who?'

'Barbara.'

'Barbara. Ah, it's a long time ago.' Alex bit his lip. 'Myself and Barbara … she was …'. He looked out the window and said nothing for what seemed like an eternity. Kavanagh went to say something to break the silence and then thought better of it. He took another sip of eggnog and looked at the rim of the glass.

'Sure what does it matter now anyway?' said Alex finally in a small voice. 'It's a long time ago, Kav.'

'Yeah, of course. Fair enough.' He was suddenly aware of how very little they really knew about each other. 'So, what are we watching?' Kavanagh asked, steering the conversation back to familiar territory.

'A selection of Christmas treats. I thought we could kick things off with *It's a Wonderful Life*.'

'Oh right,' said Kavanagh.

'Ah no, only messing, I've got *Evil Dead* One, Two and Three.'

*

By three o'clock the ashtray was full, the eggnog was long gone, and Alex was in the kitchen searching through presses.

'There must be food in here somewhere.'

'No, nothing. Sorry. We could order a pizza?'

'It's Christmas Day, Alex. Everything's closed.'

'Oh yeah.'

Then Kavanagh remembered the set of keys to the restaurant. Simon had given them to him in case of problems with the pipes over Christmas. Last year a couple of businesses on Quay Street had burst pipes due to the cold snap, and Simon was worried something similar might happen this year. Everyone else was going home for Christmas, and Kavanagh was the only one who was staying in Galway city, so he had been entrusted with the keys.

'How about a steak?' Kavanagh said. 'I never did get my Christmas bonus.'

'I'll get my coat,' said Alex.

They trudged along the footpaths. Kavanagh, so unused to seeing Alex outside the confines of his flat, felt like he was chaperoning an anaemic child on a rare day-trip. He almost stuck out his hand for Alex to hold as they went to cross the road. It wasn't until Alex, walking slightly ahead of Kavanagh, grabbed the branch from a low-hanging tree, causing snow to fall on Kavanagh's head, that he retaliated by pelting a snowball at his head and they both ran through the quiet streets, giddy like schoolchildren, pushing and shoving each other. The tourist Mecca of Quay Street was quiet, the blinds drawn over the shopfronts.

Inside, Kavanagh grabbed an apron and threw it on. When he first saw the kitchen, it wasn't at all like he had expected it to be from seeing cooking programmes on television. For the most part, everything came from packets. Not even the soup was home-made: there were large white buckets of the stuff in the storeroom. Kavanagh looked in the fridge. 'No steaks,' he said. He checked the freezer and found sausages and a bag of chips.

Alex came in holding two cocktail glasses. 'My own invention. The Evil Dead Two.'

Kavanagh took a tentative sip. 'That's actually nice. What did you put in there?'

'Vodka, rum, cranberry and …' Alex waved his hand in the direction of the bar, 'you know, the green one and some other stuff.'

Kavanagh fired up the deep-fat fryer and threw in the chips. They crackled and spat up hot oil. 'Is it meant to do that?'

'Ah yeah, that just means it's hot,' said Alex.

He fried the sausages in a frying pan and opened the industrial-sized tin of baked beans. 'I hope you like beans,' he said, as he turned the tin upside down and a mountain of them plopped into the saucepan. He hit the bottom of the tin and the slimy stragglers slithered in.

'Fucking love them,' said Alex. 'Here, I'll set the table. Where's the cutlery in this place?'

'It should be in that cabinet in the dining room,' called Kavanagh.

He slopped the beans and sausages onto two plates. The chips weren't drained so they sat in a puddle of grease on the side of the plate. He carried the plates into the dining room where Alex was sitting, sipping his cocktail.

'Dinner is served.' Kavanagh unceremoniously plonked the plates on the table.

Alex looked at the plate of food and started to applaud. 'Bravo!'

'Tuck in,' said Kavanagh. 'My first Christmas dinner as a chef.'

'I think you missed your calling.' Alex raised his glass. 'Merry Christmas, man.'

'Merry Christmas.' Kavanagh clinked his glass. 'Here, remind me to call my mam after this.'

'Okay,' mumbled Alex through a mouth full of food. 'Chips and cocktails. This is the best Christmas ever.'

'Do you think I should give Stevie a ring as well?'

'Ah yeah, why not?'

'She's probably with her family. I might leave it for a bit. I'm thinking maybe I should have gotten her a present or something.'

'You didn't give her anything?'

'No. See, she ended up leaving a day earlier than she planned, so …'.

What he really wanted was to paint her something. He had decided this weeks before, but somehow he couldn't bring himself to start. The more he thought about it, the more the feeling of quiet panic rose up. He could give Alex an old painting he found under his bed, but with Stevie it had to be right.

'You're nearly out,' said Alex, pointing at Kavanagh's glass. 'Top up?'

'Sure,' said Kavanagh.

Alex rose, unsteady on his feet, and lumbered toward the bar. He picked up a bottle of tequila. 'How about an Evil Dead Three this time?'

'What's that?'

'It's much like an Evil Dead Two but eviler.'

'I'll take two,' said Kavanagh.

'I'm really happy you're painting again, Kav. I really am. That painting you gave me is class.' The alcohol sloshed out of Alex's glass and onto the table, which was covered in rogue baked beans, as he made effusive hand gestures.

'I'm glad you like it.' Kavanagh didn't have the heart to tell him that the painting he had given him wasn't new work.

It seemed such a peculiar and distant object to him now. He felt so removed from it that it was like taking credit for someone else's work.

Back when he had painted it, he had been trying something: to render images of Galway City without the chocolate box aesthetic they were usually painted with. He wanted to show the usual picture postcard landmarks in a new light. The boats of the Claddagh, the imposing red sails of a Galway Hooker, the swans, the cathedral, the River Corrib, the Salthill Promenade, Mutton Island Lighthouse, the whole place surrounded by water, the pub fronts – Neachtain's, Freeney's, Murphy's. He wanted to take these familiar images and make them identifiable but somehow different, to show people how he saw the city.

His plan was to integrate these recognisable images with the other images he associated with Galway, the ones that didn't make the tourist brochures: the canal overflowing with discarded cans and Supermac's wrappers, the imposing steel structures of the giant oil tanks on the docks – the cause of so many protests – the midnight pubs spewing drinkers onto the cold night streets as they slammed their shutters and left their ejected guests to fend for themselves. A headless Pádraic Ó Conaire would feature in another of his paintings, that great lost son of Galway who had been honoured with a statue that stood pride of place in Eyre Square until some unknown assailant had taken a notion to decapitate the poor fucker. Another would feature the fourteen family crests of the Tribes, the merchant families who had brought Galway to prosperity and been referred to as 'the tribes' in a disparaging way, but took on the name as a badge of honour and displayed it proudly, spin-masters of their day.

At the time, Kavanagh could see all of these images in his mind, lined up and waiting their turn to come to life. His head was filled with blue swirling ink. He had grand notions of this series. He daydreamed a solo exhibition, newspaper articles, his mother and brother travelling up from Clare to see it, commissions, sales. He used to talk about this series over pints with others who told him about the books they were writing or the plays they would stage or the albums they would record. Then, after a year or so, he was meeting these same people and hearing these same plans about these things that never materialised. Still, he told himself that he wasn't like them. As time went on he heard about his classmates, fellow art school graduates who had made good. They had moved to London or the States. Some had solo shows or lecturing positions in art departments of universities while he was still sitting in Neachtain's and talking about all of the things he hadn't done yet. Years were going by and he still told himself and everyone else that he was working on this series. But he talked about it so much that he talked the desire out of himself. Even though the paintings hadn't materialised, they felt old. He was bored of them before he had even started. It got to the stage where he was fooling no one, not even himself. So, if anyone asked about his art, he gave a vague wave of his hand and said he was working on 'this or that'.

The painting he had given Alex was the only one from the proposed series that he had completed. When he had discovered it under his bed, he realised with a sense of shock that he had painted it two years ago and done little else since. Where had the time gone? He felt ancient.

'Ah, it's nothing, Alex.'

'It's not nothing, Kav. You actually have something. You could really do something with it. I wish I had something like that.'

'How about some music?' said Kavanagh.

'Tunes! Tunes!' Alex chanted as he banged his glass off the table. 'We need some tunes. Give us a song, Kav.'

'Nah, nah, less of that. I know there's a radio in here somewhere. Hang on a sec,' and he went into the kitchen to find it.

'One more tune! One more tune!' Alex chanted as he laughed to himself and his head lolled to the side like a rag doll … and something stirred from somewhere within the depths of Kavanagh; he found to his surprise that he was singing 'Will Ye Go Lassie Go', the old song pouring out from him and filling the empty restaurant.

When he finished the room was silent for a good minute. The only sound was the hum of the refrigerator.

Finally Alex broke the silence. 'Fucking hell, Kav. Where did you pull that one out of?'

'My dad used to sing that. I never really liked it.'

'Wow.' Alex wiped his eyes with the back of his hand. 'Jesus. I didn't know you could sing like that.'

'It's some maudlin' cunt flap of a song, isn't it?'

'No, not at all. It was …'.

Kavanagh coughed hard and cleared his throat. 'Here, I'll go find that radio.'

He pushed back his chair, the sudden movement making a loud squeaking noise in the now silent room.

Chapter 19

On Stephen's Day, Stevie headed into town on the bus. The snow was starting to thaw, but small patches of ice remained, little islands clinging to their fast-dissolving pavement kingdoms. She was meeting Donal and some old friends of theirs from college in The Welcome Inn. Any reservations she had about meeting up with Donal were overshadowed by her desire to get out after being cooped up in the house for the last few days. When Stevie and Donal had been together, The Welcome Inn was their 'go-to' pub.

It was near Trinity College, where they were both studying at the time. Sometimes they would join the crowd in Doyle's, which was directly opposite the university and always full of students during the week, but more often than not they would walk the short distance over the Liffey to O'Connell Street and across to The Welcome Inn on Parnell Street, where the crowd was a mix of locals and student types and you could always get a seat, even on a Saturday. It was best to stick to pints because if you ordered a short it was rarely accompanied by anything as extravagant as ice or lemon. So they would be sitting there drinking Guinness on cold nights, and talk would turn to warmer climates where people had tanned legs and sat on patios and ate barbecued food, or cities with bars that never closed and people partied all night without being turfed out onto the cold streets to maraud like the ghosts of Vikings. They talked about moving to another country when they both graduated. They could go to Canada – they both had friends who had moved there – or Australia. But then something or other always stopped them. There were student loans to pay back, or a rental deposit on a flat that they needed to save for. One of them would get a job, or lose a job. Or they would say, *we'll start saving money and we'll go when we have enough.* Or *we'll go when this contract finishes* or *after this or that friend's wedding.* Or *well, at this point sure we may as well wait until after Christmas.* And so it went for six years.

So they contented themselves with talk. They traversed the entire globe together during those nights in The Welcome Inn. Papua New Guinea was at the bottom of their pint glasses. The packet of crisps torn open and left on the table was a passport to everywhere, and when they licked the crumbs from their fingers it was not MSG they tasted but the healing salt of the Dead Sea.

Stevie opened the door of The Welcome Inn, filled with déjà vu that was tinged with a peculiar feeling of nervousness. Inside it was the same old place, the pub the Celtic Tiger forgot, all flocked wallpaper imprinted with a thousand nights of cigarette smoke – a relic from before the smoking ban – low wooden tables and threadbare carpet. The windows had a stained-glass design in draughty, cracked blotches of yellow, green and red, like some disreputable church. Unlike a lot of other pubs, there were no cosy snugs, no turf fireplaces, just a long hall, a solid rectangular shape so you could see everyone and everything in the place. A tiny television over the bar unobtrusively offered ice-breakers for lone men sitting on barstools to talk about whatever match happened to be on, or the latest economic woe, or this or that gobshite of a politician that was in the news that day.

She saw Donal and the rest of their friends at one of the tables near the back of the pub. They all stood up to hug her hello and the room was filled with a chorus of *long time no see*s and *great to see you*s. Donal gave her a kiss on the cheek.

'It's good to see you,' he said.

'You too. How've you been?'

'Great, great.'

His new girlfriend didn't appear to be with him. He sat back down and she noticed he was wearing his green Fair Isle jumper with the leather patches on the sleeves that she used to jokingly call his substitute teacher jumper. In their old house in Stoneybatter that refused to keep in the heat she had often worn that jumper when she was sitting reading in front of the fire. She pulled up a stool and joined them. They settled into a pattern of rounds, cigarette breaks and anecdotes. There was comfort in this collective recollection, filling in the gaps in each other's memories, holes in each other's stories, a repetition of events that gave them a collective mythology. *Do you remember the time when …? Do you remember your man who …?* The stories became embellished with each retelling. Certain parts were glossed over, others exaggerated or invented entirely until they formed new shapes, which everyone nodded and smiled at and accepted as the originals.

Throughout the night Stevie could see Donal trying to catch her eye, but there wasn't a chance for them to talk alone. She started to think that maybe that was for the best. Safety in numbers. Still, some remnant of that old pull was there. He still had those same kind eyes. The way he played with his beer mat or ran his fingers through his hair, all of these gestures were familiar to her. She knew him. He knew her. And yet there was something new here now, a distance.

They hadn't seen each other in months, hadn't been in touch, had only heard what the other was up to through snippets of conversation, mentions by mutual friends.

Suddenly she wanted to sit beside him, to tell him everything about Galway and about living on her own and how terribly strange it had felt to wake up in her new flat and not in their little house in Stoneybatter. She was sure that he would laugh when he heard about her crappy car and her research trips to the back-arse of nowhere. And maybe, just maybe, back then if she had said, *this isn't what I want* or he had said *we can make this work even if you move away* then they would still be together now. But neither of them had said anything, the silence was pervasive, and then she was packing all of her things into cardboard boxes and dismantling the life they had made together.

All of this was running through her head as she sat on the opposite side of the table from him.

'Donal, how was Paris?' asked George. 'I'm thinking of heading over there some time next year.'

Donal stole a glance at Stevie. 'Yeah, it was great. We enjoyed it a lot.'

'Excuse me.' Stevie pushed back her stool and headed outside for a smoke. She stood shivering on the footpath outside. The freezing air felt welcoming as she lit up, inhaled deeply and tried to get her thoughts in order. *Paris.* It had become a running joke towards the end of their relationship. When it came up in conversation, Donal always gave her that smile. 'Well,' he'd say, and recite the story. This became something they trotted out, this funny anecdote, to polish and shape into a more acceptable thing, to render it comical and gloss over what it meant about her, about him, about them. And it nearly worked.

'It's like the reverse of *Casablanca*,' Donal would say. 'We always *won't* have Paris.' They laughed at it and wanted to make others laugh at it too. But they knew that it was hollow, a fragile thing that could break and shatter and cut them both to shreds.

Stevie would inevitably shrug and say, 'I'm sorry. I just couldn't do it.' So she repeatedly had to apologise for her fear and make light of it. Sometimes she used to imagine the scenario if she had stayed on the plane. She could see it clearly, the Paris of films: black and white shots of the Louvre; a lift to the top of the Eiffel Tower; herself and Donal together and in love, arm in arm, roaming the avenues and boulevards. It was a nice film reel, but it hadn't happened.

Her sense of foreboding had started on the bus to Dublin Airport and intensified during check-in until she and Donal were sitting in the departures lounge. When they were called to the boarding gate and Donal turned to her and said, 'Are you right?' all she could do was nod. She tried to speak, but no words would come out. She was underwater. Strangely removed from herself. She heard the faint noise of an announcement, muffled, distant, barely filtering through. Everything was slowed down. She felt Donal's arm on her shoulder. 'That's us. Got your boarding card?'

The couple boarding ahead of them had their arms entwined, kissing. They told the girl at the desk that it was their honeymoon.

'Oh, congratulations, you two lovebirds. We'll have to see about getting you upgraded.'

Someone walked through the boarding gate and had her passport checked, but it wasn't Stevie. Someone was greeted by the air hostess as she boarded the plane, but it couldn't have been Stevie because she couldn't feel her legs. Some puppet-master was controlling her movements.

'I can't breathe,' she said to Donal during the safety announcements. Or at least that's what she tried to say. What actually came out was just a gulping noise. The fish was now on dry land. Panicked, she fanned her hand in front of her face, trying to breathe in air.

The air hostess came over. 'You're okay. Lean forward for me and take deep breaths. Does she have asthma?'

'No,' said Donal. 'No, she doesn't. Stevie, are you okay?'

She could hear the panic in his voice but couldn't form the words to reassure him.

'Okay, long, slow breaths for me,' said the air hostess. 'In through your nose and out through your mouth.'

And slowly Stevie's breathing began to return to normal, but she was still gasping and crying.

'I want to get off,' said Stevie. 'Please.'

'We can get you off the plane,' said the air hostess. 'I'm going to radio them to meet us with a wheelchair. Do you have luggage on board?'

'No,' said Donal. 'Just our carry-on bags.'

When she got off the plane, even when she was on the ground, she wasn't grounded enough. Her head was swimming with thoughts that this could not be the real ground. It would tear itself open to reveal a chasm. The eternity of time would not be long enough for her to reach the bottom. She would plummet, waiting for the ground to meet her, suspended forever in that fall. Her legs weren't hers. Her tears weren't hers. *Never again. Never again.* She said it aloud. Repeated it like a mantra.

And so it was that they found themselves in The Welcome Inn that night and not on the Champs Elysée.

'I don't know what happened,' said Stevie in a small voice. 'I've flown before and that never happened.'

'I didn't want to go to Paris anyway,' said Donal. 'Sure, we couldn't miss a night in The Welcome Inn.'

Weeks before, her friends had been slagging her. 'So he's bringing you to Paris to pop the question.'

'No, not at all,' Stevie said. 'It was my idea to go to Paris. I booked the flights.'

'Not very subtle, Stevie.'

Her mother had said the same thing, as had the girls in the office. It had irritated her. It was as though they could see no other reason to go to Paris, as if the food, the wine, the art and architecture were all a smokescreen, a pretty sideshow. She laughed it off, but it started to niggle at her. This parasitic thought, an earworm burrowing deeper into her brain, whispering, *but what if he does? Jesus, what if he does? What then?* That would be it. Forever. They would buy a house, get married, have children. That was the other thing. She hadn't discussed any of that with Donal. It was so many years ago. The doctor had said something about it at the time, that she may have trouble conceiving as a result of her not eating, due to the strain her body had been under at a time when it was still developing.

'But there's options,' he had told her. 'So I don't want you to worry. I'm sure that's not something you're thinking about right now anyway.' She was only half listening at the time, looking out the window.

Back at her seat, Stevie looked at the faces around the table, suddenly feeling at a complete remove from everyone. She realised she had never spent time with any of these people on her own. They had been her and Donal's friends when she had lived in Dublin and now they were his friends, not hers.

'I need to take off,' she said. 'Some relatives are in town. You know how it is. It was great seeing you all.'

She said her goodbyes, doing the rounds of hugs, refusing to meet Donal's eye as he looked at her.

It was pouring as she walked towards O'Connell Street to hail a taxi home. The rain haloed the streetlights and melted the freeze, washing away the last of the snow. Stevie took out her phone and called Orlaith. The noise was loud on the other end.

'Hey, are you out somewhere?'

'Stevie? I can't hear a fucking thing. I'll just head outside.'

The phone became muffled. Then she could hear the sound of Orlaith lighting a cigarette and taking a deep drag. 'Sorry, Stevie. I'm outside now. What were you saying?'

'I just met up with Donal in The Welcome Inn. You were right. I've been holding onto a piece of juiceless orange.'

'Hah?' laughed Orlaith. 'What are you on about?'

'I need to throw it away, it's done. Remember you said … never mind. Look, I'll give you a ring tomorrow, okay? I'm gonna head home now.'

'Wait, you're in town, yeah?'

'Yeah.'

'Come and meet me. We're in Whelan's.'

'Thanks Orlaith, but I really feel like just going home.'

'Fuck that. Stop feeling sorry for yourself and get your arse over here.'

'Wow, such kindness and compassion.'

'Shut your hole and jump in a cab.'

'Okay, fine. I'm on my way.'

Chapter 20

The image had haunted Kavanagh that night, and he woke up early with it searing his brain. He searched under his bed for his long-abandoned art supplies and easel. His fingers tingled as he set them up. He drew back the curtains and morning light flooded the room. For good measure he opened the window and shivered in the fresh air, invigorated and primed. He couldn't get started quickly enough, but then he took a closer look at his supplies. Everything was stuck together and looking the worse for wear. It was obvious that he hadn't put his brushes or palette away properly whenever he had last used them. He tried to recall when that would have been, but couldn't.

Shaking his head, he looked at them sadly. 'Rode and put away wet.'

It didn't matter now. He was long overdue some new supplies, but he would have to make do for this morning. Already he was making an inventory in his head of things he would get: sketch pads, paint brushes, paint, turps. Some of the tubes of paint were congealed at the lid making them impossible to open. He scraped at the hardened paint impatiently. Eventually they were open and he couldn't mix the paint quickly enough.

Then he was in it. It flowed – the fluid movement of the line drawing, the sketch taking shape, the ink, and the layers of paint. They had entered his consciousness, those stone figures Stevie was studying. Somehow or other they were like her: luring him in, yet simultaneously keeping him out, inviting him to understand, and then backing away before he had a chance to. It made a change from the tattoo imagery he had been working on, the clean black lines and bold inked colours. This was altogether more elusive. The sheela-na-gigs were emerging from the shadows – mysterious and primal, yet not sinister.

'Kav!' There was a knock on the door.

'I'm busy,' he called.

He heard it again, Gary's voice. 'Kav! Are you not even out of bed yet? Ya lazy prick! Can I come in?'

'I said I'm busy!'

'Do you want anything from the shop?'

'No!' Kavanagh kept his eyes on the painting as the sound of retreating footsteps echoed in the hallway.

It felt strange to be working in this way, like the painting was already there. He usually painted from his surroundings or from sketches or photographs. There was usually a degree of preparation, but he found that today he didn't need it. He could see the figures in his mind's eye. It was a leap into the dark, but he had no fear, only excitement. When he checked his watch he was surprised to see that hours had passed. It was thrilling to lose himself or to find himself lost, his hands covered in paint, the smell of turps and the feel of the brush in his hand. It all felt so right all of a sudden. He wondered why he hadn't been doing it all along, why he had stopped. All those hours he had wasted when he could have been spending time doing this. It didn't get any better: watching something evolve out of nothing, the lines, the shade, the paint taking shape. Always the terror of the blank canvas, but something came to life there, was born, once that leap of faith was taken, that first mark made.

His phone rang. He grabbed it from where it was plugged into its charger and resting on the bedside locker. 'Simon – Flanagan's' flashed up on the screen. Oh God, what could *he* want? He was probably ringing about the keys, or maybe just to make sure the place hadn't spontaneously combusted in his absence. That reminded him, he would have to go back to the restaurant at some stage. He'd go later today. He and Alex had left it in a heap, but he had a few days to get the place tidied before it would be opening for business again. It would have to wait for now. He switched off his phone, leaving the smudge of a black fingerprint on the 'off' button. He threw the phone onto the bed and got back to his painting.

*

Kavanagh let himself into the restaurant. He was surprised to see that the lights were on. Had they left them on? No, he didn't think so. As he stepped further into the kitchen, he heard muffled noises coming from the dining room. He stopped and stood still and tried to make out what he was hearing. Someone had broken in. He listened, holding his breath as his heart thumped in his chest. Straining to hear, he could just make out a lone voice mumbling and the sound of a chair being moved on the tiled floor. Adrenaline coursed through his body. He tiptoed over to the counter and grabbed a long-bladed knife from the magnetic strip on the wall. Some distant part of him was far away from this scene, already imagining the headlines in The *Galway Advertiser*: 'Canny Kitchen Porter Foils Robbery!'

Simon would be so grateful he'd throw him a party. There would be champagne for him and all of the kitchen staff. They'd slap him on the back and finally speak to him in English. The catering would have to be brought in from outside. Lacklustre soup would not hold up to the occasion. They'd have those tiny sandwiches on gilded plates – miniscule squares of bread topped with slivers of salmon.

'Oh, I'm not brave really. Just doing my duty,' he would say to the onlookers as he accepted his award from the mayor. The image bolstered his confidence. It helped him to puff out his chest and creep around the corner into the dining room. It was dark. He could see the intruder silhouetted against the light coming in from the window. Fat fucker. Kavanagh grasped the knife in his hand tighter. The intruder was hunched over one of the tables. Kavanagh was suddenly unsure of himself. How did an intervening hero proceed in such a situation? Should he just run up and wave the knife about? Or stay where he was and yell something like 'Stick' em up, punk'? His legs ached from the tension in his muscles. He waited for his eyes to adjust to the dark room as he shifted his weight from one leg to the other.

He cleared his throat – *Ma hem hem* – as though politely to announce his presence.

The intruder spun around. 'Who's there?'

Kavanagh brandished the knife. 'Hold it, hold it!' he shouted.

The look of fear on the intruder's face evaporated into one of rage. 'You!' spat Simon Dudley-Tompkinson, looking up from the table he had been cleaning.

'Simon, Jesus.' Kavanagh lowered the knife and backed away. 'I thought you weren't back for another few days.'

'Yes, I can see that.' Simon gestured at the mess. 'I thought a bloody bomb had gone off in this place.'

'Em, yeah, sorry about that. I was coming here to tidy up.'

'I've cleaned most of it now. I've been calling you all morning.'

'Em, yeah, I was kinda busy.'

'Kinda busy. Looks like you were kinda busy drinking the bar dry and smoking in here. The ashtray was full of cigarette butts and God knows what else. Drugs and the whole lot.'

Kavanagh felt a sudden desire to laugh. This whole encounter had a surreal feeling to it, heightened by the fact that he'd been painting all morning and this was the first proper conversation he'd had all day. He tried to suppress the grin from spreading across his face.

'Do you think this is funny?' Simon spluttered, his jowls wobbling in rage.

'No, no …'. Kavanagh realised he was still gripping the knife in his hand. He placed it on the table. 'At least now I don't have to stab you.'

'Stab me?' Simon recoiled in horror.

'No, I didn't mean … see, I thought you were a burglar.'

'I trusted you, Joe. Christ, I would have been better off leaving the key with one of the Polish lads.'

'Why didn't you then?' said Kavanagh. Some old reflex was kicking in. He felt like he was at school again, playing out the old familiar scene of the authority figure versus the petulant teenager. 'It's not that bad. I said I'd clean it and I'll replace the booze we drank.'

'Just get out of here and leave the key I gave you.'

Kavanagh took the key from his pocket and placed it on the table.

Simon picked it up and put it in his pocket. 'Count yourself lucky I'm not calling the Guards.'

Chapter 21

Stevie boarded the DART in Monkstown and looked out the window as the train travelled towards the city, taking in the familiar scenery of a trip she must have made thousands of times over the years: the expanse of beach at Sandymount, clouds reflected in the flat shiny surface of the pale brown sand, and the Poolbeg Towers standing guard in the distance, their red and white stripes on the horizon. She found herself looking forward to getting back to Galway and back to work. If she thought about everything she had to do in the next few months, she started to feel swamped and overwhelmed. There was the meeting with Dr Bodkin to discuss her progress. Then there was the research trip to the south of Ireland where many of the sheela-na-gigs were grouped, particularly in and around Tipperary. She would be living out of a suitcase for at least a couple of weeks. Then there was the dreaded question of why the sheela-na-gigs were there in the first place. Why were there so many in that area and not others? To attempt to get to the bottom of it would necessitate hours of poring over records, annals, and books, looking for any mention of the figures to try to piece together their history.

She had discovered that the best approach to keeping her stress levels within the non-heart-attack-inducing range was the use of lists. Writing lists made her feel in control. The world was manageable if it was broken down into neat handwriting and underlined twice in blue ink. Then, with each task completed, she could strike a line through another item on the list. *One thing at a time,* she told herself. It had become her mantra.

Thankfully, she could get to this sheela-na-gig easily, and afterwards she was heading back to Galway. She got off at Malahide station and walked towards the castle. The sheela-na-gig was built into the corner of a wall of an old abbey on the grounds. Stevie had seen an illustration of it in a book and had a rough idea of where it was located on the old building. The Malahide sheela-na-gig was the only one *in situ* in the Dublin area. There was another figure in Stepaside beside a holy well that at one time was believed to be a sheela-na-gig. It had been in dispute for a number of years, but was eventually ruled out as an example. Many sheela-na-gigs had been moved from their original locations to the National History Museum in Dublin. There, the sheela-na-gigs gave no hint of disappointment in their new dwellings: they leered down from their pristine plinths, shiny marble underfoot in the high-ceilinged museum, far from the wind-chilled walls and muck-strewn hills of their origin. Stevie realised that once she visited this sheela-na-gig in Malahide she could cross all of the Dublin sites off her list. She was already looking forward to striking her pen through that information.

The car park was full and the grounds were busy with visitors and people out for walks. Two park rangers in high-viz vests stood on a hill and silently surveyed their kingdom. A gardener trimmed the hedges, the mechanical drone of the strimmer filling the air. Tourists in raincoats and young mothers with prams made their way into the visitor centre through two gateposts topped by loyal stone dogs. A plane loomed large in the skyline, flying low to touch down at Dublin Airport.

The abbey stood behind a wall with a padlocked gate. It was missing its roof and stood in mossy grounds filled with old headstones, like crooked teeth in an old gaping mouth. Stevie shielded her eyes from the sun and looked at the gable end of the building where she had read that the sheela-na-gig was built into the wall. She ran her eyes up and down the area but couldn't see anything. Then she noticed that one of the stones higher up was a different colour, a faded reddish sandstone instead of the grey granite of the rest of the wall. She aimed her camera upwards, zoomed in and took a picture. Looking at it in close-up on her camera screen, she could just about make out the figure. It was badly worn and a good deal more faded than the photos she had seen of it. This sheela-na-gig was definitely not something a passer-by would spot. Even if you knew exactly what you were looking for and where to look for it, it was still difficult to find. She wanted to get in and have a closer look.

She headed for the castle. Unlike the abbey, it was beautifully maintained. A group of tourists stood to one side of the reception desk clutching maps and chatting to each other.

'Hello,' smiled the receptionist. 'Are you here for the tour?'

'Em, no. I'm actually a history student and I'm studying sheela-na-gigs. There's one on the wall of the abbey. Is there any way I could go in to have a closer look at it?'

'Oh, well we wouldn't have a key for the gate ourselves. I can't really say to jump over the wall because then you'd have everyone jumping over.'

'Sure,' said Stevie.

'Dermot?' she called to her colleague. 'Who would be in charge of the gate for the abbey? Would that be the local council?'

'The key for the abbey?'

'Yes, this girl is interested in the graveyard. There's some kind of statue in there.'

'If you ask one of the rangers they might be able to open it for you.'

'The rangers? Are those the guys in the vests?' said Stevie.

'Yes. They look like Guards.'

'Oh yeah, I saw them on my way in. Great, thanks for your help.'

She walked back along the path towards where she had seen the men on the hill, thinking how strange it was that she had come to spend her days like this, ogling old churches. *This girl is interested in the graveyard.* The two rangers were walking along the path in her direction.

'Excuse me. I'm doing a bit of historical research and I'm interested in the old abbey here.'

'Ah yes,' said one of the park rangers. 'The figure on the wall is it?'

'Yes, exactly.'

'No problem. I can open the gate for you now.' He reached into his pocket and took out a giant set of keys.

'Oh brilliant, thank you.' They began to walk together toward the gate. 'Do you get many people coming to look at it?'

'Oh yes,' said the park ranger. 'We've had people from all over the world coming to take photos of it. Of course, it's become very faded in recent years.'

'Yes, it's hard to see all right. It's a shame.'

He opened the padlock for her and pulled back the bolt. 'If you can just pull the bolt after you when you're finished?'

'No problem. Thanks so much.'

The mossy ground felt bouncy under her feet. She could see the blue sky filled with small white clouds through the gap in the walls where the windows used to be, but were now long gone. In the distance, the hedge-strimmer hummed, birds chirped and flitted through trees and people chatted as they made their way into the visitor centre, but everything faded away as she approached the figure on the wall. She craned her neck and looked up at the sheela-na-gig as she zoomed in with her camera and took some photos. Even at this close range it was still hard to make out.

As she walked back to the DART station, her phone rang. She took it out of her bag and was surprised to see Donal's name displayed on the screen.

'Hello, Donal?'

'Stevie, hey. Is this a bad time?'

'Eh, no. It's grand. Is everything …'.

'So how was your Christmas?'

'Oh, yeah it was nice. Quiet enough, you know. Yourself?'

'Yeah, same, same. I'm heading back to town today. Families are great in small doses.'

'Yeah, I know what you mean. So …'.

Stevie was thrown by the call. Something about it rang false, as though they had been having a casual chat and he was picking up where they had left off.

'Look, the reason I'm ringing, well … I didn't really get a chance to talk to you the other night. I just wanted to make sure we were okay. I mean, everything was okay between us.'

'Oh right …'. So this was why he was calling. 'Yeah, everything's fine.'

'Are you still around Dublin? Would you be free to meet up for a coffee or something?'

'I'm actually just about to head back to Galway.'

'Okay. Well, look. I'm gonna be in Galway as it happens in the new year for George's stag party, so can I call you when I'm there?'

'Yeah, okay,' said Stevie.

'I have some stuff belonging to you. Some books and stuff.'

'Really? I thought I took everything.'

'There's a few novels and some gloves …'.

'Oh, okay.'

'So I'll call you?'

'Yeah, that's grand. Talk to you then.'

She headed towards the station, past a playground where children bundled up in warm coats played on the swings. A giant brown dog bounded past followed by its panting owner. The winter sun hung low in the sky, a piercing white orb. Its light beamed through the gaps in the tall thin trees as she walked along the path, the bright stuttering beam of a projector seeking her out in the shade.

Chapter 22

Alex peeked at Kavanagh, his hands covering his face to shield him from the horror of what he was hearing as Kavanagh recounted the story of Simon and the restaurant.

'Oh man, oh no, oh man …' Alex repeated as Kavanagh revealed more and more details about the knife and his misguided attempts to foil a burglary that wasn't taking place.

'Oh man, we should have gone back there the day after and tidied up. Shit.'

'Yeah, I know,' said Kavanagh, 'but he wasn't supposed to be back 'till the thirtieth. I thought I'd loads of time and I was all caught up in this new painting.'

'Okay. There must be something …' Alex made a steeple of his fingers and rested them on his chin. 'How about this? I could talk to him, say it was me.'

'What, you mean take the rap for me?'

'Yeah, I mean if it would help. You might get your job back. I could say it was all my idea, that you were staying with me and I found the keys.'

'If it was just you, that'd be breaking and entering. He'd definitely call the Guards then.'

'Well, I could say you were, like, there with me, but I talked you into it and you felt sorry for me because I've no family to spend Christmas with and you were only doing a good deed kind of thing.'

138

'I *was* only doing a good deed: feeding the stoned and the hungry on Christmas day.' Kavanagh mulled the idea over for a moment. 'Nah, man, thanks,' he said finally. 'I appreciate it, but that bridge is burnt. No use going back to it now with a tiny cup of water.'

'Shit. I feel really bad, Kav. This is partly my fault. I drank a shitload of that guy's booze.'

Kavanagh shrugged. 'Look, the guy didn't even throw us a staff Christmas party. He's a fucking scabby prick. I was just taking what I was owed really when you look at it.'

'Yeah, at least you were employed by the guy though. I didn't even work there, Kav.'

'You were my plus-one.'

A reluctant grin spread across Alex's face. 'Shit. It was a good night though, wasn't it?'

'Yeah. Best Christmas I ever had by a long shot.'

'Well, I guess we won't be going back there next year. That's a pity. We said we'd make it an annual thing.'

'We'll have to break into some other shitty Irish restaurant and make Evil Dead Twos. Actually, no. This time next year I'll be living it up in Thailand, tattooing the great and the good on the beach. You should come out. We could open our own Irish restaurant.'

'Cabbage and sunshine. Living the dream,' Alex laughed. 'What are you gonna do now though? Will you sign on?'

'Yeah, I called into them today. It's gonna take a while though. There's a massive backlog of people whose claims haven't been processed yet. But it's grand. I'll get it eventually and at least now I'll have more free time for my apprenticeship in Dúch.'

'Hang on there a sec.' Alex left the room and came back with a wad of twenty Euro notes. 'Here.' He pushed the bundle into Kavanagh's hand.

'Jesus, Alex. I can't take this.'

'You can and will. I'm partly responsible for you losing your job.'

'It was a shit job.'

'Still …' said Alex. Just take it.'

'Jesus.' Kavanagh looked at the money. 'You keep this kind of cash in the house? What, do you have it stashed under the mattress?'

'It's for emergencies. Sure you can't trust the banks these days.'

'I'll pay you back.'

Alex batted the idea away with a wave of his hand. 'Actually, I've been thinking you might be right about selling some more weed.'

'Seriously?'

'Yeah. I'm growing way more than I actually need, you know? May as well spread the love a bit. You said you knew some people who were interested?'

'Yeah, there'll be no shortage of people, seriously. There's fuck all around at the moment.'

'Not like last time though,' said Alex.

'No. I won't try to sell drugs to Pajo's friend.'

'I think that would be wise.'

Kavanagh laughed. 'It's kind of funny now, looking back on it.'

He could see himself, his drunken swagger at the party in Shantalla. Thinking he was the shit and playing at being the dealer. Too drunk and stupid to realise he was right in the middle of someone else's territory. Pajo and his two goons had followed him out to the back garden. He was flat on his back with blood pumping from his lip before he even had time to know which end was up. Then the massive one, the one they called Hulk, was rifling through his pockets, taking his money and the rest of the weed.

'What the fuck, man?' he tried to say, but the blood filling up his nasal passage made it come out as *wann nhh nhh nnn*. He turned on his side and spat blood onto the ground before trying to stand up. Then he saw a boot coming for his face and he was flat on his back again.

'Where did you get this?' Pajo's ice-blue eyes pierced through him. How was he supposed to reply with Hulk's boot on his throat?

'Did you get it here?' Pajo gestured for Hulk to move back. 'Who grew this?'

'I don't know, man,' Kavanagh coughed and clambered up on his side.

Then the little weasel-faced guy snuck in a kick to his ribs and he fell back down again.

'Back off, Walshy,' said Pajo. Walshy ran back behind Hulk, squealing with shrill laughter. Pajo focused his attention on Kavanagh again. 'I asked you, who grew it?'

'I haven't a clue, man. I got it off some guy in Dublin.'

Satisfied, Pajo signalled for his goons to follow him back into the party. Kavanagh shuffled to his feet. The ground was wet and his jeans were covered in mucky rainwater. He shivered in his T-shirt in the cold night air as adrenaline drained from him.

'You better watch yourself,' said Hulk. He shoved Kavanagh's shoulders with his two giant hands. 'Consider this a warning.'

Talk about stating the obvious. Where had this moron got that line? *Oh, that was a warning? I thought you were just pleased to see me* was what Kavanagh bit back on his tongue. If he were less terrified, the whole situation would have been hilarious. If only it had happened to someone else, he would have laughed and laughed. As Pajo and his heavies disappeared back into the welcoming noise and bustle of the party, there was nothing Kavanagh could do but slink off into the night. Already shock was making way for intense pain. Everywhere hurt. His eye was closing over. He could still taste blood in his mouth, a sickening metallic tang. All he could do was try to get home without bumping into anyone he knew, wait for the bruises to go down and hope that not too many people had witnessed his public humiliation.

'No, Kav, that really wasn't funny at all,' said Alex. 'That guy could have killed you. He's a fucking degenerate.'

'I know, I know. I'll stay out of his way.'

'Be careful who you sell to, that's all.'

'Yeah, no worries,' smiled Kavanagh. 'Just close friends and total strangers.'

*

Kavanagh was walking home when his phone rang and he saw 'Colum' flash up on his screen. It was such a rare occurrence for his brother to ring him that he did a double-take before pressing the receiver button. 'Hello? Colum?'

'Joe?' said his brother.

'Colum. Hey, how are ya?'

'I've been better, Joe. I've been better.'

'What's wrong?' said Kavanagh, an icy feeling spreading over his flesh.

'Mam asked me to ring you,' said Colum. 'She's having the operation tomorrow.'

'What operation?'

'She's having a ...' his voice dipped lower into a hushed tone, an almost whisper, 'a hysterectomy.'

'What? Jesus, is that serious? Will she be okay?'

'Yeah,' said Colum, 'I know it sounds bad, but it's not cancer or anything.'

'Oh,' said Kavanagh. That hadn't even occurred to him.

'She has fibroids so she's having elective surgery. The doctor thought it would be best, and I happen to agree with him.' The words from his mouth were not his, but his wife Anne's, the medical expert. They even had that same clipped, slightly put-upon delivery. 'She should make a complete recovery but she needs to take it easy for at least four weeks. Keep her feet up, no heavy lifting, that kind of thing.'

'Right,' said Kavanagh. 'But when … this is the first I've heard of it.'

He heard Colum sigh loudly but couldn't tell if it was from tiredness or disdain. 'Well, it's been on the cards for a while. She was going to tell you over Christmas, but you didn't bother your hole coming down here, so what could she do?'

Kavanagh smarted at the comment, mostly because he knew it was true. 'I couldn't come down. The snow …'.

'Sure, that only lasted a few days.'

There was a testy silence on both ends of the phone, both men waiting for the other to speak.

'I really wanted to come down, but work was manic.'

'Work?' said Colum. 'Is that what you're calling your PlayStation these days?'

'No. I got a job in a restaurant here in town. I'm the assistant manager actually.'

'Right. Anyway, I'm here. I'm only up the road and so is Anne, so we can look after Mam. There's no panic or anything. But she'd like to see you so I'm just letting you know.'

'I'll come first thing tomorrow,' said Kavanagh.

'Leave it until the weekend,' said Colum. 'She'll be out of hospital and settled back in at home by then.'

'Okay, I'll see you at the weekend then.'

Chapter 23

'**Y**ou look really familiar. Have we met?' asked Finn as he prepared the ink.

'I don't think so,' said the woman sitting in the chair. 'I'm Jacqui.'

'Finn.'

She looked small sitting there with her legs stretched out in front of her and the leg of her jeans rolled up.

'Probably just seen you around.'

'Yeah, I'm around all right.'

Galway was that kind of place. Strangers started to look familiar after a while. Passing the same faces on Shop Street, or at the market on Sunday, or in the smoking area of the Róisín Dubh week in, week out, made them start to feel like friends after a while, or if not friends then at the very least accomplices.

'Okay. So you're happy to go ahead?'

'Yeah, definitely.'

She had chosen a sunflower for her right ankle.

'As I was telling you, this can be a painful spot, just to warn you so you're prepared. Not much fat there, close to the bone.'

She didn't look in any way nervous. 'I can handle a bit of pain.'

'Good woman. It'll be worth it, definitely. I think it's a really nice design. I love sunflowers.'

'Me too.' A smile flitted over her face. She looked pretty when she smiled but it was gone all too soon.

'You know it's one I don't get asked to do too often. Lotus flowers have become popular recently, and of course roses would be the most common.'

'It's good to go for something a bit different.'

'Yeah, definitely. Okay, I'm all set here. Just try to relax. I'll start with the outline. Now, feel free not to watch if you like.' He sterilised the skin on her leg. 'Sometimes it can look a lot worse than it is.'

He had got her to sign the agreement form even though it was just a straightforward design. It was the policy of the shop. He had learned to play it safe in San Francisco. Eight Ball had told him horror stories of names being spelt incorrectly, shops being slammed with lawsuits. He'd seen a tattoo of 'Stregnth' and even one of 'Angle' underneath a halo and a pair of wings, not to mention the countless mistakes with translations into foreign languages. It was mind-boggling how little thought went into the preparation of tattoos for some people. They were left with warnings against impulsiveness inked on their flesh as a permanent reminder.

Jacqui didn't flinch during the outline, just smiled as it started to take shape. Finn never asked his clients questions. If a client wanted to volunteer information about the tattoo and its significance to them he would listen and talk to them about it. If not, he didn't bring it up. He chatted to them when they were in the chair and when he was preparing the ink to keep them relaxed. Bedside manner is what Eight Ball called it. 'Dude, you should have been a fucking surgeon,' he used to say. Finn's approach was in sharp contrast to Eight Ball's, whose motto was, 'I'm not here to hold anyone's fucking hand.' He was not for the uninitiated.

When Finn had moved back to Galway, there was only one tattoo shop in the city at the time and he worked there for a bit. It was mostly teenage girls coming in to get their belly buttons or eyebrows pierced. The designs were the usual predictable ones: roses, broken hearts, Celtic bands, kanji symbols with their English translation underneath that said *Love* or *Friendship* or *Honour*, but for all they knew they could easily have meant something else. The place lacked the panache of Eight Ball's shop. It all seemed so arbitrary. Looking at a menu and picking out something on a whim. The place lacked the panache of Eight Ball's shop. He had been into the history of the art of tattooing and he often spoke about the Japanese masters, the *hori*.

'If they didn't like you, man, they wouldn't tattoo you. They had to get to know you first, suss out your personality. If you weren't the right kinda person who deserved their artwork on you, they'd tell you to take a god-damn hike.'

Finn started to think the *hori* might have had the right idea.

He stuck it out for as long as he could, saved his money and then opened his own place, right on the docks, which he felt was the rightful location for a tattoo shop. He liked looking around Dúch at the designs. All of human experience was there: love, death, joy, sadness, family, patriotism, humour, travel and adventure. Finn's hero was Sailor Jerry. He had taken classical American designs and used Japanese techniques to take them to another level with his use of colour and shading. He had pioneered new methods, discovered new colours. Before him, there was no purple. Finn applied the same aesthetic to designs of an Irish origin. Japanese style, bold Sailor Jerry-colours and shading applied to Celtic bands and ornate *Book of Kells* lettering. This was something new, and as a result his reputation spread. Now people travelled from across the country and beyond to get their tattoos done at his shop.

The sunflower was coming along nicely. He was enjoying the shading, giving the flower a three-dimensional effect. Jacqui seemed delighted with it. It wasn't one he got asked to do a lot, but he could vaguely remember reading about its meaning in one of his books on symbolisim, something about unrequited love and a Greek god. Hel something....

He said goodbye to Jacqui and she headed out the door. Then it came to him: Helios. A young woman fell in love with him and she stood staring at him day after day, but he didn't notice her. Eventually, she turned into a sunflower and stayed stuck there forever, worshipping him from afar as he shone down indifferently.

Chapter 24

On the bus home, Kavanagh looked out the window at the passing scenery and found his mind drifting as he thought about old friends he had grown up with, but grown apart from over the years. It was hard to stay in touch with people when you only saw them maybe once a year. He found himself thinking of Lizzie. Back then, she was his sort-of girlfriend. She was small and pale, with eyes so dark that the colour of her irises blended with her pupils, giving her a wide-eyed, amiable expression, like a Japanese cartoon. She would cast glances at him from behind her long eyelashes, and when he looked back at her she would look away. Up close you could see that her eyes weren't black after all. They were dark, dark brown. He didn't remember talking to her alone. They were always part of a group. They drank cider down by the river and smoked rollies or hash the odd time if one of them could get their hands on some. Sometimes they drove to Ennis and tried to get into the nightclub where they weren't known and their fake IDs wouldn't draw as much attention. If they didn't have enough money to go to the nightclub, they got buzzed down by the river and went to the under-18s' disco in the town, sneaking in naggins of vodka and adding it to the cokes they bought inside. Sometimes someone's parents would be away and they'd have the luxury of a free house, a tantalising glimpse of drinking indoors, blessed freedom from midge bites and grass stains. The sound of ice clinking in their glasses of vodka was a beautiful music to them. They danced in the sitting room to CDs. If not, it was the river and the bench and the tinny sound of the music from the speakers of the portable stereo.

Lizzie laughed loudly whenever Kavanagh said something funny, or whenever he said anything at all really, funny or not. The drunker she got, the more frequent and intense her glances became until she was openly fixing her eyes on him. Then she would ask him for cigarettes that she never smoked when she was sober, or stumble in her heels and steady herself by grabbing his arm – any excuse to make contact with him. Towards the end of the night the couples would pair off, and he and Lizzie would be drawn together, two ends of opposing magnets. Her perfume was sweet and fruit-heavy, the smell reminding him of the overripe strawberries he had picked during summers in Wexford. Their alliance was one of discomfort. She was always shivering, leaning in to him. They pawed at each other, hands groping, fingers finding their way through layers of clothes, flimsy cotton defences, buttons and zippers. She let him touch her, cupping her breast under her top, his hand roaming down the front of her jeans, but she never touched him back.

The first time he rode her was on the floor of a dark room at a house party. He hadn't known it was going to happen. They were kissing and next thing they were on the floor, still frantic and half-dressed for fear someone would come into the room, their hips grinding. He had carpet burns on his knees. It was only afterwards that he thought about protection. The condom he had been carrying in his wallet was still there, untouched. There were a few other times after that. Once in the back of Dave's car after they drove home from a night out. This time he had got johnnies from the toilet in the nightclub, and he fumbled with the wrapper in the darkness of the car. The last time was up against a wall coming home from the pub when he had decided not to be with her again. He had barely talked to her all night, but when he was leaving she trotted after him in her heels.

'I'm just gonna go home,' he said.

She had grabbed him, pressed her mouth against his. She was fumbling with his trousers, grabbing at him.

'Here?' he said. 'I don't have any …'.

'It's fine.' Her breath hot on his neck. 'Just pull out.'

He told himself afterwards that he had pulled out, but he knew that even in his drunken haze there was no pulling back when every atom of his being was charging forward, forward, forward.

He remembered the plummeting sense of horror he had felt when she had looked at him, her face wet, tears mingling with snot. 'I'm pregnant. I just took the test.'

His life stretched out before him, images of drudging around town, of his family's lack of surprise, this only confirming all of their beliefs and expectations about him.

'Do you love me?' she asked him, and the look she gave him was raw with need. He managed a nod. It was all he could muster and she accepted it, grabbed it while it was on offer.

'It will be fine. It will be fine,' she said to him, or maybe to herself, he didn't know which.

And he fled soon afterwards. Called his cousin Peadar and told him he was getting money together for college, was there any strawberry-picking work going? And he took off to Wexford without saying a word to her. He called her from a payphone. Her voice sounded small on the other end.

'You were supposed to come with me to tell my parents. You said you would.'

She was right. He had expected her to be angrier, to ball him out of it, but she just sounded small and lost. He felt inexplicably angry. It was churning away at him. He was unapologetic, indignant. 'I thought we'd need money. I'm working here for you, making money for you and … the baby.'

'When can I see you?'

'I'll be up the week after next. I'll call you, okay?'

After what had happened happened, he tried to justify it to himself. He would convince himself he would have come back and faced up to things. He would gloss over that evening in his mind when he and Peadar went out on the town. It was Leaving Cert results night and he had got enough points to go to art school in Galway. Peadar would be doing repeats, but he couldn't give a flying fuck and they were both drinking cider and it was a hot summer night, like being abroad. Nobody was wearing coats. The girls were in their short skirts. They met up with some friends of Peadar's and they were all buzzing with plans to head off to college. Peadar's friend Julie asked him for a cigarette and he rolled one for her. She giggled all the time and found reasons to touch him. She twirled a lock of blonde hair around her finger and looked at him from beneath long dark lashes. He didn't even fancy her, not really, but he wanted to fuck Lizzie out of his system, erase her with this other girl. Afterwards, in the bushes, he clung to her, this stranger, sticky and terrified.

When he rang Lizzie the next day, she sounded far away as static crackled over the line. 'I lost it. I lost the baby.'

There was nothing to say after that. He never went to see her, used starting college as an excuse. When he moved to Galway, he came home as little as possible. When he did come home, he avoided their usual haunts to avoid bumping into her. He heard shortly afterwards that she had a boyfriend, a local guy, and later still that they'd had a child together.

*

Kavanagh let himself into the house and the dog bounded over, barked, ran in circles and jumped up and down.

'Hi, Kitty.' He reached down to pat her black and white head. The dog's full title was Kitty O'Shea the Third, but she didn't seem to mind the abbreviation. Her predecessor, Kitty O'Shea the Second, the dog they had growing up, had met with an unfortunate accident under the wheels of a four-by-four. Kitty O'Shea the First was a sheepdog they had as children who drowned in one of their neighbours' slurry pits. Of course, Kavanagh didn't find this out until years later – his mother had told him the dog had run away to join the circus. She couldn't use the standard line about the dog going away to live on a farm because they already lived on one.

Their farm had never been a moneymaking venture. It was more about the tradition of the place. His father and his grandfather had both been teachers, and the farm had been passed down. They kept a few cows, some hens, and some geese that Kavanagh had been terrified of as a child. In fact, all of the animals had been terrifying to Kavanagh. They seemed to be biding their time until they could tread on him, run at him or bite him. It was not his farm but theirs. They were horrified by his presence. The geese hissed at him. The hens flapped. The cows looked at him out of the corners of their eyes with deep suspicion. Only Kitty O'Shea, the black and white dog, seemed happy to see him.

'I'm ho-ome!' Kavanagh called as he removed his key from the door and threw his rucksack down in the hallway. He had wanted it to come out breezy and lighthearted like in a film, but the words got caught in his throat and came out sounding strange. He coughed loudly to cover his embarrassment.

'Joe?' called his mother. 'Is that you? We're in here.'

He walked into the front room where his mother and brother were sitting in front of the fire. His mother was propped up on the sofa with cushions behind her, and his brother was sitting in his father's armchair, the TV guide in his hand, glasses at the end of his nose.

'Joe!' said his mother. He went over to her and kissed her on the cheek.

'The prodigal son returns, hah?' said his brother.

'How are you, Mam?'

'I'm grand, Joe. Colum and Anne have been taking care of me. Anne hasn't let me on my feet at all.'

Anne was a no-nonsense woman who worked at the local nursing home. She seemed to dislike Kavanagh even more that his brother did.

'Lucky you.' He exchanged a look with his mother and he thought he caught a glimpse of merriment in her eye. 'How are you feeling? Are you in pain?'

'No, I'm on painkillers, Joe. Strong ones. I'm a bit zonked out to be honest, but I feel fine, really. Sure amn't I spoilt rotten here? Lady Muck.' She pointed to a box of chocolates that was beside her on the table. Kavanagh reached over and grabbed them and handed them to her. She took one and offered them to Kavanagh. Take a few I'll have them all eaten now if you don't take them off me.'

Kavanagh ate a chocolate and put them back on the table. He sat down in the rocking chair, and the dog ran over to him. He stroked her head, and she lay down on her back.

'Ah, Kitty. You missed me, didn't you?' he said, rubbing the dog's belly.

'You're lucky she remembered you at all.' Colum nodded towards the dog. 'I'm surprised she didn't attack you, a stranger coming in the door.'

Kavanagh continued to rub the dog's belly, not looking up at his brother. 'Well, at least someone's happy to see me.'

He wished Colum wasn't there. He was always saying shit like that: just enough of a dig to let you feel it, but not enough to call him on it. If he did, Colum would plead ignorance, say it was a joke, or worse, call him 'over-sensitive', that word he had come to dread when he was growing up. Colum was like the mosquitoes in Chiang Mai: a small annoyance Kavanagh would bat away at the time and think nothing of, but that would resurface later as an itch that would scratch and torment him, one that he couldn't help but pick at.

'So, you're feeling okay, Mam?'

'Ah yeah, Joe. Sure I'll be back on my feet in no time.'

'Well, I'm here now for the next few days. If you want me to do anything around the house just let me know.'

'The windows need cleaning,' said Colum. 'And the gutters need clearing.'

Right …' said Joe.

'Ah no, sure that can wait until the weather is warmer, Colum. Just relax, Joe. It's nice to have you home.'

Chapter 25

Stevie could hear Gavin from down the hallway as she walked towards the postgrad room.

'And I must insist that I think creating a fully operational medieval slingshot is a perfect use of my time … health and safety? Oh, for God's sake! That's all you hear about these days. I tell you, they were more forward thinking in medieval times. We are positively regressing.' He thundered past with Adrienne at his heels. He was wearing a snot-green T-shirt printed with the slogan 'Archaeologists: Can you dig it?'

'Um, hi, Gavin. Doctor Bodkin wants to see you in her office.'

'Oh, marvellous. Here.' Gavin placed the clunky wooden weapon into Adrienne's arms. 'Mind this, will you? Don't touch that lever, whatever you do.'

Gavin bounded towards Dr Bodkin's office. Modern weaponry was dishonest, that was how he saw it. You shouldn't kill anyone unless you could look them in the eye and let them know who was doing the killing. He was horrified – *horrified!* – by modern warfare: snipers, drones, fighter jets and bombs. There was a cowardice to it. He lost interest in military history with the invention of the gun. He liked He liked plucky swordsmanship and battle yells of *death or glory!,*. He liked maces, crossbows, slingshots. Yes. To attack someone with one of these weapons was no accident. No *oops, I didn't mean to pull the trigger.* No heat-of-the-moment *my hand slipped* nonsense. There was no question about the intent, no hiding behind anything. It was altogether a much more honest business. The Gardaí didn't have guns. That was a good thing. Did the country run wild? Not really. Besides, you should never underestimate the power of a truncheon. People did not want to risk getting battered over the head with that. It was both painful and unseemly. All the same, times It was strange to think that if he were a medieval man, he would be wed by now and perhaps he would have children, maybe even grandchildren. Modern women were very … orange. He wasn't sure what to make of them at all.

'Do you need some help?' said Stevie as Adrienne wrestled with the contraption gingerly.

'Em, sure, if you could take … em …'. Stevie reached out and helped Adrienne support the weight.

Stevie laughed at the absurdity of the whole thing. 'What is this? Jesus!'

Adrienne looked at her with a hurt expression. 'He's quite brilliant, you know.'

'Who?'

'Gavin!' It was the loudest word she had ever heard Adrienne say.

'Is he?' said Stevie. 'Oh yes, I'm sure he is …'.

'Geniuses are seldom recognised in their own lifetimes.'

'Mm hmm.' Stevie cast about for something that was non-committal but inoffensive. 'That's what they say. Yup. They sure do.'

They placed the weapon with great care down on one of the desks. Suddenly academia appeared to Stevie as something that was the last hope for those who couldn't function in the real world, damaged souls who paced university corridors instead of psychiatric wards. As ridiculous as Adrienne and Gavin appeared to her, was she that different? She was one of them too.

'How was your meeting with Dr Bodkin?' Adrienne asked.

'Yeah, it was okay. She was talking about this conference coming up at Trinity she wants us to go to.'

'Did she talk to you about your critical assessment?'

'A bit, yeah. I'm still working on it.' The truth was that the more Stevie read the various research on sheela-na-gigs, the more confused she felt, not less. She kept waiting for one clear pathway to emerge through the forest of ideas and theories, but they all sounded plausible to her in some way.

'I have mine here.' Adrienne patted a hefty tome of printed sheets on the table in front of her.

'Wow,' said Stevie.

'I hope it's okay. I'm hoping it can be my first chapter and that I can present it to the graduate research committee.'

'That's not until the end of the year though,' said Stevie, more to reassure herself than anything else.

'Oh, I know, but it's better to get a head start on it. If they think your research isn't going anywhere they can recommend that you don't continue on to second year.'

'Yeah, well there is that.' Stevie glanced at Adrienne's stack of papers and found herself shaking her head and laughing, although she wasn't quite sure why. Adrienne looked at her in surprise, then also started to laugh.

Adrienne stopped laughing abruptly. 'Do you like poetry?' she blurted out, looking at Stevie and fidgeting with her sleeve.

'Em, yeah sure. Some of it.'

'There's a reading on this Friday in the college bar. It's Bardic poetry.'

'Oh …' said Stevie. 'Great. Are you reading?'

'Yes, I do a bit of writing, you know …' said Adrienne. 'I just … I don't know if anyone will show up.' She looked at Stevie with sad eyes, her caterpillar brows furrowed.

'Oh, sure, well count me in.'

'Okay. Thanks, Stevie.'

Chapter 26

Kavanagh found his old bike in the shed. He spent the best part of the morning working on it. He brushed off the cobwebs and evicted a family of spiders that had taken up residency on the handlebars. He filled a basin with hot soapy water and gave it a good wash. One of the tyres had a puncture, so he used the repair kit to patch it up. He oiled the chain and pumped up the tyres.

He brought his mother a cup of tea. 'Mam, I'm gonna head into town for a bit. Can I get you anything?'

'How are you getting in? Your brother's on his way down. Sure hang on and he'll give you a lift.'

'Nah, that's okay. I got my old bike up and running. Gonna take her for a spin.'

'That heap of rust in the shed? Jesus, I thought we'd thrown that out.'

'Can I bring you some more chocolates?'

'I'll turn into a bloody chocolate at the rate I'm going.'

'The paper?'

'Oh, the paper would be good. Thanks, love. Take the money from my purse.'

'Would you stop,' said Kavanagh. 'Sure it's only a paper.'

He was on the verge of saying *it's the least I can do*, but thought it best not to point out how little he had, in fact, done.

159

It was exhilarating to be back on the bike, out in the cold air. His father used to give him a lift to school when he was in first year. Kavanagh would look around furtively as he got out of the car for fear of being seen arriving to school with old 'Spittalfields'. That summer he stayed with his cousin Peadar in Wexford and picked strawberries. They would come home in the evening to his aunt's house, exhausted, with backs aching and fingers stained red with juice. He saved up enough to buy himself a second-hand racer, just like the ones the cyclists in the Tour de France used. From then on he didn't need to take a lift to school with his father. He set off every morning on the bike before his father left the house, rain or shine, to cycle the six miles to school. Every day he set his stopwatch and tried to beat his personal best time. It was a game he played where he was his only competitor, pushing himself to go faster and faster as the muscles in his legs burned and his lungs felt like they would explode. He loved the wind in his ears, his legs going a mile a minute. There was nothing better than speed. His father would beep and wave as he overtook him on the road and Kavanagh would cycle even faster, pumping his legs so fast he felt sure he'd take off into the air.

Kavanagh parked his bike by the church railings and locked it with his old rusty U-lock. He walked towards Madigan's, the village newsagent where he used to buy penny sweets as a young lad, and later tobacco and cigarette papers as a teenager. He saw that the old sign was no longer outside the shop and the ubiquitous Centra was there instead – sad, but not surprising. It was rare to see an independent corner shop these days. The red of Spar and yellow and green of Centra had colonised the old façades. He picked up a copy of the newspaper and bought himself a pack of tobacco. Jesus, there really was nothing for doing in this

town. Should he just cycle home again? He sat on the wall
beside the church and rolled himself a cigarette. Just like old
times, he thought to himself, when they would hang around
and scope out the girls, trying to inject some drama into
their humdrum lives, filling in the hours and days until they
were old enough to leave.

As he stood smoking by the church railings, a woman
walked towards him. She caught his eye, did a double take.
Her hair was different, shorter, but he would have recognised
those dark eyes anywhere.

'Lizzie?' he said.

She looked at him and turned her face to the side,
pretending she was looking at him for the first time and
figuring out who he was. 'Oh, Kavanagh. Wow. Long time
no see. What are you doing here?'

'Just visiting the family.'

'Same as myself. Mam's looking after Séamie for me.
I've to go to the chemist.'

'Séamie's your son?' said Kavanagh.

'Yeah, my young lad. He's 8 now, would you believe?
Making his Communion next year. I heard you're living in
Galway now.'

'Eh, yeah. Ended up staying there after college, you
know.'

'Right,' she said. 'Right.'

'So you're still living here then?'

'No, out the country a bit. Kevin, that's my fiancé, he
has a bit of land out there.'

'Great. Well, you're looking great.'

'Thanks,' she said, fiddling with her hair.

'Well, it was nice to see you …'.

'Would you have time for a coffee?' she blurted. 'A proper
catch-up. I don't have to be back for an hour or two, so …'.

'Oh,' said Kavanagh. 'Yeah, sure. Why not?'

They headed into Reilly's bar. It was empty apart from the barman, who was watching a hurling match on the small television in the corner of the room. She sat in a seat in the corner, shrugged off her coat and took off her scarf.

'So, a coffee, is it?' he said.

'Oh, I don't know. Are you having a *drink* drink?'

'A pint might be nice.'

'Okay, in that case I'll have a glass of white wine. A Shiraz if they have it. It's a special occasion after all.'

'Is it?' said Kavanagh with a laugh.

'Yes,' she smiled. 'Two old friends catching up.' There was a hint of something in the way she said it, a barbed edge, that made Kavanagh feel uneasy. He smiled and backed away, the way you might from a dog you're not sure is friendly or not.

She smiled at him sweetly. 'Thanks, Kav,' and the uneasy feeling retreated.

'Howya? A pint of Guinness and a white wine,' he said at the bar.

The barman observed him and then pointed a finger at him. 'You wouldn't be Míchael Kavanagh's son, would you?'

'Yes, I am,' said Kavanagh.

'Ah, you have the look of him. Colum, is it? He used to talk about you.'

'No, Colum's my older brother. I'm Joe.'

'Joe, is it? Good man. I'm Dinny. Dinny Reilly. I knew your father well, the Lord have mercy on him. You have the look of him.'

'Do you think so?'

'Ah yes, that's a Kavanagh face all right. He used to sing in here, you know.'

'Yeah, he was fond of this place all right.'

'Are you a man for the songs yourself?'

'Me? Ah no.'

The barman smiled and handed him the drinks and resumed watching the match. Kavanagh placed the drinks on the table.

'Sláinte,' said Lizzie, as she knocked back most of it in one gulp. 'So what has you home? Do you come home often?'

'Probably not as often as I should. Mam had an operation there, a hysterectomy.'

'Ah, God love her. My mam had the same thing. Takes a while to get back on your feet after that.'

'I can imagine,' said Kavanagh, for want of something to say.

'Can you?'

'Well, no. I suppose not.'

She knocked back the rest of her wine. 'Same again?'

'Em, sure. One more I suppose.'

She marched up to the bar and came back with two drinks. They continued on, drinking, talking, but avoiding anything relating to what had happened. They shared stories about their friends from back then and what they were up to now, who had headed off to Australia, or America, or the UK.

'It's sad,' said Lizzie, 'to think of them all away. You'd feel sorry for them.'

Kavanagh laughed. 'I'm sure they feel sorry for us, still stuck here.'

'Yeah, I suppose so.'

Kavanagh went out for a cigarette. He was feeling a bit lightheaded. He hadn't eaten any lunch. It was still very early. He would finish this pint, make his excuses and then leave. When he sat back at the table, Lizzie had a lopsided smile on her face.

'Thought you'd done a runner.'

'Course not,' he laughed. 'Just having a smoke.'

'No, you wouldn't do a thing like that, would you?'

Was it his imagination or was her speech slurred? 'I probably should be getting back soon though. I only popped out to pick up the paper.' He pointed at the paper that was thrown across the table, a Guinness stain at its corner. She was looking at him, a smile creeping over her face. There was a look in her eye that was familiar.

'Joe Kavanagh,' she said. 'If it isn't Joe Kavanagh.' She looked directly at him: a dare, a challenge, and slapped her hand down on his thigh in a way that could have been considered playful had they been close friends, but given their relative distance seemed to come out of nowhere. He smiled at her, cleared his throat. Her hand was still resting on his leg. She moved closer towards him, looked directly at him: a dare, a challenge.

'Lizzie, I ...' he said, taking her hand and removing it from his leg.

'It's Liz,' she said. 'Liz. Nobody calls me Lizzie any more.' 'I'm sorry, I didn't realise. Liz. Look, it was great catching up but I better be getting back home.'

'Why don't I give you a lift?' she said, suddenly all smiles again as she reached for her coat.

'Ah no, you're grand, thanks, Lizzie ... I mean, Liz. I have my bike.'

'A bike,' she laughed. 'One for the road then?'

'No thanks, Liz. It was great to see you though.' He knocked back the dregs of his pint, put on his coat and picked up the newspaper.

'Oh, it was great to see you too,' she spat, her voice dripping with sarcasm. 'To have a nice cosy chat here like we're friends.'

Kavanagh stood uncertainly, a sudden urge to run out the door overcoming him.

'We were never friends,' she said. 'You only wanted me for one thing. That's all you thought I was good for.'

He wanted to say 'That's not true', but he found he couldn't form the words, couldn't look at her.

'Liz, I'm sorry,' he said eventually. He looked at her as she stood up, her fists clenched. 'Sure, we were only kids.'

'Do you know something, you haven't changed.' Her eyes flashed with anger. 'You were a selfish prick then and you're still a selfish prick now.' She picked up her glass and threw the remainder of her wine at him. He felt the cold liquid splash his face before he had time to raise his hand. 'You'd want to grow the fuck up, Joe. I have a child. I'm getting married. I have responsibilities. I don't have time for the likes of you.'

She wobbled past him, storming out the door. He sat back down on the seat, shell-shocked, the sound of her retreating footsteps on the stone floor reverberating in his head as he took off his wine-splattered coat and wiped his face with the sleeve of his jumper. Dinny Reilly wiped the bar with a cloth and looked at the match on the small TV in the corner. If he had heard the altercation he gave no sign.

'Same again, Joe?' he called.

Kavanagh nodded. 'Thanks, Dinny.'

He thought he heard a kindness in the way Dinny spoke to him, but maybe that was wishful thinking, his need to feel that not everyone in this town hated him. 'And one for yourself too, Dinny, if you'll have one.'

'Sure, I might have a small one so, Joe,' said Dinny, pouring himself a whiskey.

'Grand. Just popping out for a smoke.'

'Right ya are, I'll drop it over to you.'

Kavanagh followed the arrow on the handwritten sign on a piece of A4 paper that said 'Beer Garden' out to the sunless yard filled with empty beer crates. A plank of wood was held up on two empty kegs, a makeshift bench. He sat down and rolled a cigarette, his hands shaking. He inhaled the tobacco and breathed out long streams of air and smoke. He rolled another one straight after and continued to smoke until finally he could feel his heart rate starting to slow, his hands no longer shaking and returning to normal.

All these years he had told himself that he had done nothing wrong and avoided Lizzie so that he never had to face up to it. As the years flew by he had thought about her less and less. She had almost become a phantom. He had convinced himself that there would be no repercussions, but now he was faced with the horrible truth – she hated him. *Grow up, Kavanagh.* She wasn't the first person to say it to him either. Colum had been saying it for years. Simon from the restaurant said the same thing and now Liz. *Grow up, Kavanagh.* He smoked the rollie down to the quick and headed back into the warmth of the pub. The drone of the match on the telly in the corner and the stout in his glass were pleasant forms of distraction he could sink into: a meditation where his mind could rest easy, safe in the foggy moment of now, free from the troubling thoughts of the past. They quelled the tormenting repetition, that sneering chastisement: *Grow up, Kavanagh.* It grew quieter and quieter until it was completely silenced.

Chapter 27

'Are you still milk and one sugar?' Stevie called from the kitchen.

'Yup,' said Donal. 'A good bit of milk.'

'Okay.' Stevie splashed the milk into the cup, seeing the familiar pale-fawn colour appear. They had gone through an unnatural amount of milk in their old house in Stoneybatter thanks to Donal's milky coffee habit. Stevie seldom drank coffee, preferring tea, but when she did she took it black. She carried the two cups into the sitting room.

'Nice place you have here,' said Donal.

'Yeah, it's not too bad,' said Stevie. 'So, George's getting married. Wow.'

'Yeah. I know. The wedding's in Florence next March.'

'Nice.'

'Yeah, I've never been to Italy. It should be good.'

'So, where are you headed later? Are there many of you down for the stag?'

'We're going for a meal and then to some pub on Quay Street. They should be arriving soon. They got the eleven o'clock train down, brought a load of cans with them.'

'Jesus, they'll be baloobas.'

'Yeah, it's gonna be messy. I guess that's why these things are always in another city. It's inevitable you're gonna make a complete show of yourself. Anyway, I bought myself a bit of time with this designated driver carry-on.'

Donal had never been much of a drinker. Even in college when their classmates were drinking like it was going out of fashion, he was happy enough just to have the odd sociable pint.

'So, this is your stuff I brought down.' Donal handed her the cardboard box. 'Sorry, I meant to give you a ring about it before now.'

'That's okay. I didn't even miss anything. I thought I brought everything when I moved out.' Stevie looked through the items in the cardboard box.

'It was just a few bits and pieces around the place.'

'Oh, these. I forgot I had these.' She pulled out a pair of black sandals she had bought for a summer that had never quite arrived. There was one sunny day that May, and she had gone out and bought the black-studded leather shoes. Although flat they were deceptive in the level of comfort they suggested, and the first and only time she had worn them she got a nasty blister on her heel. The weather had turned and she had left them in the spare room, where she promptly forgot about them and spent most of the summer in black Converses.

'Maybe not the best weather for them.'

'Well, I've time now to break them in for the summer.'

She pulled out a couple of books from the box. There was her archaeology textbook from her degree, covered in black ink doodles and a dog-eared novel.

'*Confederacy of Dunces*. I thought I gave this to you one Christmas?'

'You did,' said Donal. 'That's your copy.'

'Oh yeah,' said Stevie. 'Did you read it?'

'Never got around to it, but I will.'

'So … how's everything going with Amy?'

'Yeah, good. It's going good.'

'I heard you moved in together.'

'Yeah, we did. I know it seems sudden, but she needed a place to live and I needed someone to move in, so …'.

'Sure,' said Stevie. 'I'm happy for you.' As she said it, she realised it wasn't an empty platitude. She genuinely meant it.

Donal smiled at her. 'Thanks. That means a lot. You seem happier now too. You seem really good.'

'I am, yeah. It's nice to be able to talk like this.'

Towards the end of their relationship they were like two ghosts haunting separate rooms, never going to bed at the same time. They had drifted that way and neither of them had made the effort to right it. Unemployment had taken its toll on them: no money coming in, an endless round of job application rejections. Somewhere along the line, they went from lovers to room-mates. Then Donal had got a job and he was up early in the morning. Each night Stevie stayed up late and crept into bed when he was asleep. She slept on her side of the bed and he on his, an invisible line drawn down the centre of the mattress.

After he left for work she sat in the house by herself, trawling through job websites. For no apparent reason, she would find herself crying. Anything could set her off – an ad on TV, a song on the radio. Some days she couldn't bring herself to leave the house. She knew that if she could get outside and move her limbs it might clear her head, lift her from the fog that had settled around her, but moving from the sofa seemed impossible.

Eventually she started to go for daily walks. She tried the Phoenix Park, but it was too wide and the green vastness of it terrified her somehow. Instead she would walk by the Liffey, down the Quays and into the city centre. She liked the bustle and noise of town where you could be surrounded by people, but still be alone. It was on one of these walks that she found herself in the National Archaeology Museum on Kildare Street. She hadn't been in the building since the time she visited it on a class trip. It felt like a sacred space to her – the cool air of this marble-pillared hall with its mosaic-tiled floor – and she was suddenly aware of the dirt on her shoes, of her tangled hair, the grime under her nails. She wanted to go home, to shower, to put on some clean clothes. She decided that she would, it was time for a change. As she walked around the exhibition she felt herself filling up with joy. This was more nourishing than any meal. It started to come back to her, her old feeling about history, about exploration, about everything – a kind of unexpected homecoming. Then she saw the sheela-na-gig on the plinth, the one that had sparked her interest all those years ago. It hit her then, a definite thought through the fog: *this is what I should be doing.* She would study these stone carvings.

Donal placed his cup on the table. 'Okay, I better get going. I've to catch up with these eejits. I'd say I'm about ten pints behind at this stage.'

'Okay, have a great night. Enjoy Galway. Try not to get arrested.'

'Thanks, I'll try. So we're okay then?'

'Yeah, of course,' said Stevie.

'I'm glad we can be friends. It feels wrong not to be. Sometimes I think of things that I really want to tell you but I can't ring you up because I don't know if that would be weird.'

Stevie smiled. 'Yeah, I know what you mean.'

'Okay. Well, let me know when you're in Dublin the next time. We can meet for coffee.'

Stevie smiled. 'Okay.'

They hugged and she walked him to the front door. She watched him walk away, already knowing that she wouldn't be contacting him when she was in Dublin again. That was something people said and didn't really mean. It was kinder than saying *we won't see each other again and that's okay with me.* Orlaith had been right all along, but this was a good ending. One she could be happy with.

Chapter 28

Kavanagh stood out by the shed smoking a one-skinner joint. He had come outside to refill the turf bucket that lay at his feet. Off in the distance a cow lowed as the breeze whispered through the tall trees behind him. A familiar kind of music. His breath was visible in the cold night air. Above him the stars shone, bright pinpricks of light in an endless blanket of darkness. The only other light visible was from inside the house, seeping out from the edges of the curtains of the sitting room window.

Kavanagh came into the sitting room and set the turf bucket down by the fireplace. He threw another couple of pieces of turf on the fire.

'Thanks, Joe. That'll keep us going for a while.'

His mother was watching *The Late Late Show*, a cup of tea in her hand.

'I usually have a glass of wine when I'm watching this, but I'm not supposed to with these antibiotics I'm on.'

'Ah, it won't be long now,' said Kavanagh.

'Help yourself to a drink, Joe, if you'd like one.'

'Ah no, Mam. I'm grand here with my tea.' Kavanagh refilled his cup from the pot on the table and grabbed a couple of biscuits.

'Are you still smoking, Joe?'

'Em, ah, I'd have the odd one, you know?'

'A social smoker, as they say.'

'Yeah, that's it.'

'And what about the other stuff?'

'What other stuff?'

'The whacky tobaccy.'

Kavanagh laughed and cleared his throat.

'I used to smell it in your room you know.'

'That wasn't me, Mam. It was Colum.'

His mother laughed at that. 'Nice try, Joe. Sure he's straight as an arrow. Just like your father. I always wondered what it was like. I almost tried it once, you know.'

'Did you?'

'Yeah, years ago. It was before your father and I were married. We were at this party and there were these hippies at it, like you'd see in a film or something. I remember one of the girls had long hair all the way down her back. It was so long she was sitting on it, and it was so straight I think she must have ironed it or something. I wanted to ask her about it, but it seemed rude to. Anyway, they were passing this joint around. They were very generous. They weren't trying to hide it or anything. It was no big deal to them. I know it would be no big deal now, but back then in this little town, well, I don't need to tell you it was quite conservative still. People did not know what to make of this. And it came around to me, this joint, and I took the thing in my hand and your father was looking at me. Agog, he was.'

Kavanagh laughed. 'I can imagine.'

'So I just sat there staring at the thing. The girl came over and she took it from my hand. "Thanks, dear," she said, and she walked back over to the other side of the room, her long hair swishing. I always wondered …'.

'What stopped you?'

'What your father would have thought of me. Would I be a ruined woman?' she laughed. 'I think if I'd been on my own it would have been different. Maybe I would have felt more free, but we were all so frightened back then of everything. Not like it is now. Sure, in parts of America they prescribe it to sick people. California, I think it is. There was a documentary on about it not so long ago.'

'That's right,' said Kavanagh. 'They should bring that in over here.'

'And what would it do exactly for these people they prescribe it to?'

'Well, it can help people who are terminally ill, you know, who may not have any appetite.'

'Oh, well I wouldn't need any help now with that. Is it good for pain as well?'

'Yeah. I suppose so,' said Kavanagh. 'It definitely makes you feel, I don't know … lighter or something.'

'I wouldn't mind trying it, you know. If I could get my hands on some.'

'Are you in pain, Mam? Are the painkillers not strong enough?'

'No, I'm not in any major pain. Nothing more than you'd expect. It's more … uncomfortable than anything else. I was just curious more than anything. At this stage of my life it's hardly going to lead me to ruin, is it? Sure, what harm?'

'It is illegal though.'

His mother shrugged. 'Sometimes rules are made to be broken. If only I'd realised that when I was younger.'

'I mean, if you want to try it I could …'.

'Do you have some here?'

'Yeah, I have a bit,' said Kavanagh.

His mother nodded. 'Right so, let's see what all the fuss is about.'

Kavanagh rolled a joint and lit it up.

'You smoke this like a cigarette, is it?'

'Yeah,' said Kavanagh.

His mother inhaled the smoke and coughed. 'Oh, that hit the back of my throat. I haven't had a cigarette in twenty years.' She inhaled again and blew out the smoke in a steady stream. 'Ah,' she said. 'You know, back then they didn't even let women drink in the pubs, would you believe that? I had friends who had to give up their jobs when they got married. There was no choice, that's just how it was.'

'It's crazy to think it, isn't it?'

'It is in this day and age, but it was a different time. Sometimes I wonder is it really that different at all?'

'Well, I suppose at least women have the choice now to stay in their jobs if they want.'

They do, but who minds the kids then? The grannies. Don't get me wrong, I love my grandchild, but I already raised my children. I see it with my friends too, you know. Oh, I can't meet you for coffee that day, I have to mind the grand-kiddies. They're having to raise children all over again, but I don't know. I don't know what the answer is.'

'Wouldn't it be great if we didn't have to work?' said Kavanagh. 'I don't know. I feel like people are too defined by the jobs they do. They get all of their self-worth from their job title. I mean, where does that leave people who can't find jobs? Are they not worth anything?'

'How's your job going in the restaurant?'

'Yeah, pretty good.' Kavanagh felt a twinge of guilt for lying, but it was easier than having his mother worry about him. 'But you know, it's just a means to an end so I can save some money.'

'To head off travelling again, is it?'

'Yeah.'

'Good for you, son. Colum thinks you're daft, but do you know something? I think he's only jealous. He's a homebird like your father. You're like me, Joe. You want to get out and see things. There's a whole world out there.'

Kavanagh nodded.

'You know, I wish I'd travelled more when I had the chance.'

'Sure, there's still time,' said Kavanagh. 'You can come over and visit me in Thailand.'

'We should have gone in the summer when your father had all of those holidays, but then there was always the farm. If I could do it over again I'd head off with my paints …'.

'Your paints?'

'Yeah, I used to do a bit. Way back.'

'You never told me that.'

'It was never much encouraged back then. It wasn't a thing you could make money from. Dressmaking on the other hand … but you must have got it from somewhere, Joe. Sure, you didn't lick it up off the stones.'

When he was younger the kitchen table would be covered in dresses and shirts – buttons to be sewn back on, hems to be altered. He would come in from school and his mother would be beside the fire, her measuring tape around her neck, a pin in her mouth, the needle weaving in and out of material. Or there would be some person from the village standing there, arms outstretched, Christlike, as she took their measurements and marked the clothes in chalk.

'There's no money in it now. Sure why would anyone get a dress made? They can go into a shop and try it on there or order it online. Even the repairs now, sure why would you pay someone to fix a ripped seam when you can go into Penney's or one of them places and buy something new for half nothing? Clothes aren't built to last these days, and people don't expect them to either. It's all … different.'

'Are you okay, Mam?'

'I don't know. I'm feeling a little sad I suppose, after the operation and everything. I mean not that I was planning on having any more children or anything,' she laughed. 'I'm gone well past that now. I don't know. It's just the idea of it, that that's all over with. You probably think that sounds daft …'.

'No, not at all,' said Kavanagh. 'I think that sounds completely understandable.'

'Promise me one thing though.'

'What's that?

'If you do go off travelling, promise me wherever you are that you'll come home for Christmas. We missed you this year.'

Kavanagh nodded. 'I promise.'

'Are you hungry at all, Joe?'

'Yeah, I'm a bit peckish all right.'

'I'm starving. Have we any crisps or anything in the house? Do you know I don't think we do.'

'How about some toast, Mam?'

'That'd be brilliant, and a cup of tea. Can you manage?'

'Sure, I think my culinary skills can stretch to tea and toast.' Kavanagh made his way into the kitchen. 'What with my professional restaurant experience and all.'

'Thanks, Joe. And we don't need to be saying anything to Colum about this.'

'Oh, God no,' said Kavanagh. 'Course not.'

'I don't know if he'd approve.'

'I can safely say he definitely would not approve.'

'He means well,' said his mother. 'He's just …'.

'A dry-shite.'

His mother nodded. 'You know, he might be. Just a little bit.'

Chapter 29

Adrienne was wearing some sort of purple robe covered in Celtic spirals. She stood at the top of the room, although to describe it as a room wasn't entirely accurate. It was a dimly lit, curtained-off section of the college bar. The noise from the DJ in the other room seeped in and the smell of the bar food that had been served earlier still hung in the air. A couple of students screeched and popped their heads around the curtain, frowning into the darkness.

'Is the cigarette machine in here?'

'No. This is a poetry reading,' said Adrienne, contrite as the microphone hissed and made noises like a thing possessed.

'Oops!' The curtain swished closed with a loud giggle. 'Oh my GOD! What the hell was that?' The girl's voice floated back to them.

'Em, can everyone hear me?' Adrienne said as the microphone farted and she looked at it in fright. She tapped it with her fingers and it boomed back.

'I just wanted to say thank you everyone for coming tonight. It's nice to see so many people here.'

Gavin began to applaud loudly. Kavanagh looked around the almost empty room and threw Stevie a bemused look.

'Em, yes, thanks. I want to say a special hello to a couple of people. I'm honoured to be joined tonight by my colleagues from the Medieval History Department, Gavin and Stevie.'

Gavin stood up and waved at the meagre gathering. 'Thank you. Pleasure to be here.' Stevie felt her cheeks flush, her plans to sit unnoticed at the back of the room ruined.

'So this evening is a celebration of poetry in the Bardic tradition. We will have readings of some traditional poems, and we are also lucky enough to have some poets with us this evening who are still writing in this style and keeping the Bardic tradition alive. I'd like to introduce our first poet for the evening, Conall McIonomara.'

A small bearded man shuffled on from the wings and cleared his throat for what seemed an eternity. He fiddled with a large sheaf of paper in his hands.

'Thank you, Adrienne. It is great that some people are still supporting the Bardic tradition of poetry, a once lauded style of traditional verse. I believe it is long overdue a revival.'

'Hear, hear!' yelled Gavin.

A couple of people tittered.

'Here is my first poem this evening. I wrote this poem a few years ago … excuse me …'. He cleared his throat again as if something had died in there that he was trying to dislodge. Adrienne rushed up to him with a glass of water.

'Thank you.' He took a sip and placed it on the table next to him. His coughing seemed to have set off a series of coughing from the sparse audience. Suddenly everyone was horribly aware of the itch in their own throats as a chain reaction of coughs spread around the room, punctuating the silence as they waited for the man to start reciting his poem. He cleared his throat one final time, looked down at his paper and spoke into the microphone. What then emerged from his mouth was a series of strange garbled noises. Kavanagh shot Stevie a startled look. She leaned closer and concentrated.

'Is this in Irish?' said Kavanagh.

It sounded like Irish, but she couldn't make out any of the individual words. It was like someone who had once heard Irish and was now doing a phlegmy gibberish impression of it in an impassioned reading.

'It must be old Irish,' she whispered back to Kavanagh.

'Jesus. Here, I'm going out for a smoke.'

'You can't go now. He's in the middle of a poem.'

'When can I go?'

'When he's finished.'

'How long is the poem?'

Stevie shrugged. This is exactly what she had been worried about. She had told Kavanagh she would meet him another night, but he had insisted. 'No, I'll come. I want to see you. I haven't seen you in ages.' To sit quietly and listen to a poetry reading she had no interest in when he was sitting beside her was almost torturous.

'Now?' whispered Kavanagh, gesturing towards the door.

'Just wait!' Stevie's voice came out unintentionally loud at the exact moment the poet had paused dramatically. All heads turned towards Stevie, who suddenly became very interested in the exact contours of her wine glass as Kavanagh tried not to laugh.

At last the poet finished his phlegmy delivery and Kavanagh leapt up from his seat and headed outside.

'This next poem is a bit of an epic in duration ...' said the poet. Stevie sighed and knocked back her wine.

*

Outside, Stevie lit up her pipe and inhaled deeply. 'Look, if you want to go, feel free, but I'm going to have to stay 'till the end.'

'No, I want to stay. It's hilarious. How did they let these people out? They're mental.'

'They're not mental,' said Stevie. 'Besides, you shouldn't say things like that.'

'Like what?'

'Calling people mental. How would you feel if someone said that about me?'

'Why would anyone say that about you?' said Kavanagh with a confused look on his face.

'They've said worse.'

'Who has?'

Stevie took a deep breath. For a moment she thought it would all come tumbling out about her time in the psychiatric unit. 'Let's just forget it, okay?' she said.

'I just meant that they're funny.'

'No, I know. It's just, I don't think they're trying to be. That's the problem. Look, I know it's a bit ... naff, but I work with these people. I have to show support, you know?'

'I'm sorry if I ...'.

'No, it's fine.'

'Look, I just want to spend time with you, so whatever you want to do is cool with me. I was thinking about you a lot over Christmas.'

'Really?'

'Yeah, I ... missed you.'

'I missed you too.'

Kavanagh cupped her face with his hands and kissed her. 'So, will we go back in?'

'Do we have to?' said Stevie, kissing him again before breaking off reluctantly. 'Yeah, I suppose we do. I'll get us another drink on the way back.'

'That would help things,' said Kavanagh.

The atmosphere was heating up back in the student bar. The DJ was playing more energetic songs and a group of girls were dancing on the floor, flinging their arms up in the air with an abandon reserved for the heavily intoxicated. On one of the couches a girl was straddling a boy, pressing her body against his as his hands roamed all over her body.

'Jesus,' said Kavanagh. 'Maybe I should come back to college.'

'Would you rather wait for me here?' smiled Stevie.

'Jesus, no. Those girls look like they'd eat you alive. And the music … Christ. I think it's possibly even worse than the poetry thing.'

'Stuck between a rock and a bard place,' said Stevie. 'I'll get us a drink and meet you there.'

Back inside it was still the interval and Kavanagh wasn't in his seat. Stevie spotted him sitting at a table with Adrienne and Gavin. He must have gone over and introduced himself. As She sat down to join them, Kav was smiling at Gavin, 'So you actually make these weapons yourself? Wow, man. That's deadly.'

Stevie tensed, waiting for Gavin to make a blustering retort, but he beamed and looked down at his hands on the table then looked back at Kavanagh shyly as Adrienne looked on adoringly. Kavanagh had that warmth, that unassuming charm that put people at ease and made being around him so easy. It seemed to Stevie that it was something he wasn't even aware of.

'Time to start the second half,' said Adrienne as she stood up. 'Thanks so much for coming, guys. It means a lot.'

Chapter 30

The first sunny day of spring hinted at the summer that was on its way. A favourable sign. A sneak preview of the main feature that was coming to theatres soon. Finn loved this time of year when everything was filled with the promise of the new. Birds from foreign climbs rested their wings, on land again at last after weeks of sky. Daffodils poked their heads through soil and feasted their eyes on the cars encircling the roundabout. The grass never looked so green. The particular slant of the sunshine illuminated dust on counter tops and shelves. All of a sudden, everyone was mad for cleaning. Spiders became unseated from cobwebby windowsills. Everyone opened their doors to the fresh air.

In Dúch, sun spilled in through the slanted blinds casting shadows on the polished wooden floor. The bell over the door tinged, and Kavanagh arrived in with two takeaway coffee cups.

'White coffee, one sugar, right?' He placed one of the cups in front of Finn.

'Holy shit.' Finn smiled and shook his head. 'That's it. That's it exactly. I never thought I'd see the day.'

He had noticed a change in Kavanagh lately. The last few mornings Finn had arrived to find Kavanagh already waiting outside for him to open up. There was no more disappearing. He was present, focused. He saw what needed to be done and did it without being asked. Maybe Finn had redeemed himself as a mentor after all.

As Finn drank his coffee he glanced up to see a dark shape making its way past the door. He looked out the window and saw a short, wiry man dressed head to toe in black standing opposite the shop and shooting furtive glances in. Something about the presence of the man unnerved him. He was conspicuous in his attempts to appear inconspicuous. Finn realised he had seen him a few days before, hanging around the shop as Kav was getting ready to leave.

'Hey, Kav. Do you know yer man across the road there?'

'Who?'

Finn moved closer to the window and Kavanagh followed. 'He's staring in here.' He raised the blinds and they both looked out, but all Finn could see was the back of the figure as he made a hasty retreat.

Kavanagh peered out the window. 'Where? I don't see anyone.'

'He just left. I think I've seen him before though, hanging around, scoping the place out.'

'Maybe he's working up the nerve to get a tattoo?'

'Yeah, maybe.' He lowered the blinds and turned to Kavanagh. 'Speaking of which, how's the one you did on your leg? Did it heal up okay?'

Kavanagh cringed. 'Yeah, it's grand. Look, about that, I don't know what I was thinking. It was a stupid thing to do and it was … it was disrespectful to you.'

Finn nodded. 'I appreciate that. That was my idea of an apprenticeship, I guess, watching and learning. Maybe it was too old-school.'

'No, not at all. I was impatient. I should have waited. I really am sorry about that.'

'Could you do it better now, the same tattoo?'

'Oh yeah, definitely.'

'Okay, let's see.' Finn sat in the chair and rolled up his trouser leg. 'Same tattoo, same spot, but this time on me.'

'Seriously?'

'Yeah, and after this you can consider your apprenticeship over. You're ready.'

'I ... I don't know how to ... '

'I haven't got all day here,' smiled Finn.

Kavanagh nodded. 'Okay, let's go.'

Chapter 31

'In this country we've gone from boom to bust, and now we have another boom – a boom of knowledge! I think that will become apparent throughout the course of our conference here today. Each speaker will present their paper for twenty minutes, with a five-minute slot at the end for any questions.'

The first speaker was a young American woman who presented a paper on the drúth in Irish writing. When she pronounced some of the words in Irish, Stevie could see Adrienne squirming uncomfortably in her seat as though hearing the words spoken incorrectly caused her physical pain. Stevie had her pen in her hand to take notes but ended up doodling on her notepad, drawing a series of increasingly larger spirals.

The second speaker looked very young and very nervous. She dropped her notes, and her hands shook as she apologised and picked them up. She read from them and barely looked up. She seemed to forget entirely about the projector until the end, when she clicked through all of her slides in a flash. Nobody asked her anything during the alloted question time and she sat back down and looked relieved. Everyone clapped loudly, as though they had been collectively holding their breath and were celebrating the fact that her presentation was over.

The final speaker was a man who was researching the velocity of medieval catapults. He had charts, which he explained in intricate detail. Stevie shifted in her seat and tried to focus on the speaker as he droned on in a monotone. What struck her was the specifity of the presentations. She began to wonder if this was what her future held. Were all academics some version of this man, focusing their entire life on a subject in minute detail, buried so deeply in it they couldn't recognise their own esoterica as they tried to convince everyone of its worth and value? For every tiny pocket of history it seemed there was that one person who would embrace it and make it their life's work. What was any of it for? She imagined herself in the speaker's position, facing a sea of bored faces, a life of disinterest and lukewarm responses.

They couldn't find three seats together earlier, so Gavin and Adrienne were sitting in the row ahead of her. Adrienne turned around and gave Stevie a wave, and out of nowhere Stevie felt a desire to laugh that threatened to escape from her mouth. Adrienne caught her eye and grinned, a look passing between them. Stevie covered the laugh with a cough and a sharp clearing of her throat as Gavin turned and glared. Adrienne saw this and stifled her own laugh. She put her head down and Stevie could see her shoulders shake. She felt like she was in Mass again, alternating between head-nodding waves of tiredness and barely contained hysteria that threatened to explode if the priest said something inadvertently funny or some poor unfortunate unwittingly broke the silence with a fart.

After the lecture they filed out of the room and headed like zombies in the direction of the strong aroma of coffee that was wafting from the common room. During the coffee break there was a flurry of chatter with people meeting old friends and colleagues. The mood was upbeat as people of all ages and accents mingled and chatted.

Stevie smiled at Adrienne. 'Jesus, that was tough going.'

Adrienne nodded. 'I feel bad for laughing.'

They both started to laugh again, unleashing all of the laughter they had held back.

Gavin came bustling over. 'Well, that catapult one was fascinating, wasn't it? Highlight of the conference thus far I would venture.'

'Yes, very interesting,' said Adrienne.

'Hmm,' said Stevie.

'There's a lecture on ring forts up next' I want to get a seat near the front. Are you coming?'

'Well, I'm gonna head out for a smoke. I'll see you back in there.'

'I'll come with you,' said Adrienne. 'I could use some air.'

'Very well. I'll try to save you both seats.' Gavin bustled off.

They made their way outside and the cold blast of air hit them, reviving their senses. The courtyard of Trinity College was filled with tourists lining up to see *The Book of Kells*.

Stevie filled her pipe with tobacco and lit up. 'So how's everything going with you?'

Adrienne bit her lip. 'Yeah, okay I suppose. I'm a bit nervous about this meeting with the graduate committee.'

Stevie nodded, 'Me too.'

'I'm just worried I don't have enough done. I mean it's not from lack of effort …'.

'I know what you mean. You'd be spending days on something and it would lead absolutely nowhere. Jesus, it'd break your heart sometimes.'

Adrienne nodded. 'I suppose that's the nature of it though. It's so rewarding at the same time when you get a good run at it and the pages almost write themselves.'

'Oh definitely, yeah.' Stevie smiled as if she knew what Adrienne meant. *Pages writing themselves — what the hell?* She was hoping Adrienne might express some doubt or difficulty, that they might bond over how they were both struggling, but she could see now that it was just her, only her, that wasn't getting it. 'So you reckon you'll stick it out then?'

'The conference?'

'No. Your Ph.D.'

Adrienne blinked hard and tried to process the question. Dropping out was a possibility that hadn't ever occurred to her. She loved university she was always the first over to the library when essay questions were set. She couldn't understand why students complained about exams. Wasn't that what they were there for? Wasn't that the whole point? People actually asked her why she bothered studying ancient history. It seemed they could understand studying modern history — just about — but ancient history, when people lived differently, why bother with that at all? They didn't get that there was a connection there, something magical between the ages. She read these ancient Irish poems and she recognised them, she knew them, she felt them. How could you explain that in logic? It was something inside of her, like her senses had a memory. Maybe if she could let others know about it they would recognise it too: the collective Irish consciousness. It was part of their make-up on some primal level, like grain on wood.

'Yes, I mean.... Why, do you think you won't stick with it?'

'Oh no, I definitely will,' said Stevie. 'There is a really high drop-out rate though. They don't tell you that, you know, but it's true.'

'Really?'

'Yeah, I was reading an article about it. Maybe it's all those hours by yourself, and then of course it's the question of what do you do afterwards. You can call yourself 'Doctor', and that's all well and good, but what does that even mean? There's no guarantee you'll even get work. They say that if finding work is your reason for doing it, to choose something else.'

'I don't know what else I could do,' said Adrienne.

It was true. The medieval world she was studying had become her life. Things were better back then, they just were. Everyone had a place and knew what that place was. They knew what was expected of them. They had the right idea about poetry then too. Not like today. These days they just made it up as they went along. People found shopping lists left in supermarket trolleys and they called that 'found poetry'. Ridiculous! If you knew the rules it was fairer for everyone.

'Me neither,' said Stevie. 'So, do you have much done?'

'No, hardly anything. Just a few chapters.'

'Oh, great. Yeah, I'm sure that will be …'. Stevie didn't have anything. Just some photos of the sheela-na-gigs, some scribbled notes and an entire forest of crumpled-up bits of paper. She had allowed herself to become distracted in the heady newness of being with Kavanagh. When the enormity of her research loomed, it was much more satisfying to escape into him. This need to be with him was like a drug that made her forget about anything else. She would have to ween herself off him. Turn over a new leaf. Gain some focus from somewhere, grab it from the ether. She would start by going back into the conference, even though every atom of her being wanted to walk out the front gates of Trinity College and merge with the crowds on the Dublin streets.

She turned to Adrienne. 'Ready to head back in?'

Adrienne smiled. 'Sure.'

Chapter 32

Patrick's Day was bright and sunny Stevie had been planning on doing some study, but Kavanagh had convinced her to come out. 'Come on, it'll do you good. Besides, you can't work on a national holiday. I'm pretty sure that's illegal or something.' She tidied away her books and went to get dressed. The weather was so warm it made her think of the sandals Donal had returned to her. They were still in the cardboard box in the sitting room. She had put it in the press when she was tidying and forgotten about it. She took out the box and searched through it. Maybe wearing the sandals wasn't a great idea. They were planning on going for a walk. She should probably wear them around the house for a few days first to break them in. She put them on and paced back and forth a few steps.

She sat down on the floor and took the other items out of the box. There were some books, an old jumper she had forgotten about. At the very bottom was a shoebox. She opened it up to find old concert tickets, holiday photos, and a pile of old birthday and Christmas cards. Underneath were some letters held together by a thick elastic band. She saw the brightly coloured envelopes, faded now – some covered in stickers – the familiar childish handwriting that spelled out her name and address. It came flooding back to her: Pam, the letters.

Stevie suddenly felt ancient as she sat holding the letters, relics of a bygone era, before email or social media, before mobile phones. Not that long ago, but it may as well have been a different universe. They had written to each other. They lived at opposite ends of the same city. They talked about meeting up in town one day, going to McDonald's or to the cinema. But they never did. They spoke on the phone once, but were both suddenly shy. All the openness of their letters, all that they had poured out in writing – their feelings about themselves, about therapy, about feeling at a remove from the worlds they inhabited – was now bottled back up again, unsayable.

It was easy to forget the intensity of those feelings, Stevie thought as she opened each of the letters. It was tempting to look back on it and minimise it, call it growing pains or teenage angst, but reading the letters again she could feel it all. She was immersed in it. The pain was a physical thing. She remembered that day when Pam did her hair and how they had talked about what they would do, who they would become. Stevie found that she was crying then, big tears plopping onto the letters. She put them aside, not wanting to smudge them.

And there was the second bunch of letters, the ones she had written in her neat handwriting, that precise cursive font in neat rows. She wrote on pale blue Basildon Bond writing paper with her fountain pen and she made sure to never smudge it. Every word was spelt correctly, and if she was ever unsure she consulted a dictionary. Even this casual exchange between two friends was ordered and exact for Stevie. In contrast, Pam wrote little poems with childish bubble-letters, drew silly pictures, and signed her letters *Luv you lots n jelly tots.*

Stevie shouldn't have her own letters too. Dr Doyle had given them to her. She had continued to attend as an outpatient once a week and there they were one day, sitting on his desk. Her heart jumped in her chest when she realised what they were. She couldn't comprehend it. Was Pamela angry with her? Had she written something in the letters that had upset her, made her give them to Dr Doyle? Frantically, she cast her mind back over what she had written. They had written about Dr Doyle, called him a creep. Pamela had drawn a picture of him with stink lines around his face, giant glasses and goggly eyes. They had written about what a kip the clinic was, how it stank of boiled cabbage, how they were delighted to be out of there.

'I have some bad news, I'm afraid.' Dr Doyle adjusted his glasses. 'These came from Pamela's mother. She wanted you to have them.'

'I don't understand.' A wave of panic washed over Stevie. Some part of her already knew.

'Pamela passed away.'

They sat in silence as Dr Doyle waited for this to sink in. Stevie knew she was supposed to say something, but she couldn't think what. Dr Doyle was looking at her sympathetically. She hated him, didn't want to hear another word from him.

'Her mother thinks it was an accident,' he continued. 'She cut herself.'

Stevie stared at her hands. She would not cry in front of him.

'Her mother wanted you to have this.' Dr Doyle handed her a Mass card. 'Would you like me to call your mother or father to come collect you?'

She shook her head. 'Mum's picking me up outside,' she lied.

'Okay. We can talk about this next week. You can schedule an extra appointment with me. You can give this to the receptionist.' He handed her an appointment slip.

Stevie walked straight past the reception desk and outside. They wouldn't notice that she hadn't made the appointment. Dr Doyle already had too many patients and people on waiting lists to see him. Then guilt consumed her as she realised that she hadn't responded to Pam's last two letters. She hadn't replied because it brought her back to that time, those feelings of self-consciousness and being set apart. She was studying and hanging out with friends now. She was training herself not to listen to that voice and trying to leave that part of herself behind. When Stevie reached the bus stop she took the Mass Card out of her pocket and examined it. The girl in the picture was Pamela, but not Pamela. She was younger and her face was rounder with baby fat. Why didn't they have a more recent photo? Stevie realised that there were probably no recent photos of her either. There were few Kodak moments when someone is sick, especially when they were not the type of sick that their family can discuss without whispering, or shifting uncomfortably, or blaming themselves in some way.

There was a sharp knock on the door that pulled Stevie back to the present. She put the letters back in the shoebox, placed the shoebox into the larger cardboard box and returned it to the press. 'Coming!' she called as she wiped her eyes and blew her nose.

She smiled as she opened the door. 'Sorry, I'll just be two secs. Come on in.'

'Are you okay?' said Kavanagh. 'Your eyes are red.'

She thought of telling him, but how could she even begin? 'Yeah, I know. It's this bloody hay fever back again.'

She made her voice breezy and light. Glancing at his face she could read him, and could tell that he believed her completely. She had forgotten what a convincing liar she could be.

The Spanish Arch was thronged with revellers drinking in the sun. Some dangled their feet over the edge of the embankment, almost touching the slow, swollen black river below as an occasional swan floated past, contrasted in brilliant white against the dark water. Every so often someone would let up a cheer and it would carry and travel along the crowd as people held their cans and bottles aloft. Stevie and Kavanagh made their way through the throngs of people, Kavanagh nodding and stopping to exchange a few words with this person or that. He seemed to know everyone and everyone seemed to know him. He gripped Stevie's hand tightly as they navigated their way through the crowds.

They walked out towards Salthill, away from the whoops and roars of the crowd. The sun beamed on the shallow water, illuminating the yellow sands and the clumps of brown seaweed that danced here and there like submerged ballerinas. The water in the sun's path glittered and shone like scattered diamonds. Dogs trailed their owners' feet and snuffled in pools that had collected all along the jagged rocks lining the smooth promenade. Everything smelled of the sea and sunshine. Mothers pushed prams, children cycled, a man passed by on rollerblades. People ambled or ran or sprinted, arms swinging, everything in motion. Stevie had the sensation of being elsewhere. This was not the west of Ireland but France or Italy, the Mediterranean sun shining on them. A feeling of contentedness embraced her. Thoughts of the letters tried to intervene but she forced them from her mind. She focused on her breathing and enjoying the moment. Kavanagh held her hand and smiled at her.

On days like this, when all that mattered was the sun that shone and the birds that swooped, it was difficult to remember why she worried about any of it: the research, the books, the piles of scrawled notes. The thing she liked about history was the idea of leaving a mark. Sometimes it seemed like you could go through your whole life and never really do that. But recently it had started to feel like academia was an avoidance of life and living and the real world, some type of Narnia of parchment and book.

They found a free bench and sat down and looked out to sea. Kavanagh fished a hip flask from his pocket, unscrewed the cap and took a swig before offering it to Stevie.

'Sure, for the day that's in it.'

'Ah, I dunno. I've a load of work to do later,' she said.

'It would be unpatriotic not to.'

She smiled and accepted the flask, shuddering involuntarily as the whiskey hit the back of her throat.

'The sea is beautiful today.' She passed the flask back to him.

'You should see the sea in Phuket.'

'Yeah, yeah, Thailand this, Thailand that. Change the record, Kav,' she teased.

'I'd love for you to see it is all,' he said. 'The two of us there together.'

'You know I can't.'

'Because of your research? Stevie, you know they have temples and shit over there. Really fucking old ones. You'd be right at home.'

Stevie laughed. 'Wow, old temples and shit? You're really selling it to me, Kav.'

'I mean it though,' he said. 'Just think about it. That's all I'm asking.'

They bought ice-creams and sat looking out to sea. She tried to push from her mind the thought of all of the work she had to do in preparation for her trip the following day. Kavanagh was still talking about Thailand, but she couldn't take in what he was saying. She looked down at her ice-cream, imagining the fat molecules suspended in frozen liquid. The thought of having to eat it made her feel sick. She stood up and dumped it into the bin.

'I think it was off,' she said as Kavanagh looked at her in surprise.

'Really?' he said. 'Mine tastes fine.' It was melting fast, dribbling over the cone.

'I'm sorry. I really have to get back. I've so much to do,' she said. 'You can stay here if you like.'

'No, don't be silly. I'll walk back with you. Are you okay?'

'Yeah, I'm fine,' she said. 'I'm fine'

Chapter 33

Pajo hadn't intended on staying at the party, but after he made the delivery he found himself getting into the spirit of things. He'd received the good news from Walshy and he felt like celebrating. Jacqui had shown up and she was wittering on about a tattoo she'd got.

'It's on my ankle.' She smiled at Pajo. 'Do you want to see it?'

'Hmm?'

'My tattoo.'

'Go on, show us it then.'

'I don't know if you'll like it.' She was playing coy all of a sudden, hiding behind her scraggly mop of yellow hair.

'Don't show me then.' Pajo looked away and scanned the room.

'Okay.' She rolled up her jeans and stuck out her leg. 'Here it is.'

He peered at the yellow flower that spread across her ankle, its petals reaching out almost three-dimensionally like some kind of optical illusion.

He grimaced. 'I fucking hate sunflowers.'

'What?!' she laughed. 'You're not serious?'

'I am.'

It was true. He couldn't stand those flowers. Seeing them brought him back to his childhood when his mother would grow them in the back garden. He could see them when he looked out of his bedroom window. All the hours she spent fretting over them, and for what? They were fickle, only blooming when it was hottest, completely unsuitable for an Irish climate. What were they even doing here? They turned their giant stupid faces to the sun, begging it to notice them, reaching up higher and higher on their obscene stalks, which were taller than he was. You never saw that part of the flower in pictures or in the neat bunches at the florist's – those thick, green monstrosities bursting through soil, lifting those idiotic black-seeded heads and piss-yellow petals further and further upwards towards the sun. When the weather got colder, as it invariably did, they withered and drooped, their un-petalled heads shrivelling up like dead spiders. They repulsed him.

'How can you not like sunflowers?' Jacqui was looking at him in disbelief. 'Everyone likes sunflowers.'

The yellow of the flower on her skin was the same artificial yellow as her hair.

'Well, I'm not everyone.'

She was looking up at him with her don't-hurt-me eyes, the ugly flower still on display.

'I think it's lovely, Jacqui,' said Hulk.

Pajo had never been a fan of tattoos. Girls with their fairies and their stars and their flowers, treating their bodies like colouring books. He couldn't imagine liking anything enough to want it inked onto his flesh forever. Some lads saw them as a badge of honour, showing off tattoo sleeves on pumped-up biceps in tight T-shirts at the gym. It was the footballers' fault, most likely. Now you had some gobshite from Rahoon thinking he's Beckham because he has the same tats. Some lads in school used to give themselves DIY tattoos, scraping compasses across their arms at the back of class and filling the cuts with Indian ink. The tattoos rarely took though. They'd scab and the ink would shed along with the skin. A total waste of time.

Walshy nudged her with his elbow. 'He's not pulling any punches, hah, Jacqui? He was giving me awful abuse earlier too.'

Jacqui scowled at Walshy. Pajo could tell she didn't want his sympathy. She didn't like the fact that he was trying to equate them as the same in Pajo's estimation. Everything seemed very hilarious all of a sudden. He was so tickled by it that he let out a belly laugh.

'What's so funny?' said Hulk, worried he was somehow the cause of the laughter, as was frequently the case.

Pajo grinned. 'Oh, just in a good mood is all. We have him. We have our man. Now we just have to be patient and bam!' He smacked his palm with his fist. Walshy and Hulk laughed. Jacqui looked at them in confusion.

'To catch a sneaky little mouse, Jacqui, a quiet little mouse that's hiding away up to no good, what do you use?'

'A trap?'

Pajo shook his head. You use a weasel.' He grabbed Walshy around the neck and rubbed his hair with his knuckle. 'Little Walshy Weasel gets his man.'

Walshy let out a high-pitched laugh.

'You don't mind me calling you a weasel, do you, Walshy?'

'I'll take it as a compliment.'

'Good weasel. Good little weasel.' Pajo got him in a headlock and started to run around the room with 'Pajo...' squeaked Walshy.

'What is it?' Pajo laughed. 'What is it, Weasel?'.

'Pajo, wait,' said Hulk.

Pajo stopped dead in his tracks. 'What?'

Hulk held out the plastic bag of MDMA. 'Have some more of this.'

Pajo nodded and released Walshy from his grip. He slapped Hulk on the shoulder as Walshy recovered his breath. 'We got him, we got the fucker!'

*

'So, do you still hate my tattoo?' Jacqui giggled.

'Hmm?' said Pajo, pulling the covers up to his chin.

'You're gonna change your mind about it. You'll end up loving it, I bet.' She wrapped her leg around his. He edged away closer to the wall until his face was almost touching the smooth coldness of the plaster. Had she told him about her tattoo? She might well have done. He couldn't get a grip on his memory of the night before. It came back to him in flashes. There had been a party in Knocknacarra. He'd gone there on business to make some deliveries, but found himself drawn into the spirit of things. He normally kept himself at a remove, even at parties. He liked to keep his wits about him, but last night he'd been in a jubilant mood. He was snorting coke and dabbing great wads of MDMA on his gums, reaching for the plastic bag again and again. He was grinning like a loon and dancing, dancing, dancing. Usually he never danced. And there was something else … *Party Pajo*. That's what they had called him, the crowd of people that had gathered around him. They had chanted it as he danced and danced and picked Jacqui up and swung her around. He cringed at the memory. They weren't scared of him. They had laughed and chanted *Party Pajo*, delirious like schoolchildren getting away with something.

Jacqui's voice brought him back to the present. How had she ended up back here? He couldn't even remember.

He turned to face her. 'I'm gonna have a shower.'

'Are you okay?' Jacqui asked.

'Yeah, yeah. Grand.'

She'd never seen him so distracted, but he obviously wanted her to stay. He hadn't said anything about her leaving. She lay back in bed, luxuriating in being there. She thought of the previous night when he'd finally told her how he felt about her. *I love you, Jacqui.* She had known all along that he did. He was just one of those fellas that had trouble revealing their true feelings.

He had taken some photos last night on his phone, including one of the two of them together, his arm around her like a proper couple. She saw that he had left his phone beside the bed. He wouldn't mind, she told herself, if she had a look. The photo was dark, an outline of two blurry black shapes, a halo of refracted light. She was disappointed, but she told herself that there would be other parties, other photos of the two of them together.

She went to put the phone back but something stopped her, some curiosity, some impulse. She glanced toward the door, heard the sound of the shower, then scrolled through the rest of his photos. A picture of a girl, then another, then…. Her skin turned cold. Confusion, disbelief, and then the gut-punch realisation of what she was seeing. Photo after photo. Girl after girl. On their knees. A succession of pale faces and bodies in badly lit rooms. Some of them looked so young, so vulnerable, so out of it. Nameless. She saw that they weren't people to him, just things to be used. Something for him to manipulate and control because that's what he did. He had no feelings for her. He had no feelings for anyone.

She placed the phone back on the locker. Her hand was shaking. Reaching for her clothes, she got dressed as quickly as she could. She let herself out of his apartment. She didn't look back.

Chapter 34

Stevie wasn't expecting anyone, so it took her a few minutes to realise that the sound she could hear was someone knocking on her front door. She opened it to see Kavanagh standing there holding a pizza box, his hair plastered to his head.

'Surprise! I thought I'd surprise you …'.

'Oh. Oh, great.'

'Are you surprised?'

'Well, yes, this is definitely surprising. I thought we'd arranged to meet tomorrow?'

'Shit. I should have called first, shouldn't I? You probably hate surprises. You do, don't you? I can see it in your face. See, I love surprises but …'. He glanced into the sitting room where Stevie's notes were spread out on the table. 'Ah, you're in the middle of something. I don't want to disturb you.'

'No, it's fine. I could use a break.'

'Well, I brought you the holy trinity of Friday amazingness: pizza, wine and a little something-something for afters.'

'Well, now I'm intrigued. What's the little something-something?'

'A spliff.'

'Ah. I thought you meant …'.

'You thought I meant what? Oh, well that too.' He leaned forward and kissed her. 'It could be the holy … what's like a trinity but made of four things?'

'A square?'

'The holy square of Friday awesomeness. No, that doesn't sound right. Triptych?'

Stevie shook her head. 'No, a triptych is still three.'

'Ah, I'll think of it again,' he waved his hand. 'Seriously though, if this is a bad time, I can just leave this stuff here and let you get back to it.' He backed away and made an elaborate bowing gesture.

Stevie laughed. 'Come on in,' she grabbed him by the arm and kissed him. 'So, is it raining or are you trying out a new hairstyle?'

He placed the pizza down on the counter top and ran his fingers through his hair, which was slicked back, flattened by rainwater. 'Both,' he said. 'I got the pizza from the new Italian place on Cross Street. It's meant to be lovely. Dan said it tastes just like the pizza in Naples.'

'Have you been to Naples?'

'Me? No. But I'd say they make some pretty decent pizzas.'

They sat down and Stevie moved her notes out of the way.

Kavanagh put the pizza box in the middle of the table. 'Look, I won't stay long if you need to get back to work. Have you been working all evening?'

'Nah, just a couple of hours.'

The truth was that she had been staring into space for an hour. Then, when she dropped the pencil she had been chewing on, she had noticed how dusty it was under the sofa. She decided she needed to clean it immediately. Once she had tackled that bit of dust, the entire apartment looked filthy so she had to clean it from top to bottom. Then she'd become lost in an internet rabbit hole. What had started innocently enough with her checking the location of a sheela-na-gig in Tipperary had somehow ended up with trying to find out whatever happened to the fat kid from *The Goonies*. Then she wondered what all of the rest of the cast were up to and had started looking them up too. But the knock on the door had been a distraction. She was just about to get back into her studying mode, really she was, so she could convince herself she would have got loads done if it wasn't for Kavanagh's unexpected visit.

The rain was falling heavily on the roof as Kavanagh opened the pizza box. 'Help yourself.'

Stevie broke off a slice, the gooey cheese stretching as she lifted it. She took a small bite and placed it back down.

'What do you think? Best pizza in Galway?'

'It's great,' Stevie smiled.

'Wow, it's really coming down out there. Glad I'm not still out in that.'

Stevie went to take another bite of pizza, but out of nowhere she realised she couldn't eat any more. She didn't even want to hold the slice as she imagined the pores of her skin absorbing the calories from the oil. She tried to push the thought from her mind, but it remained there, insistent and urgent. She placed it down and turned to Kav. 'Would you mind getting wine glasses?'

'Sure.' Kavanagh headed off towards the kitchen.

Stevie broke off most of her slice of pizza and hid it in a napkin.

Kavanagh sat down and poured her a glass of wine. 'This is nice.'

Stevie wiped her hands. 'Yeah, it's times like this I wish I lived in a house with a log fire. Sitting in front of the storage heater doesn't really have the same romance to it.'

'Want another slice?'

'No thanks, I'm stuffed.'

'You don't like the pizza? I'll kick Dan up the hole for recommending the place.'

'No, no. It's great. It's just I already ate so I'm still pretty full.' She tensed, waiting for him to pick her up on it, but he just reached for another slice.

A light flooded the dimly lit room and they heard the loud noise of a rasping engine.

'What is that?' said Stevie.

They looked out the window but couldn't see anything. Stevie switched off the sitting room light so that they could better peer into the darkness outside. Then they saw what was making the noise: a helicopter hovered over the river. It beamed a searchlight up and down the length of the Corrib.

'Jesus,' said Stevie. 'Does that mean …'.

Kavanagh nodded. 'Yeah, someone's in the river. I passed it earlier and the water was crazy high.'

Stevie shuddered. 'I can't imagine how cold that water must be. And it's so windy tonight. Do you think someone could have been swept in?'

Kavanagh thought this over. 'It's possible I suppose, but usually these things are deliberate.'

Stevie moved away from the window and sat back down on the sofa. She ran her hand over her arm and her skin felt goose-bumped. She could almost feel the intense coldness of the water surrounding her. Kavanagh sat beside her and put his arm around her. Stevie moved closer to his warmth. 'Do you want to stay over?'

'Sure, if you're certain I'm not keeping you from your work.'

'It can wait until tomorrow. I'm glad you're here.'

'I'm glad I'm here too.'

*

She is alone on a hill surrounded by shadows, frozen with terror. She can feel rancid breath on her neck. A crow flaps by, black wings inches from her face. *Caw aw caw!* She is trespassing, should not be here. A cold panic grips her. She needs to find the way out – looks for a door, a window, but everything is cloaked in black. *You're late, you're late,* says Dr Bodkin. Pamela is in the corner, blood dripping from her wrists. She looks at Stevie, a pale face with hollow eyes. *Why won't you help me? I thought you'd help me, Stevie.* She tries to reach her. *Pamela....* She tries to call out but she can't make a sound. The baby photos from her mother's fridge are scattered all over the ground. She is treading over them but they are gum on a sunny day, sticking to her shoes.

Stevie? She hears Kavanagh's voice. If she can just get to him she knows somehow that she will be safe. But she can't see him. And she is on a ledge now, high up over a sheer drop to the black sea below. The noise of crashing waves roars in her eardrums. The cliff edge is filled with carvings. She tries to see if they are sheela-na-gigs. She leans over, some part of her not registering the danger. They are carvings she has never seen before. She hears Dr Bodkin: *An invaluable find, a stunning contribution to the field.* Stevie reaches for her camera around her neck. *Stevie, no!* Looking up, she sees Adrienne standing on the cliff edge, her purple robe billowing about her. Stevie reaches for the camera and knocks off the lens cap, trying desperately, *desperately,* to focus the blurry image with hands drenched in sweat. She sees it in her viewfinder. It is not a sheela-na-gig. It is just a stone. Smooth, blameless. She raises her head above the viewfinder, looks at the spot where the carving was. *It's gone,* she says. Adrienne reaches out her hand. *They tricked you, Stevie.*

Ladies and gentlemen, please fasten your seatbelts as we prepare for landing. The plane's engine roars in her ears. One side of the plane is a sheer cliff drop. She clings to the edge with all the force she can muster, digging her nails into its surface. If she can make it to her seat, if she can fasten her seatbelt, she will be okay. She has never felt fear like it before; She has never felt fear like it before. The rocks under her feet give way. She looks down at the sheer drop below and she is falling, falling, falling....

'Ow!' Kavanagh sat up in bed, his hand over his face. 'Stevie, you just whacked me!'

'Oh God, sorry.'

'Were you having a nightmare?'

'No, I … I can't remember.'

He reached to put his arm around her waist, but she sat up abruptly. 'What time is it?'

'Hmm?' Kavanagh yawned and reached for his phone. 'Just gone nine.'

Shit.' She jumped out of bed and grabbed her towel. 'Gotta have a shower and get going to the library.'

'But it's Saturday. Do you have to go already?' He gave her a lazy grin. 'Why don't you come back to bed?'

'I can't. I've so much to get done.'

All of the ease of the previous night, how close she had felt to him, evaporated in the light, and in the imminent hangover that threatened at her temples. He was too charming, too distracting. Everything was so easy for him. He never seemed stressed or overwhelmed, and even though that was one of the things she liked most about him, now she found herself resenting his carefree approach, envying his calm.

'Okay, well we can do something later.'

'Yeah, I'll see how I get on and call you, okay?'

'Mm.' He was already drifting back to sleep.

She sighed and headed for the bathroom. She felt heavy as she walked, the approaching workload weighing on her shoulders.

Chapter 35

The train juddered and shuddered noisily along the track, rocking from side to side. Stevie had planned on writing up her notes but everything was a distraction: the noise, the movement, her view of the countryside as she moved through it. The landscape here was like something from a Bórd Fáilte advert – all fields dotted with dandelions, lambs frolicking in lush fields, hedgerows prickled with brambles. The bright yellow flower of gorse added a splash of colour to the green, leading to mountains in the distance. Roscrea, Cloughjordan … she had never been to any of these towns … and on and on the train swayed. The day was bright and clear, bathing the countryside in a warming glow. Sunlight lit up half the plastic table in front of her as the other half was eclipsed. She watched as the light crept over, inch by inch, until it had commandeered the entire table. Further along the track, the train became less jerky and fell into a predictable rhythm.

Stevie stretched her arms over her head and yawned. She would love to sleep, to give in to the lulling movement of the train along the tracks and let her body sway loosely, but her mind was alert despite the tiredness of her body. In the fields all of the cows were lying down, which meant that it would rain soon. This was something Stevie remembered from childhood trips to visit her father's relatives in Wicklow. He would point at the cows lying in the fields and say *rain's on the way*. He told her that the cows lay down to keep the patch of grass underneath them dry. She wondered now how true it was. Perhaps it was just an old wives' tale, or two separate unrelated events, correlation mistaken for causation. As she was thinking about it, the sky darkened and spatters of rain landed on the carriage window.

It would be great to listen to some music, but the battery of her iPod was dead. So she listened to the symphony of the train on the track, the drone of the engine, the faint hint of voices further up in the carriage, the *cla clunk, cla clunk* of the forward movement. She sipped on black tea from a paper cup. The woman with the drinks trolley had placed two sachets of sugar and two tiny containers of UHT milk on her table along with the tea when she had ordered it. The thought of drinking milk made her stomach turn. She wrapped the containers in a napkin and pushed them to the other side of the table. She hadn't eaten anything in days, not since the accident, but her thoughts felt clear, focused, unclouded. Her car was a write-off, and she wasn't sure if her insurance would cover the full cost of her buying another one. She couldn't bring herself to think about dealing with that now. The important thing was that she had now visited all of the sheela-na-gigs in the whole country. It had taken her two weeks longer than she had planned due to the car troubles and having to rely on patchy public transport. It struck her how very, very remote some places in Ireland were, but at the same time how complete strangers were willing to help you. She had been offered lifts, given names and numbers for local taxi drivers and even offered a bed for the night when she was having trouble finding her B&B. This helpfulness en masse was like the universe at large was willing her to succeed.

But there was something else in all of that helpfulness. *Are you alone, love? Where are you headed? Is there someone you can call?* There was something that made people uneasy about a woman on her own. That's what gave them the right to approach her like they already knew her, to ask her questions about herself, to suggest how she travel or where she should stay.

Maybe that's why she lied following the accident. After she hit the tree, she watched as her car was towed away and, in a detached way, she heard the man who had helped her out of the car: *It's a miracle, you know. You're lucky to be alive. Not a scratch on you.* She didn't like being in the hospital even though they were only examining her as a precaution. She didn't want to be stuck there having to answer their questions. But some part of her took over, reassured them. When they asked her if she wanted to call anyone to let them know what had happened, she invented some relatives in Ennis. She said they would come to the hospital to collect her and she would stay with them tonight.

Stevie took another sip of tea. Her end-of-year meeting with the graduate research committee was on Monday and she didn't feel prepared at all. She would have to sit in front of them and talk about her research so far. If it wasn't up to scratch, they wouldn't approve her for continuation. They could recommend that her research stop. She tried to push the thought from her mind, and the image of the crash appeared again. She had surprised herself with the lies in the hospital that had come to her out of nowhere. There was nobody she wanted to tell about the crash, nobody she wanted to have worrying about her. Saying it out loud would be admitting that something was wrong, that she had made a mistake.

The accident didn't mean anything, she knew that, but others might not see it that way. It was because she had too many ladders in a row. It was inevitable that a snake would appear. Roll the dice, up the ladder, roll the dice, move forward, roll the dice, down the snake. Arbitrary. No grand plan, just dumb luck. It was simply life carrying on regardless around and around the board. She remembered the games of snakes and ladders that she and Pamela played in the common room. They had played so many times that they became bored, so they changed the rules. They travelled up snakes and plummeted down ladders.

'It's more like real life,' said Pamela. 'How do you really know who is a friend and who isn't?'

Stevie agreed. It all depended on your perspective and what way the board was facing. She would have to lock herself away over the weekend and prepare something for her meeting. Anything. The answer was there somewhere, she could feel it.

Chapter 36

Jacqui sat quietly on the sofa, her hands resting on her stomach as Pajo paced in front of her. This was the first she had heard from him since the morning she had left his house after the party. She could see now how wrong she had been – how very, very wrong. For the first few weeks she had been expecting something. He would explain, apologise, say things would be different from now on. He would show up on her doorstep. He would surprise her in work. He would call her, text her: something, anything. Despite all the evidence to the contrary, despite the fact she could now see that she had been fooling herself all along, perhaps some tiny part of her was still hopeful. Perhaps this part of her conjured up a scene where he would embrace her and tell her how happy he was. She saw this in her mind's eye and held it there, despite the contradictory feeling of dread in her stomach. But that had changed now.

'Why don't you sit down?'

'I don't want to sit down. This won't take long.'

'How did you hear?'

'Walshy said he'd heard something. So it's true?'

'Good news really travels fast around here.'

He took an envelope out of his pocket and went to hand it to her. 'Here …'.

'I don't need your money.'

'But do you not need to take care of it? While you still can?'

'Don't worry about it. I'm not asking you for anything.'

All she wanted was for this conversation to be over and done with so that he would leave. Her head no longer had space for Pajo. It was full of plans for when the baby arrived. She was counting down the days in her head. It was still early but she could feel the little life growing inside her. She didn't care that she would have to do it on her own. She would go for her scans, continue to eat properly. Already she had cut down on the junk food since she found out. She had cravings for fresh fruit and salads. The morning sickness didn't bother her. Even work was better. Her co-workers no longer irritated her. She asked them questions about themselves. They made jokes together.

'You're like a new person, Jacqui.'

'She must have some new fella on the go,' they teased.

But she wasn't a new person. She was her old self, the self she had allowed to get lost. It was funny to think that it could have been like this all along.

She felt more herself than she ever had before. There was a tenderness to her that she had tried to bury by cackling and drinking and egging Pajo on. But there was something about her even then, a softness that people saw, despite her best attempts not to let it show. Strangers told her their sad stories. They always had, like the girl in the toilet of Sally Longs that night who told her she was going to London the next day to have an abortion. All of her sad story came out and they both cried and held each other. They were like sisters that night, she and this girl she didn't know.

'I'll help you, luveen,' she said, and she meant it and she meant it and she meant it. She saw the girl in there again a few months later when she was sitting at the bar, but if she recognised Jacqui, she gave no indication.

Pajo's voice was louder now and his pacing more frantic. 'Don't be fucking stupid, Jacqui. What are you gonna do, bring a baby into work with you? Have a pram in behind the checkouts?'

'I'll manage,' she said.

He continued to roil and rage, but she didn't react. She remained still, quiet, unshakable. He was a storm she would wait out.

Eventually, he stopped shouting. 'I'll see you out,' she said.

'This isn't over,' he said as she closed the front door, but she knew that it was.

Jacqui was unafraid now. She could already sense the huge reserves of strength she contained within her. Her mother was gone, but she still had family. That's what mattered, really. All of a sudden, she wanted to see her brother.

She found him in Eyre Square, sitting with the winos, drinking from brown-paper-wrapped bottles.

'Sis!' he called as she approached.

'Is that your sister, Maloney?' one of the winos said. 'Fuck off, it's not.'

'How've you been?' she asked him, ignoring the others.

'Sound. Try this. It's unreal. We got some of that high-powered weed that's going around.'

'I can't be smoking that stuff,' she patted her stomach. 'I have some news. You're going to be an uncle.'

'Sis Sis Sis!' he said and flung his arms around her in a hug, and the drunkards followed his cries with a chorus. *Sis, Sis, Sis* they called, and flung out their arms and swooped around her, laughing like some deranged dance troupe as she stood laughing at the centre, holding her brother's hand.

Chapter 37

There was something apocalyptic about the weather. It battered the roofs and swelled the Corrib. Giant waves crashed onto the prom in Salthill. A storm warning was in place, and sandbags lined the houses by the river. Wind whistled against the windows of Alex's flat.

Kavanagh turned to Alex. 'So is this it do you reckon?'

'Is this what?'

'The end of days.'

'Sounds like it,' said Alex. 'Ah well, sure. It was good while it lasted.'

Kavanagh smiled and passed the joint to Alex. 'It reminds me of this religion teacher I had years ago. He said, "Boys, ye should live every day like it's your last," and I couldn't get my head around that at all. I think the idea was that if you thought you were about to die and be judged with the possibility of eternal damnation facing you, you would walk around being extra nice and charitable to everyone. I sat there thinking, if this was really my last day on earth, I wouldn't be sitting here in this classroom filled with BO, that's for fucking sure. I'd go out and break each and every one of the windows and piss on the shards. I'd take whatever drugs I could get my hands on and fuck anyone who would have me. If this is it, I mean really it, then why not?'

Alex laughed. 'Is that still what you'd do?'

Kavanagh shook his head. 'Nah, I was angry back then. I don't even know why. I hated everything.'

'Ah, adolescent angst,' said Alex. 'You're too old to be an angry young man any more. So, what would you do now, if it was your last day on earth?'

'I don't know. Stay in bed probably.'

'With Stevie?'

'Yeah. If she'd have me.'

'Things not going well?'

'Nah, things are fine. She's just been busy with this research she's doing. I'm sure it's ...'. He checked his phone to see if Stevie had replied to his texts. Nothing. He had tried to ring her over the last few days, but she never answered. Maybe she was immersed in studying and she had run out of credit. Yeah, that was probably it. He would call over to her on his way home. He put his phone back into his pocket. 'So, last day on earth. What would you do, Alex?'

Alex looked around the room at the film projected onto the wall, the joint in his hand, the cup of tea on the table. 'I dunno. This?'

'There's nowhere you'd want to go? Nothing you'd want to see?'

Alex shrugged. 'Nah.'

'You know who you remind me of?'

'Who?'

'Monet. I mean, don't get me wrong, I fucking hate the impressionists – bland leading the bland – but I have respect for Monet, just painting those water lilies in Giverny over and over again, striving to capture the essence of that one tiny place. You'd think it'd be boring but it's not, man. It's really beautiful.'

Alex smiled. 'I think people think if they go far away they'll leave the parts of themselves they don't like behind.

But it doesn't work like that. They're on the other side of the world but they're still themselves. There's no escaping that.'

'Hey!' Kavanagh feigned a hurt expression.

'Oh shit, but I'm sure it won't be like that for you in Thailand.'

Alex didn't need to go out and discover the world. His world was right there in that room, and in truth there was something beguiling about it. Sometimes Kavanagh struggled to leave that room. Some of his happiest moments had been spent there. It would never occur to Alex to go out into the world, to *find himself*. There he already was. But that wasn't enough for Kav. He had glimpsed the possibility of something different, something else. Why did he have to be *this* Joe Kavanagh when he could paint over it, start afresh? But maybe Alex was right. Maybe he was just lying to himself. Maybe over there he would be just as lazy, just as clueless, just as scared.

'You know I had a religion teacher like that too,' said Alex, 'and I think he meant well. I mean, he honestly believed that he had the answers. He had *an* answer, but nobody has *the* answer, and the people who are convinced that they do, who go to such great lengths to force what they believe onto other people, those are the most dangerous ones. I don't believe that there's one true path. There's endless paths stretching out to infinity. You just have to choose one and walk down it and see where it leads. We're all stumbling in the dark, but how we stumble is our choice, nobody else's.'

*

As Kavanagh headed towards Stevie's place, he remembered the peculiar feeling he'd had on his way to Alex's that someone was following him. He had promptly forgotten about it once he had plonked himself down on Alex's sofa. Now it came back to him, the sensation of being watched. He glanced back and saw a small, shadowy figure duck into a doorway and light a cigarette. *I'm being paranoid. Just keep going,* he told himself. But he had the sense that he had seen this figure before, a panicky feeling of déjà vu overcoming him. Kavanagh picked up his pace. *It's grand. Just get to Stevie's.* He looked back, but the dark figure had evaporated into the night.

The rain continued to hammer down. Umbrellas were defeated in this weather. Some brave souls tried to ignore this fact as their umbrellas were whipped inside out. Icy droplets continued to pelt from a sky that roiled with looming slate-grey clouds. Traffic had slowed to a turgid pace as the cars and buses snailed alongside gutters overflowing with dull grey water, leaves and pieces of floating debris: cigarette butts and crisp packets. Kavanagh pulled out his phone and called Stevie. He thought it was about to ring out again. Then he heard her voice on the other end.

'Hello?'

'Stevie? Hey, it's me. Is everything okay? I've been trying to call you.'

'Sorry I missed you. I'm just ….'.

'Are you home? I'm heading that way now. I thought I could call in to you for a bit.'

Silence on the other end. He thought the line had gone dead. Then he heard the faintest intake of breath.

'Hello? Stevie?'

'I've been studying.'

She sounded strange, distant, barely audible. Her voice was flat and lifeless.

'Okay. Can I see you tomorrow?'

'I don't know…. Look, I have to go now.'

'Stevie?'

Something wasn't right. He called her back but her phone rang out. He would call over to her. If he could just see her, even for a few minutes he could reassure himself that she was okay.

*

There was a loud knock on Alex's front door. Kavanagh must have forgotten something. Alex made his way to the hallway and turned the latch. He squinted into the darkness, trying to make out the black shapes of the men standing on his doorstep. Instinct told him to close the door, but it was too late. As he went to slam the it closed, the door kicked with force from the outside. Next thing he knew he was on his back, the metallic taste of blood filling up his sinuses. It took a while to register the pain. But then it came. *Oh, Jesus.*

He heard the voice of the man standing over him.

'So this is Kavanagh's friend. We meet at last.' He heard the figure close the front door behind him. Then to the men: 'Take the plants and load them in the van. Take everything.' He heard the sound of footsteps thundering past his prone body.

There was a voice above him. He tried to make out what it was saying. How long had he been lying here? Time was gloopy. He was wading through the marsh of it.

'I said where's the money?'

He tried to reply but blood was filling up his mouth; a sharp pain in his temple; a weight on his chest; a snapping sound like kindling.

'Don't worry, we'll find it. Don't you worry yourself about anything.'

Chapter 38

A light was on in Stevie's house. Kavanagh knocked and waited, but she didn't come to the door. The wind howled and the drizzle gave way to a deluge. He shivered on the doorstep.

'Stevie?' he called through the letterbox. 'Can you let me in?'

Finally, she opened the door a crack. She looked like she hadn't slept in days. There were dark shadows under her eyes. She looked at him wordlessly and didn't open the door any wider. He was suddenly uncertain of everything between them.

'Can I … is it okay if I come in? Just for a second. I know you're busy. I won't stay long. I promise.'

She opened the door for him and stood back as he came in. He went to kiss her and she accepted the kiss, but didn't return it.

'Are you okay? I haven't heard from you in days. I was worried.'

'I'm fine. I'm just trying to get this work done, you know.' She glanced back at the table where her textbooks and piles of notes waited.

'How's the work going?'

She shrugged. 'Yeah, okay.'

'I'm worried about you. Maybe you should take a break. How about some dinner? Have you eaten yet? We could order some takeaway.'

'No, I ate already. Thanks though.' She gave him a tired smile. 'Look, I'm fine, honestly. I just need some time to get this done.'

'Okay. If you need anything, just call me, okay?'

'Okay,' she said.

'Just think, this time tomorrow your meeting will be long over. I'll bring you out to celebrate.'

'I mightn't have much to celebrate.'

'Of course you will. You've been working so hard. I know you're going to do great.'

She walked him to the door and kissed him goodbye.

'So, I'll see you tomorrow?'

She nodded. 'Okay, see you then.'

Chapter 39

Kavanagh headed back into the hostile night. It was teeming rain, the kind that made you gulp for air like a fish on land. He remembered then that Alex had said once that it was only a matter of time before the people of Galway evolved to form gills. How else could they survive in this city with forty shades of rain? It fell at impossible angles, foiling the tightest raincoats, snaking its way down necks, rendering umbrellas useless. It seeped through the soles of shoes into the soles of feet. It crept into bones and marrow where it festered, causing unshakable colds and dark thoughts and an unquenchable thirst for drinking pints in front of warm fires.

He and Alex had joked about it being the apocalypse, but that's exactly what it felt like to him now. It made sense that the end of the world in Galway would have no flames, no molten lava spewing, no earth ripped open with Kavanagh flailing towards its burning centre. Just the splish. Just the splash. Just the splish, splash, splish of constant rain. That constant sound like the repetition of a whining child: but why, why, why, but why? Bucketing down. Fucketing down. It should drown him and be done with it. Sweep him away and put him out of his misery for good.

Kavanagh followed the path of the river walk, with railings to his right and a drop to the river below. On the other side was the canal and a grassy bank. From his elevated spot he looked down at the fast-flowing water. He continued on to where the path met the bridge and the main road. The river surged forward – relentless, angry, brown. The colour of stew gone cold. The colour of unloved shoes. It formed white-foamed waves that crashed in on each other from all directions. A heron stood on the bank, its shoulders hunched, as though to protect itself from the elements. In the canal, salmon swam against the fast-flowing stream, throwing themselves in vain at the closed sluice, their bodies making dull thudding sounds before they splashed back into the water. Ducks waddled, unperturbed on the bank of the canal, or sat, heads tucked down, in a line like a cosy shooting gallery. The water smashed off the stone at the base of O'Brien's Bridge, determined, or so it seemed to Kavanagh, to make it collapse and be swept out to sea, taking the cars with windscreen wipers squeaking and pedestrians doing battle with inside-out umbrellas along with it.

He checked his phone and saw that he had a text message from Alex. He hadn't heard it beep. *Can't talk. In hospital waiting room. Pajo broke in and took plants. He's after you. Stay in until it blows over. Be careful.* He tried to ring Alex but there was no reply. He felt a sickness in the pit of his stomach at the thought of Pajo hurting Alex, of taking his plants. How had they known where to find him? The realisation hit him like a smack in the face: they had followed him. Then the sickness was replaced by another feeling – a rage like he had never felt in his whole life.

A jagged rain fell as he passed the churning angry river. The water level had risen high and plastic barriers had been erected along the water's edge at the Spanish Arch to keep people from going too close. He realised he was near Pajo's house. It was well known that he lived in one of those penthouse apartments overlooking the river. If Kavanagh were sensible he would walk a different way, avoiding this route altogether, but something kept him walking in this direction, some feeling of inevitability. Sheltering now was pointless. Soaked as he was, he decided he may as well keep going, right into the eye of the storm. The wind whipped the hood from his head yet again, and this time he didn't bother putting it back up, but let the rainwater fall on him and drip down the back of his neck.

*

Pajo jumped out of the van and made his way to his apartment building. Not a bad evening's work. The lads would hang on to the plants until they could get a proper setup for them. They had their orders to keep their eyes peeled for Kavanagh. Lying little toerag, telling him he'd got the weed from some guy in Dublin when it had been right here under his nose the whole time. He'd get what was coming to him. He had his keys in hand, head down, making his way to the apartment front entrance when he saw the familiar figure approaching up ahead. No, it couldn't be … was it? This was his lucky night.

Pajo's hand was on his phone to call the guys, but then he decided against it. His adrenaline was still pumping from taking the plants off Alex, from seeing his utter vulnerability as he lay in his own home unable to defend himself or to stop Pajo from taking what he believed was rightfully his to take. He would handle this himself.

'You've some fucking nerve, Joe Kavanagh,' he bellowed.

He was half expecting Kavanagh to turn and run, but he surprised him by stopping dead in his tracks. He glared at him with fists clenched. 'Pajo. How could you do that to Alex?'

'Who the fuck is Alex?'

'My friend. My friend you put in the fucking hospital.'

Pajo laughed. 'Oh, him. Would you like to join him?'

Kavanagh looked from left to right. 'Do you not have to call your backup? Wouldn't want to get your own hands dirty.'

Pajo smiled and cracked his knuckles. He took a step closer to Kavanagh. Kavanagh stared straight back at him and didn't budge. 'He never did anything to you.' His voice shook with emotion and barely contained rage.

Pajo smirked. 'If you're looking for someone to blame, try yourself. You led us right to him.'

'It isn't my fault.'

'Isn't it?' Pajo took another step towards Kavanagh. He thought he saw a hesitation, a look of uncertainty.

'No. No, it fucking isn't. I see what you're trying to do and it won't work on me. You got what you wanted you fucking degenerate, now leave me alone.'

Kavanagh turned to walk away. He heard laughter behind him, cold and sinister. 'Oh, Joe. Poor little Joe Kavanagh. You think it's over because you say so? It doesn't work like that.' Kavanagh kept walking. Then he felt a dull thud to the back of his head. He fell forward, landing with a squelch on the rain-soaked grass.

'Get up!' the voice boomed behind him.

He scrambled to his feet and tried to back away.

'Where the fuck do you think you're going?' Pajo roared.

A smack to his jaw.

Kavanagh doubled over with the pain of it. 'Jesus.'

'This is too easy. You're even weaker than your little pal. Are you gonna start crying like him now? "Oh, don't take my precious plants. Boo fucking hoo." '

Kavanagh charged at Pajo, headbutting him in the chest. They scuffled and slipped over muck and wet grass, trying to get to each other, trying not to fall over. Then Pajo's hands were around Kavanagh's neck. He squirmed and struggled to break free. They edged closer and closer to the river. Kavanagh regained his footing, broke free and charged at him again. Pajo slipped and took a tumble. It all happened so fast. Kavanagh watched dumbstruck as Pajo went careening – Smack! – into one of the plastic barriers. Over. Down. Into the river....

Kavanagh ran to the edge, but Pajo had disappeared. No sign of him in the dark waters below. Gone.

'Pajo!' he called, but the wind and the rain stole his voice. He dug his phone out of his pocket and dialled 999. *Galway. The Spanish Arch. A man just fell in the river. No, I don't know. He's gone. I can't see him now ... I don't know. I don't know what happened. Okay, yes. I'll wait.*

He hung up. And then he ran.

Chapter 40

Stevie was drowning in photos, scrawled notes, photocopies and textbooks. Nothing made sense as she flicked through the pages. Words were random marks on paper. She couldn't process what they meant. She was trying to condense her research into something coherent, something with a clear trajectory, and she was so overwhelmed it seemed impossible even to know where to start. Exasperated, she paced up and down the tiny room as rain hammered down and the wind howled at her windows.

She was glad that Kav was gone. He had been too close, too irritating. She didn't want him to be there distracting her, taking her out of her own headspace, where she needed to be. She could hear the concern in his voice when he asked her if she'd eaten. Not him. Not him too with the worried glances and the questions. She couldn't stand it. The last thing she wanted was to stop, to lose focus. His being there had seemed to threaten everything. She needed to get to the centre of this thing, unravel it. If she could just focus. If she could just think straight....

The noise of a helicopter in the distance broke the silence. Stevie walked to the window and looked out. Another soul in the river, another light searching the dark water, and on a night like this. She felt the coldness enveloping her body.

She shuddered and wrapped her arms around herself. No, she couldn't think about that now. She had to get back to her work.

The light from the helicopter shone into the darkened room. Suddenly it seemed the light was trying to catch her, to pick her out and make her visible, to show her up so strangers could stare. *You won't claim me*, she thought. *Not tonight.* She pulled her blinds closed and switched off her phone.

Stevie sat down, closed her eyes and breathed in deeply. Suddenly everything seemed so straightforward. Somehow, the fog had lifted and her thoughts were clear and ordered. All of the pieces of work she had done, books she had read, notes she had made had added up to something. All she had needed was to step back from it in order to see it. She would have to pull an all-nighter, but she would be okay tomorrow. She would have something to present and a clear direction for where she was headed with her research. Picking up her pen, she pushed thoughts of the river from her mind as she began to write again. Her words flowed over the page until the hum of the helicopter grew more and more distant, then disappeared altogether.

Chapter 41

When Stevie woke, she searched for his heat in the bed. In the hazy sleep between dreaming and waking she expected to feel his arms around her. Then she remembered that he hadn't stayed with her. She shivered and curled herself up into a ball, searching for warmth. She felt herself retching and leaned her head over the edge of the bed. With no food in her system she could only vomit a clear liquid that burned her throat.

She got up, drank some water and brushed her teeth. Her stomach rumbled again but she couldn't face the thought of eating. She checked her watch. Her meeting with the graduate committee was in half an hour. She got dressed, grabbed her bag and headed out the door.

*

As Stevie was leaving her meeting and heading towards the door, Adrienne came running towards her.

'Stevie! How did it go?'

'Oh, hey Adrienne. Yeah, it went really well. Really, really well.'

'That's brilliant!'

'Are you up next?'

'Yeah. In half an hour.' She could see the anxiety on Adrienne's face.

'Listen, you'll be great. You know exactly what you're doing so don't be nervous, okay? It's really not as bad as you might expect.'

'Thanks, Stevie. It must be a relief for it to be over.'

'Yeah … yeah it is, I suppose.' It couldn't have gone better. She had spoken eloquently and answered any questions they had. They were impressed by the extensiveness of her critical response. 'I mean, they basically told me there and then that I'll be approved for continuation.'

Adrienne beamed at her. 'You must be delighted.'

'Yeah. No … I know that I should be but to be honest I don't really feel anything.'

'Oh …'.

'Maybe I'm just tired. I had a late night last night.'

Adrienne nodded. 'Oh, me too. Yeah, that's probably it. You'll feel differently after a good night's sleep.'

'Yeah … you know what? That's not it. I mean I am tired, I am, but that's not why I'm not feeling happy, why I can't feel anything. It's this. This whole thing. I don't want to do this. This isn't what I want to do.'

'Are you … okay, Stevie?'

'Yeah, I'm great. I actually feel … really, really good.' Stevie smiled at her and stretched out her arms for a hug. Adrienne returned the embrace awkwardly and patted Stevie on the back. 'Good luck in there, yeah? You'll do amazing.'

*

Back at home, Stevie started to take down the photos from the walls, piling them up in the centre of the floor. She looked at the photos of all of the sheela-na-gigs she had visited. Was she really any closer to understanding anything? Maybe some things were beyond logical explanations, and no amount of itemising and categorising would change that. Yet, she had given herself completely to trying to form one such explanation. It all seemed absurd all of a sudden, like trying to count the grains of sand on a beach. She pulled the map of Ireland off the wall and removed all of the index cards and notes, bundling them up before heading out into the clean, bright air. The storm of the previous night had receded. It felt good to be outside. She found herself drawn towards the river.

She stopped on the Salmon Weir Bridge and looked at the water below. The river was still swollen from the storm. She flung the papers up into the air and they scattered into the river, floating down the Corrib like lost love letters. She stood leaning on the bridge until they disappeared, a feeling of lightness embracing her.

Suddenly, she felt hungry. It was a hunger deep within her like she had never felt before. The feeling reverberated through her entire body. If she didn't eat something immediately she felt like she would collapse. She walked up Abbeygate Street and into Cooke's restaurant. She had often passed it and looked in covetously but never gone in. It had an old-world charm with its candlelit tables and heavy velvet drapes, dark wood furniture and oil paintings. The first time she had seen it she had decided that she would go there when she graduated and received her doctorate. Well, that wouldn't happen now, but she still felt like she had cause to celebrate. Something had shifted. It was the beginning of something. She didn't quite know what, but it felt like a momentous occasion.

She shook her head when the waiter brought her a menu. 'Fillet steak, medium rare, and a glass of Cabernet Sauvignon.'

He smiled at her. 'There's a woman who knows what she wants.'

A woman who knows what she wants. Yes, why not?

While she was waiting for her food, she took her notebook of to-do lists from her handbag. She struck a line through them all and flipped the pages until she reached a blank one and she began to write to make sense of her thoughts. She looked down at the words on the page.

You want us to be one thing but we are all things. You do not know the why of us. You look for an entrance but we are the entrances. Hag, goddess, hag. Blink and we are one, then the other. A blink that lasts a century. The same picture through a different lens. The snake becomes the ladder. We are the HagGoddesses and the GoddessHags. We are everything and nothing.

It was the truest thing she had written about the sheela-na-gigs. It had never occurred to her to write about them in this way before. She surrendered to the not knowing and it felt good.

She picked up her fork and cut a piece of steak. As she ate she found herself thinking back over her research, of how people lived in those times. Heaven and hell were not concepts, they were real places. Life was important, but only as a gateway to the next life. Death was not the end, but a doorway to eternal life. Those beliefs were important back then because they were needed for society to function. What better way to stop people questioning their lot in life than making them believe that it was transitory, a test of hardship and suffering before they received their just rewards? *I only have this moment*, she thought to herself. *This is it.*

There was a whole world out there. Stevie wanted to look at a different ocean, see a different shade of blue, feel the sun on her face. She wanted her ears to be filled with a language she couldn't understand. Then she thought of

Kav inviting her to go to Thailand with him. It had seemed ridiculous at the time, something to which she had not even given serious consideration. Now anything seemed possible. She would go with him. There were no confines, no limits, only the barriers she had created herself. Anything was possible now. It always had been, but she hadn't seen it before.

It was only outside in the daylight that she turned her phone back on and saw the missed calls and texts from Kavanagh. As she walked back towards her house she tried to ring him back, but there was no answer. She started to walk home, telling herself she would try him again later, but she couldn't shake the feeling of foreboding that was creeping upon her that something was terribly wrong.

Chapter 42

Kavanagh awoke in Phuket as though awakening from a strange nightmare. In a state of shock, he could barely process the sequence of events that had brought him here.

He remembered Alex handing him the sugary tea when he had called over to his house. 'Here, drink this. It'll help.'

Kavanagh had accepted the cup and drank in silence. He was shivering in his wet clothes, his eyes wide, frantic, darting. He was trying to grasp what had happened, what it meant. His thoughts were frenzied and they flew away from him.

Alex placed his hand on Kavanagh's shoulder. 'Did anyone see you? Kav, this is important.'

Alex's eye was swollen and he had stitches in his lip. 'Your face. Jesus, your face,' said Kavanagh.

'I'm fine. Honestly, it looks worse than it is.'

'I'm so sorry.'

'It's not your fault.'

'They were following me. They must have been.'

'Who?'

'One of Pajo's guys.' He realised now that he was finally giving voice to this intuition, this feeling he'd been having for some time that had now taken shape as an absolute certainty. 'I should have noticed. I should have stopped it.'

'Kav, that's not important now. I need you to focus and tell me, did anyone see you there when Pajo fell in?'

'He just fell. I didn't … I mean, I wanted to hurt him, I did, but not that. I wouldn't …'.

'No, of course not. It was an accident.'

'They were in the van, Pajo's guys. They were pulling up as it happened.'

'Do you think they saw anything?'

'It was dark … I don't know. I can't know for sure.'

'If they saw you … I mean, if they know you were there …'.

He couldn't be certain. He had run from there in a blind panic. He tried to ring Stevie again but her phone was off so he had headed straight for Alex's.

'If they know you were there, they'll come looking for you,' said Alex.

Kavanagh nodded.

'I have some money. I don't want you to argue with me. I want you to take it and I want you to get as far away from here as you can, as soon as you can.'

'Okay,' Kavanagh had whispered.

And now he was here and she was there. He was here on his own and he had left her there. He had been desperate to hear her voice, but as soon as he did he found that he had no words to explain. He could hear the hurt in her voice, the confusion. *How could you just leave like that?* The distance between them was filled with static on the phone, her voice in his ear as she said *Don't call me again. Just don't.*

He imagined that she was there with him. He conjured her in his room, stretched out on the hammock, her long limbs sprawled over its sides, foot dangling and tapping out a rhythm that only she could hear, a book in her hands. He saw the gentle encounters between Nogsy and Kannika and his heart ached: the way they shared a joke

237

that only the two of them got, the way they could say so much to each other with only a look or a smile. It struck him how much of communication was not through words but a glance, a touch, a language in which only two people were fluent. He felt the absence of Stevie like a physical pain.

Occasionally Kannika would look at him with such sympathy that he started to force himself to smile and laugh extra loud when he was around her.

'What did you tell her?' he asked Nogsy the night after he arrived when the two of them were out for a few beers.

'She asked me why you were so sad. She said you're different to how you were when you were here before for the wedding. I couldn't explain it that well. Still working on my Thai. I said you'd had your heart broken and she kind of filled in the gaps herself.'

'The universal language of the sad bastard.' Kavanagh grimaced and drank some beer. 'God, I must seem pathetic.'

'She feels bad for you, that's all. She asked me if something terrible had happened to you. If someone had died.' Nogsy laughed.

Kavanagh felt his blood run cold. 'Really?' He tried to laugh, but it came out sounding hollow.

'Is everything … I mean, if there's anything you want to talk about …?' said Nogsy with great delicacy.

'Something happened in Galway before I left.'

Nogsy leaned in closer, waiting for Kavanagh to continue, but he was silent, unable to meet Nogsy's eye as he stared down at his hand on the table.

'Want to talk about it?'

For a moment Kavanagh thought about telling him. He knew he could trust Nogsy. To say it out loud might help him make sense of the confusion in his head, the circular repetition of his thoughts, the barely contained panic that floated up when he remembered that night.

'Nah, nah I'm good. Thanks, Nogsy.' If he refused to give voice to it, it would prevent it from being real. He decided the only solution was to get rip-roaringly pissed. He ordered a round of tequila shots, then another as the night swirled around him and he laughed and blustered and bantered with the bar staff.

'You're Irish?' smiled the barman.

'Yeah,' said Kavanagh.

'Where from?'

'Galway.'

'Ah, Galway!'

'Have you been there?'

'No, no, but I want to go.'

'That's what everyone says.'

'We play song for you.'

Kavanagh smiled and sat back down.

Moments later the familiar tune wafted through the bar. *And I lost my heart to a Galway girl.* No escaping it, even on the other side of the world. He smiled to himself, raised his glass to the barman and nodded his thanks. One minute he was drinking his beer and the next he was heaving sobs, and he could feel the ground underneath him and feel Nogsy's hand touching his back. 'You okay, bro?'

'It's fucked up. It's all fucked up.'

He wanted to feel Stevie's arms around him. He wanted to hear her voice telling him that it was okay, but that was impossible now. He'd blown it.

Chapter 43

Jacqui sat in Marguerite and Richard Donnellan's sitting room, drinking tea and eyeing up the photographs that lined the mantelpiece of a young Pajo, or Patrick, as his parents called him. His mother had clutched Jacqui's hand at the funeral. 'Let us know how you're getting on. Anything we can do to help, and you must come to visit …'.

She hadn't cried at the funeral. Walshy and Hulk had come over to her and they exchanged awkward hugs.

Then Walshy had leaned towards her and whispered, 'We think something happened to him that night down by the river.'

'Of course something happened to him, Walshy. He fucking fell in.'

'Did he fall though, Jacqui? Or was he pushed?'

'He fell.'

'You seem pretty certain about that. You and him weren't getting along too well, were you?'

'What's that got to do with anything?'

'Motive,' said Hulk.

'What is this – good cop, gobshite cop? Lads, this is hardly the time or place. Have you no respect?'

They both looked bashful for a moment until Walshy piped up, 'We're gonna get to the bottom of this. It's what he would have wanted.'

She could see then how utterly lost they were without him. 'You know what you should do?' They leaned in closer. 'Start thinking for yourselves.' I've just started it recently. It's fucking fantastic.' And with that she turned on her heel and clip-clopped off.

'So, your family must be excited about the baby,' said Marguerite.

'Well, they're not really around. My mam died a few years back. Cancer. She was very young.'

'Oh, I'm so sorry to hear that.'

'And my dad was never really on the scene, so … I have a brother. He lives in Galway too. He's … yeah, he's around, you know. So that's …'.

'Patrick was an only child,' said Marguerite. 'We did everything for him. Maybe it wasn't enough …' .

Jacqui reached out and held Marguerite's hand. 'It's not your fault. There's no rhyme or reason to this. Sometimes things just happen.'

'We didn't see much of Patrick these last few years,' said Richard, shaking his head sadly. 'Was he … did he seem … happy?'

'Oh yes,' said Jacqui. 'I'm sure he meant to visit you more often. He spoke about you all the time.'

'Did he?'

'I'm so sorry that we didn't know about you, about the baby. He never told us.'

'I know. We were waiting until it was confirmed. He was planning a trip to visit you both to tell you the good news. And then, well, then the accident happened …'.

She was surprised to find how easy it was to lie, to tell his parents what they wanted to hear by recasting Pajo as the loving boyfriend, the dutiful son. It wasn't a difficult thing to do when she could see how happy it made them, how they clung to it. Sometimes there was a kindness to lies.

*

As Jacqui was getting ready to leave their house, gathering up her coat and bag and thanking them for their hospitality, Marguerite excused herself and said she'd be back in a moment. She returned with a bunch of sunflowers and handed them to Jacqui. She had admired them earlier in the back garden when they were showing her around their house.

'Oh, I love sunflowers,' she said. She was about to mention her tattoo but something stopped her. They might ask her if they could see it and then she would have to roll up her trouser leg, take off her shoe and roll down her sock. No, it was just for her now.

'Anything you need, love, just let us know,' said Marguerite as Jacqui turned to smile and wave goodbye as she headed down the driveway.

'You're family now,' called Richard, his voice shaking.

Chapter 44

Once the jet lag had subsided, Kavanagh's days took on a surreal quality. He had entered another world. Everything was different. He threw himself into his work, hoping it would distract him from the thoughts in his mind. In the tattoo parlour they were impressed with his work.

'Holy shit, man, you've really improved,' said Logan. 'I mean you were good before, but now ...'.

With the hum of the needle, he disappeared. His mind was expansive. The gnawing feeling in his stomach almost retreated. He sent postcards to Finn, to Gary and Dan. *A great job opportunity came up and I had to head over earlier than I'd planned.* He hoped that they would be happy for him, that they wouldn't question him too much, or read the lies between the lines – the false joviality that masked guilt and terror.

He nearly broke down when he called his mother. 'I'm sorry. I left without saying goodbye. I'm so sorry. How are you?'

He heard her laugh. 'Don't worry, Joe, I've come to expect the unexpected from you. I'm back on my feet and feeling better than ever. You'll never guess what I've done.'

'What?'

'Only set up a painting group in town. I thought maybe one or two would be interested but we've sixteen members. We meet once a week and we're planning a trip away to France next spring.'

He wiped away tears with the back of his hand. 'That's brilliant.'

It hadn't rained since he'd arrived. It was disconcerting. Nogsy laughed when he mentioned this to him. 'You won't be saying that come September, believe me.'

Kannika and Nogsy insisted on bringing him off on day trips when he wasn't working. They travelled to Wat Chalong with the windows down in Kannika's tiny yellow car.

He walked around the temple in his bare feet, taking in the ornate gold leaf, the displays of Buddha statues, the reverential air of the place, the scent of incense that hung heavy in the air. 'She'd love this. She really would.'

'Stevie?' said Nogsy.

Kavanagh nodded.

'Why don't you try calling her again?'

'It's no good, she's not speaking to me.'

*

'What other historical sites are here?' he asked Nogsy when they were back at the house later.

'Jesus, bro. There's tons.' He showed Kavanagh some photos of the places that he and Kannika had visited. He marvelled at the temples and laughed at the photos from the fertility shrine in Bangkok with Nogsy embracing a giant penis statue.

'It's funny. I was never that interested in any of this stuff before.' He found himself charting itineraries, trips that he would take if Stevie were with him.

'There must be a way,' said Nogsy. 'A way for you to make it right.'

'Maybe there is.'

He called Alex on Skype. His bruises had faded and he looked much better than the last time he had seen him.

'You look great, man.'

'So do you. You got some colour.'

'Any news about …'. Kavanagh couldn't bring himself to say his name.

'Our mutual friend?'

Kavanagh nodded.

'There was an obituary in the paper. I can send it on to you.'

'Oh God, no. No. I mean, that's okay. What about our mutual friend's mutual friends?'

'Those guys? Yeah, they were looking for you. I called over to your place like you asked. Gary and Dan were asking me about it. I didn't let on I knew anything about it.'

'And did you find it? Was it still there?'

'Yeah, I have it here. I'll make sure she gets it.'

'Okay, thanks. How's everything with you? How's … the shrubbery?'

Alex laughed. 'This is great. I feel like we're in a spy film.'

'You can't be too careful, I suppose.'

'Ah yeah. Well, I was upset about what happened to my last … em, garden, but I've managed to procure some new plants and I've signed up for a horticulture course.'

'Wait, is this code?'

'No, like I'm actually going back to college and training to become a horticulturist. That thing that happened, I don't know. It was a bit of a wake-up call.'

'Wow, so me ruining your life and causing you to be attacked was actually a positive thing. I'm the greatest friend ever.'

'You are,' said Alex, his voice lacking the irony to match Kavanagh's. Kavanagh felt a lump in his throat. He coughed.

'Great, so you won't mind me asking you another favour? When you go to Stevie's, I need you to tell her what happened, why I left.'

'When you say everything, do you mean … everything?'

Kavanagh nodded. 'She needs to know.'

'Okay. I can do that.'

Chapter 45

There was something familiar about him, this stranger who knocked on Stevie's door, that put her at ease immediately. She invited Alex inside.

'Kav asked me to come here. There's something you need to know. Have you seen this?' He handed her the *Galway Advertiser*. It was open on an article with the headline 'Tributes To Popular Local Man Following Funeral'. She saw a face she knew from somewhere as she scanned the article about a man who had fallen into the river and been swept away the night of the storm. Pajo ... why was the name familiar? Suddenly she remembered him from a long-ago party, the night she first met Kavanagh.

'The guy from the party. I remember him. He seemed ...'. She stopped short, not wanting to speak ill of the dead.

'Like a nasty piece of work? Yeah, he was. Kavanagh was there that night. They were fighting and Pajo fell in. It was an accident, but maybe some people wouldn't see it that way. Maybe some people would relish the chance to have someone to blame.'

Suddenly it all made sense. The helicopter searching the river, Kavanagh's sudden disappearance, his reluctance to say why he had left.

'How is he? Have you been speaking to him?'

'He's terrified,' said Alex. 'And he wants you to know that he's sorry about the way things happened. He wanted you to have this.'

He handed her the painting.

Chapter 46

That night Stevie dreamed of the ocean, an expanse of blue. She dreamed of the sun warming her pale body. She dreamed of Kavanagh. She looked around the empty flat. It looked and felt different now that the walls were bare. Kavanagh's painting was the only sheela-na-gig left. It didn't feel oppressive like the others. There was a glint of mischief in her eye, a kindness even, a warmth, despite being surrounded by all that blue. She was her own island in a vast ocean.

Stevie realised that everything had been about a closing off, a narrowing. What if she allowed herself to stop, to breathe, to say, what is it that I want? What would it feel like to relinquish control, to live and love without fear? She had clung to this idea of Stevie the Historian because without it what was she, who was she? And she had pushed Kavanagh away as a result.

And now he was gone and she had done nothing to stop it. She hadn't wanted him to go away, not really, and now it was too late. She couldn't tell him about her fear. She would set herself apart again as less-than, as weak. She didn't want to be that person. She had had enough of being vulnerable. She had been on the receiving end of enough sympathetic looks to last a lifetime. She wanted to explain to him that she had been that way because she had to be.

She started to write an email to Kavanagh. Her fingers tapped out the words, trying to make sense of everything. She told him about her fears; about the psychiatric unit and Pam; how she was waking up now from a strange dream and trying to make sense of things; and on and on. Reading it back, she shook her head. She hit delete and watched her words disappear. In their place she typed *I know I wasn't there for you and I'm sorry, but I want to be now if you'll let me.*

*

Stevie clutched her boarding card and passport in her hand. The anxiety tablets were in her bag. She fished them out and held them in her hand. She didn't need them. She felt clear-headed, determined. The last thing she wanted to do was dull her senses. All she wanted now was to feel everything. She threw them in a nearby bin and made her way to the boarding gate.

Stevie felt her heart surge as she boarded the plane. How easy it was then, after all. She looked out the window as the plane rose higher and higher until Dublin was a patchwork quilt of green below. She would soon land where he was. They would be together and they would figure things out from there. She smiled to herself, thinking about how he said he loved surprises. Stevie was heading towards her future, soaring above it all, over the fields and the churches and the many mysteries of the past. Curled up inside her, the tiny life soared too, biding and patient. Not one heartbeat, but two.

Also in the New Island Fiction Firsts Series

Forsaken
Gerard Lee

'When I was ten, my father went up a tree and never came down.'

So begins the frantic and compelling journey into the inner universe of
JJ, a child who we come to realise sees the world in a very different way.
Forsaken develops as a journey through the psychological spiral of a ten-
year-old boy's struggle, not merely to survive, but to fulfil a primal instinct
– to reunite with his family. In spite of JJ's deteriorating circumstances,
he never wavers from this mission; if anything, the rapidly unravelling
exterior world steels his determination to achieve his goal.

Inspired by the author's personal experience of the lives of the
children who lived in the Residential Homes where he worked
for several years, who persisted with extraordinary resilience and
passionate longing to somehow fix their broken world.

'One of the best things I've read this year.' – Rick O'Shea

My Buried Life
Doreen Finn

What happens when you no longer recognise the person you have become?

Eva has managed to spend her twenties successfully hiding from
herself in an alcohol-fuelled life in New York. Attempting to write, but
really only writing her epitaph, she returns to Ireland to confront the
pas that has made her what she is. In prose that is hauntingly beautiful
and delicate, Doreen Finn explores a truly complex and fascinating
character with deft style and unflinching honesty.

≈

*'Doreen Finn has created a loaded pistol in Eva Perry, an embittered poet whose
creative voice has been silenced … Finn's language showers sparks as Eva confronts
her own difficult nature and her family's clouded past.'*
– Janet Fitch, author of *White Oleander*